GHOSTS
OF ANGELS

A. E. LAWRENCE

 FriesenPress

One Printers Way
Altona, MB R0G 0B0
Canada

www.friesenpress.com

ISBN
978-1-03-913000-5(Hardcover)
978-1-03-912999-3 (Paperback)
978-1-03-913001-2 (eBook)

1. FICTION, THRILLERS

Distributed to the trade by The Ingram Book Company

ACKNOWLEDGMENTS

Writing is the most fun you can have with your pants on—what follows is an often monotonous, often heartbreaking grind: re-reading and re-writing your manuscript for what seems like a million times with an effort to keep improving the story, then undertaking the seemingly impossible task of finding an agent and publisher to believe in your words.

To get it this far I asked for and kindly received help from an army of heroes who gave me invaluable insights and suggestions to make the book better.

These truly remarkable people included, in no specific order, my wife and love of my life, Vickie, my son Adam, and Robin McCormick, whose help with everything computer was invaluable, and Margie McCallum, and Sally and Tom Davidson for their unfaltering encouragement.

Then there's the cadre of poor souls who read my first efforts: Bryan and Suzanne Smith; Irene and Greg Aziz; Tony Hillman; David Klugsberg; the two Michaels, Wiggan and McEwan; Eve Lewis; Stacey Katzman; and fellow authors, Shelley Peterson and Hugh Russel—please buy and read their books.

I would also like to thank my team at Friesen Press: Carlo Giambarresi for the amazing cover illustration and Coni Kennedy for making the finished design truly outstanding. It's no wonder she's won a multitude of graphic design awards.

I finally decided to be my own publisher and found an editor, Diane Young, who's brilliant guidance and frank honesty has been truly appreciated. Every writer needs a great editor and Diane is the best.

The book you're holding in your hands, or reading on your device, is my dream come true. I sincerely hope you enjoy the story and tell all your friends about it.

For Vickie, my beautiful wife.

and

Derrick (Ricky) Thompson
(1952–2020)
Rest in Peace, my dear friend.

Our feet are planted in the real world, but we dance with angels and ghosts.

—John Cameron Mitchell

CHAPTER ONE

Nick felt like shit.

He hadn't slept in weeks, and last night's toss-and-turn marathon had been another struggle in futility.

His personal life was spinning out of control, and his job, as a Chicago homicide detective, was throwing him more curves than he could ever possibly hit. It had been a month now, Christmas was sneaking up, and there were still no leads. In all his years on the force, Nick Palmer had never investigated such a mystifying murder.

The victim was a young woman, late teens or early twenties. She was cheerleader pretty with long, blonde hair and pale-blue eyes. A passerby discovered her frost-covered body in the early morning of November 12, near the front steps of the Holy Name Cathedral on North Wabash Avenue. The murdered girl was kneeling, her head down on the icy pavement with her elbows in front of her, as if she were praying, and covered with a coarse black robe that would have done little to keep out the freezing weather.

Underneath the robe, the victim was almost naked, dressed only in a skimpy black bra and thong. There were no witnesses, and they had yet to determine her identity. The forensic team in the Chicago Police Department had discovered a tiny filament of gold thread embedded in the bloody wound she received during strangulation.

The only other clue came from security footage. Cameras mounted in front of the cathedral showed two nuns pushing a girl in a wheel-chair. It was impossible to tell from the CCTV footage if she was already deceased. They stopped at the point where the girl's body was found, carefully placed her in the prayer position, covered her, and knelt beside her for thirty seconds. One of the nuns had then taken the victim's place in the wheelchair, and the other had pushed her around the corner and out of sight.

Police found the nuns' robes in a trash container four blocks from the crime scene. The wheelchair, left leaning next to the bin, held no clues. It had no identifying marks, and because the fraudulent nuns had worn gloves, there were no fingerprints.

The nuns' garments had been rented from a costume shop on the city's southeastern outskirts. The deposit was paid in cash, and the person who rented them had used bogus identification. The clerk who served the man had no recollection of the transaction, nor did he think he'd be able to recognize him in a lineup. Nick wondered if the costume shop's employee had been smoking something stronger than a cigarette.

Nick didn't need this kind of aggravation, not now, and probably not ever. Isabela, his wife of the past seven years, had just left him and taken Lucy, their seven-year-old daughter, back to her parents' home in Sacramento. The unsolved case, the impending holidays, and the realization that his marriage was over weighed heavily on his psyche.

ψ

Nick had met Isabela at a party in Chicago's Old Town. She'd come to the city from California to work and have fun, but mostly, to get away from the oppressive home life she'd been dealing with, living under her parents' roof—parents who harbored a sheepish devotion to an obscure religious order from their Mexican homeland.

Nick had always had a thing for Latino girls, and Isabela was hot—jalapeño hot. She was curvaceous, had raven-black hair, almond-shaped eyes, and silky-smooth skin. In retrospect, it should have been a casual fling, but when she'd gotten pregnant with Lucy, they'd gotten married in a civil ceremony that had infuriated her father and mother. Isabela's parents wanted more for their only daughter than to be the wife of a gringo cop, and they'd never forgiven him for what he'd done to their little girl.

Nick was born and raised in Chicago. His dad was a cop who'd died in the line of duty when Nick was barely out of diapers. His mom was an eccentric second-generation Italian who once, long ago, had confided to Nick that she communicated with angels. These angels she spoke to didn't seem to help much, because even with his dad's pension, Nick's mom had had to keep two jobs going to raise him and his older sister.

When she'd passed away from cancer, he'd feared his entire world would collapse around him, but on the day following her funeral, he'd felt an inner warmth. It was as if a small part of her soul had entered his body.

Growing up, Nick had always known he wanted to be a cop and follow in his father's footsteps. He was now thirty-three and had risen quickly through the ranks of the police department. He was smart, personable, physically fit, and dedicated to his job. He thought about Isabela's parting words to him: "I loved you once, Nick, but now you're more married to the force than you are to me." Deep within his heart, he knew that what she said was true. They'd grown apart, and the love they'd once shared was now a distant memory.

Their family home in Clarendon Hills, a charming Tudor-style house with a big backyard, was up for sale. The house held a lot of memories, good times and bad. Thoughts of Lucy and her friends playing on the backyard swing set filled his mind. He choked back tears for a life gone forever.

Now, besides everything else going on in his life, he needed to find a place to live.

Ψ

Nick was wide awake when his clock radio went off, the blaring sound of heavy metal reminding him that it was 5:45 a.m. It was predawn dark, and the baffling case of the cathedral murder was still sitting in a slim file on his desk. He stretched, got out of bed, and made his way to the bathroom. Flipping on the lights, he took a cursory look in the mirror… and staggered backwards against a towel rack on the wall behind him.

He rubbed his eyes and looked again. The face looking back was not his; it was a young woman's. She was beautiful, with wavy auburn hair, a pale complexion, and large hazel eyes. Her clothing reminded him of what women wore in the early films Isabela loved. He'd seen just about everything he could ever imagine while working on the force, but this was something totally different, and it scared the hell out of him. His hands were trembling, and he felt the coldness of sweat forming on his forehead. *What the fuck's happening to me?* He rubbed his eyes again, just to make sure he was awake. The woman was still there, looking back at him. She had a despondent look that reached deeply into his heart. He braced himself against the counter.

"Who the fuck are you?"

The girl in the mirror looked directly at him and started to speak with an enchanting French accent he found irresistible and a voice that was soft, like he imagined an angel's voice would sound.

"Bonjour, Monsieur Palmer. My name is Margaux Deneuve."

She paused and took a deep breath.

"I was living in Paris, on the Ile Saint-Louis, with my parents, when the Nazis occupied the city in 1942."

She closed her eyes and the memory of some unimaginable desolation washed across her face.

"C'était terrible. Food, when you could get it, was rationed, as was clothing and coal. There were curfews, but German soldiers still roamed the streets searching for Jews, girls, members of the resistance, whoever. Many of our friends left the city to try and find safety."

She took another despairing breath and sobbed. Her tears turned to

4

glistening little rivulets that trickled silently down her ghostly cheeks.

"On November eleventh, my nineteenth birthday, a group of students held a demonstration against the occupation. It was on the Champs-Elysées at la place de l'Etoile, and I was there."

She stared straight at him, the anguish he'd seen earlier now gone, replaced a look of steely determination and absolute defiance.

"There was a lot of noise, people shoving and shouting, and I was grabbed from behind, but it wasn't the Germans or the gendarmes."

Nick couldn't tear his eyes away from the apparition. He had a million questions, but he couldn't speak. It was as if the girl had cast a spell on him—a spell that compelled him to listen.

"I was blindfolded and taken to what felt like a cellar. The air was damp and cold, and I tried to struggle free. Then they ripped off my clothes and tied me to a chair. There was murmured chanting from perhaps ten or fifteen people, and a strong smell of incense. Then a rope was placed around my neck... and I was strangled."

Nick couldn't move. He was frozen in place by some unknown force that was pushing against his will. Her story was horrific—a nightmare scenario found only in the most graphically explicit films.

"The police found my body the following morning, kneeling in front of Cathédrale Notre-Dame on the Ile de la Cité."

The girl's image faded, but before she vanished, she uttered a final plea, as simple as it was impossible, *"Please, Monsieur Palmer, help us. Please, help all of us."*

Nick found himself staring at his own disheveled image. His first thought was that the stress of work, family, and just about everything else in his screwed-up life might have finally pushed him over the edge. He slapped his cheeks to double-check that he was awake.

Jesus, it's just a lack of sleep... that or my fucking imagination playing tricks on me.

He shook his head to clear away the image he'd seen, then stepped into a hot shower. The scalding water hit his body like another hard slap in the face.

CHAPTER TWO

The morning was bitingly cold. A light dusting of snow had fallen overnight, and traffic was heavier than usual. Cars and trucks crawled through the winter streets, spewing clouds of toxic exhaust that crystallized and dissipated into the sunrise. On his way to work, Nick stopped at Starbucks. His regular barista, a young African American man with an infectious smile, greeted him and handed the cop his usual double espresso.

"Good morning, chief. Scooped up any bad guys yet today?"

Nick responded, as he always did, with the third digit of his right hand and a smile. The man responded in kind; it was a private ritual they played out every morning.

ψ

The Second District's homicide division on South Wentworth Avenue occupies a stark, pale-colored brick building. It's a somber structure, with its occupants busily going about the serious business of solving murders.

Nick drove into the parking lot, pulled up the collar of his topcoat, and trudged slowly across the street to begin his shift. He couldn't get the image of the girl in the mirror out of his mind. Even the strong black coffee he'd picked up earlier hadn't helped clear his thoughts.

When he got to his desk, he flipped open the "Cathedral Murder" file and stared at photographs of the victim. His thoughts kept returning to the girl in his bathroom mirror. Then it hit him.

Holy shit, both girls were murdered on November 11, both were strangled, and both were left kneeling in front of a cathedral.

His thoughts were interrupted by Detective Gabriela Martinez, his partner in crime.

"Good morning, handsome. Penny for your thoughts."

Gabriela was tall and slim. She had glossy shoulder-length black hair, dark eyes, and a dazzling smile, and spoke with a soft Texan accent that reminded him of warm honey. She had graduated with a law degree from the University of Houston Law Center, but early in her career, had decided she'd rather be on the front lines of law enforcement than fighting it out in the dusty, crowded courtrooms of the Lone Star State.

She'd moved to Chicago after being accepted into the city's police academy, and was tough, smart, and as kindhearted as she was beautiful. She also had a secret. She was in love with her partner, Nicholas Palmer. No one knew—not Nick, not her family or friends, and not anyone she worked with on the force.

Gabriela was Nick's longtime sidekick, and their close working relationship had made Isabela jealous. Unfounded as her suspicions had been, they'd often caused arguments.

In retrospect, Isabela might have been right. Nick had an attraction for his partner that went well beyond their everyday working relationship. Sometimes he did wonder what his life would be like if he were with Gabriela instead of Isabela. Those daydreams had always ended with the same slap-in-the-face realization: *Jesus, Nick, don't be such an asshole! You're a married man.*

Gabriela smiled and leaned in. He felt the warmth of her cheek against his ear.

"Hey, Nick, I think we've got a solid lead on the identity of our cathedral girl."

He straightened and looked at her. Anything that could help solve the murder would be welcome news.

"Go ahead. I'm listening."

"We just got a missing person's report from the cops in Ann Arbor. Fits the description of the woman we've got in the morgue. A sophomore at the University of Michigan—a nice Midwestern girl. Her parents haven't heard from her in weeks and got worried."

The detective handed Nick a photograph. It looked exactly like the dead girl would have looked before the ravages of death had taken their toll.

"Do we know her name?"

"Susan Roberts, nineteen years old, born November 11, 1999. She majored in anthropology with a particular interest in precolonial Mexico. You know, Aztec, Mayan, Toltec... that kind of stuff."

The coincidence of this girl and the girl he had seen in his mirror having the same birthday, on top of everything else, shocked him. It probably showed on his face.

"What are you thinking?" Gabriela asked.

He brushed aside her question. He wasn't ready to tell her about the apparition he had seen. She might think he was losing his mind.

"Nothing really. I guess we'd better talk to the guys in Ann Arbor and perhaps notify her parents."

"Already on it. They're sending us the girl's prints and dental records to confirm her identity. With any luck, they should be here later this afternoon."

She left him and went back to her desk. Their abysmal record of arrests and convictions lately was humiliating, and the pressure from their superiors to get results was beyond intense.

At a quarter to five, the report from the Ann Arbor police was put on Nick's desk. It confirmed that the victim was Susan Roberts. She was an honors student, popular and personable. Her middle-class parents lived in suburban Columbus, Ohio.

Nick and Gabriela placed a call to the Columbus police and

relegated the unpleasant task of contacting the girl's parents and telling them that their daughter had been murdered. Now all they had to do in Chicago was continue their investigation, which still seemed daunting. This could be another unsolved murder added to the list of many others in their jurisdiction.

They checked out at about seven, went to a local bar, and ordered burgers and beer. After eating their artery-hardening meal, they said goodnight and went their separate ways.

ψ

Nick's house felt hollow and empty. He missed having a family, but mostly, he missed his daughter's laughter. This was normally his and Lucy's time. He stood in the doorway and listened for something, anything, to break the silence. Just a few months ago, Lucy would have jumped happily into his arms, and he'd hear sounds of water splashing in the kitchen as Isabela cleaned up after dinner. All the sounds of life that he'd once thought would last forever were now gone. The quiet was almost a presence, something that sucked the air right out of the room and caused a weight to settle on his chest. He kicked off his shoes, made his way to the kitchen, and grabbed a beer from the near-empty fridge. Flicking on the television, he was grateful for the voice of the local newscaster, reporting on the latest round of shenanigans from Washington, but wasn't in the mood for their political bullshit, and started yelling at the television.

"What the hell's the matter with you guys? All this petty partisan crap isn't good for the country, and the guy I voted for is the biggest idiot of them all!"

He took a deep breath.

Fuck! Now I'm even talking to myself.

He turned off the television and put on a CD. Within seconds, the smooth sound of Chet Baker playing "Dreamsville" filled the empty rooms.

After taking a hot shower, he called Sacramento to say goodnight to his daughter. Isabela's mother answered. She sounded distant and unfriendly—exactly as she always sounded when talking to him.

"Neither Lucy nor Isabela are available. Try calling tomorrow."

She slammed down the phone.

He swore under his breath, hung up, went upstairs, and crawled into his unmade bed, turning out the lights and closing his eyes. The sleep he so desperately needed would be a long time coming.

CHAPTER THREE

Nick's radio went off at the usual time: 5:45 a.m., the heavy-metal music that he hated but needed to get him going blasting out of the speakers. He threw off the covers, stumbled sleepily through the darkness, and went into the bathroom. He glanced into the mirror, but it was only him looking back. Not an attractive sight after a restless night but welcome sight nonetheless.

Suddenly his image faded and morphed into the face of yet another young woman. He blinked repeatedly to get rid of the apparition, but when his eyes were fully open and focused, she was still there, looking back at him.

The girl was bewitching, with tanned skin, almond-shaped eyes, and ebony-colored hair pulled back off her face. She was wearing a bright-orange bikini top and spoke with an Italian accent, as cheerless and unsettling as it was sexy. It was a voice that sounded as if the soul had been ripped out of it.

"Buongiorno, Signor Palmer. My name is Sophia D'Angelo. I lived with my parents, in a villa on the Amalfi Coast, and attended the American University in Rome."

Nick couldn't believe it was happening to him again. He shook his head, looked away, and turned back again several times. He thought he was going crazy, but each time he looked, the mournful girl was still there, in the mirror, looking back at him. Nick's heart was pounding like a drum. He felt like he was having a heart attack. He turned away from the mirror and tried to shake the apparition from his head. Then he finally looked directly and defiantly into the girl's eyes.

"What do you want from me?"

The Italian girl ignored his question and kept talking. Her voice trembled with every word, as she struggled to keep from crying.

"On November 11, 1972, my nineteenth birthday, I was preparing to go home for the holidays. As I was leaving my apartment, I was grabbed, blindfolded, and taken to what I think was a cellar."

Nick felt he was going out of his mind. This wasn't normal. Either he was on the verge of insanity, or he'd entered an inexplicable world he knew nothing about—though his mother often spoke about it. He tried to shut the girl out, but his innate curiosity and training made him want to hear more.

"Go on."

"It was damp and cold. There was chanting and the smell of incense. I was tied to a chair, a rope was wrapped around my neck, and I was strangled. The polizia found my body kneeling, with my head down, on the hard stones in front of the obelisk in Saint Peter's Square. I was covered with a black robe."

The girl looked into his eyes, and Nick couldn't remember ever seeing such despair.

"Please help us, Signor Palmer. Please help us all."

Then, just as before, the girl's image faded, and he was left looking at his own disheveled, unshaven reflection. His head was throbbing. He rubbed his eyes, hoping he'd soon wake up from this delusional nightmare.

He stayed in the shower for thirty minutes—much longer than normal—to wash away the apparitions he'd been seeing in his mirror. After drying himself and starting to get dressed, his cell rang. It was his real-estate agent, who was in much happier spirits.

"Good morning, Nick. It's Larry. Thought I'd catch you before you went to work. I've got some folks, a nice young couple, who want to see your place. Can I take them through this afternoon?"

"Yeah. Sure, Larry. You know where the key is. Just let yourself in."

"Okay, buddy. I'll let you know how it goes. Don't forget to tidy the place up. Last time I was there, it looked like a vagrant was camped out in your bedroom."

His friend's tone was jovial, but he got the message loud and clear.

"Oh, just fuck off, Larry."

He smiled, hung up, and raced around the house picking up, throwing out, and doing his best to make the place look more presentable. He passed on his usual Starbucks stop and still arrived at the station fifteen minutes later than usual. Gabriela Martinez was waiting at his desk. She was scowling playfully and pointing at her watch.

He sighed. "Jesus, Gabi, what's a few minutes between friends?"

She laughed. It was an infectious laugh that turned heads and made men dream about leaving their wives. He took her by the arm and led her towards to the door.

"Let's grab a coffee. There's something I've got to talk to you about."

They found a quiet corner booth in the same bar they'd had dinner in the night before. He sat staring into his coffee, wondering how to start the conversation. He needn't have worried because his partner piped in instead.

"Okay. Nick, what's been bugging you?"

Nick was still staring into his cup. He didn't know how to tell her about the apparitions he'd been seeing. Didn't know how she'd react. Didn't know if she'd think he'd lost his mind. His palms were sweating, and his heart was pounding. This was going to be one of the most difficult conversations he'd ever had, and he prayed it wouldn't affect their relationship. Finally, he looked up, took a deep breath, and told her about the young women he'd been seeing in his mirror. He told her about Margaux Deneuve in Paris and about Sophia D'Angelo in Rome. He told her about the strange coincidence of them sharing a birthday with Susan Roberts, as well as them all dying on their nineteenth birthdays. Then he described the circumstances of their murders.

She reached across the table, gently touched his arm, and spoke the words he'd been thinking but afraid to consider.

"Nick, are you sure you don't need a break? What with Isabela and Lucy leaving, trying to sell the house, and all the shit going on over at the precinct, do you think maybe you've pushed yourself too far?"

Nick rubbed his face. He was exhausted and troubled.

"Maybe you're right."

He felt he needed to change the subject and get away from talking about the girls in the mirror before Gabriela became overly concerned with his sanity—just like he was.

"My agent is taking people through the house this afternoon."

As Gabriela got up to leave, she turned and looked back at him. "Do you think you'll get more money if they know the place is haunted?"

He smiled. "Let's get the hell out of here."

ψ

They hadn't been at their desks for more than five minutes when a call came in. A domestic dispute in Logan Square. A woman had apparently taken a kitchen knife to her sleeping husband, and afterwards, called the police to report what she'd done. It was a cut-and-dried case (so to speak). Obviously very messy, but it would fill the rest of their day and a few more days to come.

When Nick got home that night, all he wanted was sleep. He pulled a beer from the fridge and a bag of potato chips off the kitchen counter. That was dinner, and once his head hit the pillow, he was dead to the world in minutes.

CHAPTER FOUR

Nick woke before his alarm went off and went to the bathroom, uneasy about what he might see in the mirror. He stared at his reflection for a few minutes and when nothing appeared but his own face, he breathed a sigh of relief. He showered, then looked in the mirror again.

"Thank God, it's just me," he said to himself.

On his way to the station, he stopped at an all-night diner and ordered eggs over easy, sausages, and rye toast. He was halfway through his breakfast when his cell rang. It was his real-estate agent.

"Hey, Nick, got you an offer. The couple from yesterday loved the house."

He was about to shovel a forkful of egg into his mouth. "How much?"

"Full asking. You should be happy as hell—and they want a fast closing too."

Nick had mixed feelings. He felt a tinge of sadness about selling the family home but was happy he could scratch another thing off his long to-do list.

"I'll stop by tonight with the paperwork. Is that okay with you?

"See you at seven, Larry, and thanks… thanks a lot."

Nick left the restaurant and was about to back out of the parking lot. He glanced in the rearview mirror and quickly slammed on the brakes. Looking back at him was the anguished face of yet another attractive young woman. She spoke with a softly accented Spanish

15

voice. It reminded him of a movie star he'd loved when he was a kid. He slid the gear into park and listened.

"Buenos días, Señor Palmer. My name is Juanita Diaz. I was nineteen and working in a women's boutique in Madrid."

She paused for what seemed like forever.

"In Spain, it is common practice for businesses to open in the morning, close in the afternoon at siesta time, and reopen again in the evening until ten o'clock."

The girl in the mirror paused again. Her face expressed the anguish of her story—a story the Chicago detective was getting to know all too well.

"I locked up the shop and was going to a nearby restaurant to celebrate my birthday with my twin sister and some friends. As I was walking, someone grabbed me from behind. It was two men and a woman, I think. They blindfolded me, took me to a cellar, and tied me to a chair. I heard my sister cry out; she was there too."

The girl sobbed, and Nick felt the heartache she was going through.

"They put a rope around your neck and strangled you. Is that what happened?" Nick asked.

"Me and my sister too. We tried to scream, but nothing would come out of our mouths. The police found our bodies the next morning. We were kneeling, like we were praying, both Adriana and me, covered in thick black robes, facing the Catedral de la Almudena."

These apparitions were becoming all too real and all too frequent. He looked at the girl in his car's mirror, and it felt as if a heavy black cloud were descending over him. He whispered to the girl.

"November eleventh?"

She put the palms of her hands together as if she was praying.

"Sí, in 1962."

Then, as the vision of the girl started to fade, she raised her head, looked directly into his eyes, and pleaded with him, *"Please help us. Please, help us all, Señor Palmer."*

Nick sat in his car for another fifteen minutes. He was trying to understand why this was happening to him. Maybe, as Gabriela had suggested, he needed a break, or perhaps it was his mother's hand reaching out from beyond the grave to connect him to the souls of these poor girls.

ψ

When he got to his desk, he went online to see if he could validate any of the stories the girls had told him. He searched "Margaux Deneuve, 1942" and "Juanita Diaz and Adriana Diaz, 1962." Several names came up, but none matched any of the girls' descriptions. Gabriela rolled her chair over to where he was siting and looked over his shoulder. Her soft hair brushed against his cheek.

"What are you up to, partner?"

"Nothing much. Just seeing if I can get any confirmation on the girls I'm seeing in mirrors."

As the beautiful detective leaned in closer, Nick noticed the intoxicating scent of her perfume and felt her soft breath as she looked at his screen.

"Let's see here, 1942… 1962… Computers, as we know them, weren't even invented yet."

"Yeah, that'll be a big problem."

"Did it happen again?"

"Yeah, just this morning in my car's rearview mirror."

Nick could see a look of concern in Gabi's eyes. She whispered into his ear so no one else could hear her. "Like I said, Nick, you need to take some time off. You've got to forget about this crazy stuff. Got to stop chasing ghosts." Nick knew what he was going through wasn't normal. His mind was in overdrive and uncharacteristically jumbled. Maybe Gabriela could see it, because she changed the subject. "Say, how's the house sale going?"

Nick snapped out of his trance. "Good, I guess. Larry's coming over this evening with an offer—full asking price."

Gabriela reached over and squeezed his hand. "That's great news, Nick. One problem solved."

"Yeah, but another one's brewing. Now I've got to find a new place to call home."

Gabriela did another quick scan of the room and whispered in his ear. "I think there's a couple of apartments available in my building. I'd be happy to check them out for you."

Jesus, he thought, *this could either be the best thing or the worst thing that could ever happen.* He smiled up at her, and hoping to sound more convincing than he felt, he said, "Thanks, Gabi, that'd be great."

Gabriela went back to her desk, and they both got down to the often monotonous, mostly onerous, task of everyday paperwork.

Yesterday's domestic homicide was in the books, the accused was in a cell, and Nick was hoping, without much optimism, that when the time came, he wouldn't have to appear in court.

He spent the afternoon going through some of his unsolved case files, but his mind kept returning to the Susan Roberts case, and the haunting images of the anguished girls he kept seeing in his mirrors.

He thought of his own daughter and the heart-wrenching guilt he felt about letting her and her mother down. Lucy was also born on November 11, and even though she was a long way from being nineteen, he imagined her face in the mirror and almost cried. He drove the horrific thought from his mind and checked out at five o'clock.

Gabriela waved and wished him good luck. He wasn't sure if she meant for the sale of his house or for his life in general.

ψ

Nick got home at six and spent the next hour thinking about, and trying to rationalize, why he seemed to be the only one seeing the apparitions. He didn't understand why these long-dead women felt he could help them. Perhaps he'd really inherited some of his mom's curious "gifts," or as Gabriela suggested, maybe he just needed a break. His thoughts were scattered and unsettling.

I'm just a fucking Chicago cop who's never been to France, or Italy, or Spain, and I haven't the slightest idea how I would help them… even if I could.

Just after seven, Larry Baxter appeared at the front door. He was carrying a thin blue folder that Nick rightfully assumed was the Offer to Purchase for his family home. They sat at the kitchen table—the very same table where he, Isabela, and Lucy had shared so many breakfasts, dinners, and happy times. All his plans felt like they'd been crushed into nothingness by the daunting realization that his previous life was now over. The agent flipped open the file.

"So, I guess this is it, then?"

Larry smiled and slid the papers across the table. Paper-clipped to the top page of the agreements was a certified check covering the deposit.

"You'll be pleased to know it's a clean deal. No conditions. No haggling."

Everything seemed in order, and Nick, somewhat reluctantly, signed the offer and pushed the file back to the agent.

"As you can see, the new owners need a fast closing. They're moving here from Pittsburgh, and the husband starts his new job in a couple of weeks. Does that give you enough time to move your stuff out?"

"It is what it is, Larry. I'll manage."

Nick shook the agent's hand and showed him out. That was it—a lifetime of memories, some bad, most he thought not too bad, all gone with a signature on a piece of paper. He pulled a beer from the fridge, sat down, and turned on the television, wondering what the next chapter in his life would bring.

ψ

At ten thirty, he went to bed. He was hoping for a good night's sleep, but instead, laid awake for hours. At a quarter past four, he got up and looked out to the backyard where Lucy's swing set sat forlornly swaying in the cold breeze. His loneliness hit him like a punch to the gut.

He went into the bathroom and looked in the mirror. There was another young woman staring back. She was different from all the others.

"Good morning, Detective Palmer. My name is Aislinn Donovan. I was born on November 11 1932 and was murdered on my birthday in 1951."

Nick was mesmerized. The girl was pretty, with freckles covering her face and shoulders. She had extraordinary pale green eyes and a mane of wild red hair so unruly that she had to keep pushing it off her face.

"I was returning home from a lecture at Trinity College in Dublin when I was grabbed from behind."

The story was becoming all too familiar to the weary detective.

"I thought they were going to rape me, but instead they covered my head, bound my arms and legs, and took me to a place that was damp and cold like a basement."

Nick looked straight into the girl's eyes, as if hoping to hear a different story from that of the others. "Then they tied you to a chair and strangled you with a rope."

The girl's face remained expressionless, but he could see the fear and revulsion in her eyes. *"Yes. The police found my body the next day—kneeling in front of St. Patrick's Cathedral."*

The girl looked at the detective, lowered her eyes, and raised her hands in prayer.

"Please help us. Please help all of us."

Then, just like all the others, the girl's image slowly faded and vanished.

Nick stood there, transfixed and deeply troubled. He knew, deep within his heart, that all these apparitions were somehow connected to the Susan Roberts case. He had to do something; he just didn't know what, and he didn't know how.

CHAPTER FIVE

Nick had no sooner sat down at his desk than Gabriela Martinez strode over.

"Well?"

"Well, what?"

"Don't give me that crap. Did you sell your house or not?"

"Yup, it's sold, and in a couple of weeks, I'll get a nice fat check. Only trouble is, I've got just fourteen days to move out."

She looked around as if she didn't want anyone else in the crowded room to hear her. "Then I've got great news. There's a fantastic one-bedroom apartment in my building, and it's available right now."

Nick's apprehension was written all over his face.

"Come on, if you like the place, it'll save you a ton of time and hassle, and hey, being neighbors could really be fun."

Nick didn't know what kind of fun she had in mind, but he told her he'd stop by later in the day to check out the apartment.

"Why wait until later? We can grab a quick sandwich and see it during lunch break."

Nick didn't tell her about the Irish girl. That could wait until later when he might have some idea about what he was going to do about the apparitions.

The morning passed quickly. Nick was online, trying to track down any information about the girls he'd been seeing. He soon got frustrated. Every entry led to a dead end, and every potential lead soon fizzled out. At a quarter to one, Gabriela marched over to his desk, placed her hands firmly on her hips, and stood there before him as if she meant business.

"Okay, buddy. Let's go see your new home."

"And a sandwich?"

"Yeah, and a sandwich too. My treat."

They took his car and drove to a neat little six-story building in Chicago's Gold Coast neighborhood. The building was clean and well maintained. It had a small gym, and the beach was just a couple of blocks away. Gabriela's apartment was on the fifth floor. His, if he decided to take it, was on the third. They rang for the superintendent, who showed up almost immediately, and gave Nick a quick once-over.

"So, Gabi, this the bum you want as your neighbor?" The man chuckled, his ample girth jiggling up and down with every breath.

"Yeah, Jake, he's pretty respectable, got a good job, and in a couple of weeks, he's going to get a fistful of cash."

"Well, honey, if he's okay with you, he's okay with me. C'mon. I'll show you the apartment."

Gabriela, Nick, and the chubby, balding superintendent took the elevator to the third floor. The hallway was spotlessly clean, as was the apartment. The view, over East Schiller Street, was like many city apartments in that it looked towards a similar building right across the street.

Nick liked the place, and it solved the immediate problem of where he was going to live. He turned to the oddly mismatched couple standing behind him.

"Looks great. I'll take it."

Gabriela looked pleased. Nick wrote a check for the deposit and the first months rent, and told Jake he'd be moving into the apartment in a couple of weeks.

On the way back to the station, they stopped at a deli on North Wells Street and picked up two corned-beef sandwiches and coffees to go. He was still wondering about two things: Was it a good idea to move into the same building as his partner? And would the apparitions he'd been seeing follow him to his new home?

It was now December 3. He still needed to get Christmas gifts for Lucy and call Isabela to tell her he'd sold the house.

ψ

"What are you doing at Nick's computer?"

"Nothing, Jack. He must have left it on. Just shutting it down for him."

The man grunted and moved on.

Detective Marcos Ruiz pulled on his topcoat, trudged through the snow to the privacy of his car, and placed a call to a man in New York.

"Tell me."

"I hacked in and checked his search history."

"And?"

"Just someone called Margaux Deneuve, 1942, and another named Sophia D'Angelo, 1972. And something else: flight information to Paris, France. Then I had to leave before anyone got suspicious. Do you think he's planning a vacation or something?"

"You've done well, my son."

Before Ruiz could respond, the man had hung up.

Hector Rodriguez opened his wall safe and removed an ancient leather ledger. He carefully turned the pages until he reached one headed "1942, Paris," then flipped forward and looked at the page headed "1972, Rome." He felt the blood coursing through the veins in his forehead.

Then he picked up his cell and called a man in Paris—a man who would obey his every command.

ψ

Nick sat at his kitchen table, in the now-sold house, with a pen and paper in front of him. He was wondering what gifts he could get for his seven-year-old daughter.

He decided to go to Walmart, hoping some nice clerk in the toy department would be able to help him. Then he showered, changed into his sweats, and placed a call to California. Isabela answered, but she sounded cold, vaguely formal, and generally indifferent to hearing from him.

"Hi, it's me. How're you guys doing?"

"Pretty good. It's a lot warmer than Chicago, and Lucy seems to like it here."

"I miss you guys."

"Yeah, I know, but it's over, Nick. It's finally over."

For once, she didn't berate him about his long hours and his indifference to her needs.

"I sold the house, full asking price. I'll send your share when it closes."

"Thanks, Nick. I know it's been hard. It's been hard for Lucy too."

"Yeah."

Isabela paused as if she didn't know how to say what she had to say next. "Nick, I've filed for divorce. You'll be getting the papers anytime now."

"I guess that's it then."

"Yeah, I guess it is. Good luck, Nick."

He was about to hang up but then added, "Oh, I'm going to send some Christmas gifts for Lucy."

"She'll like that, Nick. Goodbye."

The line went dead.

No "I miss you."

No "Merry Christmas."

No nothing.

Even though he knew this was how it was going to be, Nick had never felt so alone.

He watched the late show on television and went to bed, thinking about the money he'd be getting in a couple of weeks: $470,000. Cash. He'd managed to pay off the mortgage several years back, so even after he'd sent Isabela her half, he'd still be left with more money than he could earn in a couple of years on the force.

A nice nest egg to start my new life with, he thought, before falling asleep.

CHAPTER SIX

The following morning, Nick half expected to see another apparition in his bathroom mirror. It didn't happen, and he wasn't sure if he was relieved or disappointed. Perhaps they knew it was his day off and wanted to give him a break. He showered, dressed, and turned back to check the mirror—still nothing.

It was a typically cold December day in Chicago. Snow was forecast, and the powerful winter winds off Lake Michigan felt like daggers of ice ripping through his topcoat and plunging into the very core of his body. He coaxed his car to life and drove through the billowing haze of exhaust fumes to Walmart at the Darien Towne Center.

The store was a madhouse of frantic people, all of them shoving and shopping for all things Christmas—artificial trees, lights, decorations, electronics, food, and toys. Nick elbowed his way through the crowds to the toy department. The area was in shambles. Crazed mothers and fathers were pushing and grabbing at everything that looked even reasonably appropriate for their little loved ones.

Jesus, I should have done this weeks ago, Nick thought as he jostled his way through the shopping mayhem.

Out of the corner of his eye, he spotted a young woman in a blue Walmart vest. She was obviously trying to hide and almost ran away when she noticed Nick approaching her.

"Miss, I really need your help. I'm looking for something special for my daughter. She's seven and pretty hard to impress."

The girl looked at him with the deer-caught-in-the-headlights stare that seemed to signal real terror.

She stammered, "W-what does she like?"

"Not too sure; to tell the truth, I haven't seen her in a while."

The girl and Nick shoved their way through the crowds. She ignored the frenzied requests of other shoppers and focused her full attention on Nick. They struggled from aisle to aisle, grabbing stuff from almost-empty shelves. Finally, he said thank you to the harried girl and pulled up to the long cash line with a load of puzzles, video games, clothes, wrapping paper, and ribbons.

He drove home, narrowly missing cars, trucks, and pedestrians caught up in the insanity of the holidays. He dumped the load of parcels on his kitchen table and sat down to survey the jumble of presents. Just then, there was a knock on his door. He got up to answer it and was handed a large envelope that he needed to sign for, which he did, knowing full well it contained the divorce papers from Isabela. He dropped it unceremoniously on the table beside the gifts and then sat back. Just then his cell phone rang, and when he answered, he heard the familiar voice of Gabriela Martinez.

"Hi, partner. What're you doing?"

He gave her the full rundown of his Christmas shopping ordeal at Walmart.

"Now I've got to figure out how to wrap all this stuff and get it to California before the holidays."

"Hold on, partner. You obviously need a woman's touch. Sit tight. I'm on my way." Then, as an afterthought, she added, "If that's okay with you?"

"Yeah, thanks. That would be great. I'd really appreciate the help."

He hung up, wondering what the hell he was getting himself into, and decided to check out the divorce papers while he waited for Gabriela to arrive.

Twenty-five minutes later, Gabriela knocked on his door. She shed her winter coat and boots, came into his kitchen, and surveyed the large pile of Walmart bags.

"Do you think perhaps you might have overdone it a little?" She smiled and winked at him.

"Hey, I'm kind of new at this. Isabela always did this stuff."

He immediately regretted bringing up his soon-to-be ex-wife's name, but Gabriela didn't seem to notice, and if she did, she hid it well. For the next hour or so, she wrapped gifts while he wrote out the gift cards. While they worked, he told her about his strained conversation with Isabela and what he'd learned from the papers he'd just gone through.

"She's filed for divorce and says that her half of the money from the sale of the house is enough for her. She doesn't want any alimony or child support, and best of all, she's agreed that I can visit Lucy anytime I want."

Gabriela felt understandably uncomfortable talking about Nick's arrangement with his wife and quickly changed the subject.

"Seeing any more girls in the mirror?"

"Not today, thank God. They seem to be leaving me alone for now."

The conversation turned next to their plans for the upcoming holidays.

Gabriela smiled. "I'll be going to Houston for a few days to spend Christmas with my family. You?"

Nick sounded, and felt, abandoned and forlorn. "No real plans. I think I'll just hang around here, get settled into the apartment, maybe take on a couple of extra shifts. Give some of the guys at the station time off to spend with their families."

She looked at him as if he were a sad little boy, then replied in a sympathetic tone. "That sounds lovely… and lonely too." Changing the subject once more, she said, "I'm starving. Is there any place around here where we can get a pizza?"

The talk of food made him realize he was hungry too. His mood quickly changed. He picked up his phone and speed-dialed Dino's

Pizza, then turned to Gabriela. "What toppings do you want?"

"Pepperoni and cheese is good for me."

He gave the man the order, then hung up.

"Be about forty-five minutes. Do you want another beer?"

ψ

The pizza arrived, and while he was pulling out the plates and napkins, she rescued a couple more beers from the fridge.

It was ten o'clock when they finished eating and wrapping presents. Gabriela looked over at him.

"Do you mind if I crash here for the night? I think I've had one too many beers to be driving."

He shot her a look that said he was unsure if that would be a good idea.

"It's okay. I'll sleep in Lucy's room… if that's okay with you?"

He shrugged his shoulders.

At ten thirty they said goodnight and went to their respective bedrooms.

Thirty minutes later, he felt her slide into the bed beside him. She pushed her naked body against his back, reached over him, and murmured, "Feels like you were expecting me."

CHAPTER SEVEN

Gabriela left the house before dawn. Neither of them wanted to be called out and talked about on the Clarendon Hills grapevine, especially if the gossip managed to reach California. Nick laid in bed for a while, then got up and wandered into Lucy's room. Nothing had been touched, the bed wasn't even wrinkled. He went into the bathroom, looked in the mirror, and saw his face morph into yet another soulful young woman. Anguish seemed to seep from every pore on her beautiful face.

"I'm here, like the others, to ask for your help."

By now, Nick knew her story so well that he could repeat it almost verbatim.

"You're nineteen, and your birthday is November eleventh."

The girl looked directly at him and gently nodded.

"I lived in Mexico City and attended Simón Bolívar University. I was meeting friends for drinks in Centro, and when I left the bar, I was grabbed from behind."

"I think I know the rest of your story except your name, the year of your murder, and where they found your body."

The girl lowered her eyes and spoke in a voice that was barely above a whisper.

"My name is Juliana Cortez, the year was 1963, and they found me kneeling, as if I were praying, in front of the Catedral Metropolitana.

30

I was hidden behind the stone wall and covered with a thick black robe. We have to make the people responsible for our murders pay for what they've done."

Her face contorted, and tears of utter anguish began pouring down her beautiful cheeks. *"My parents are still mourning. They pray every night that I've found peace with our lord."* Slowly her heartbroken expression turned into one of steely resolve. *"You have to help us, Señor Palmer. You have to help us all."*

The image faded, and Nick was left looking at his own troubled countenance. Then and there, he reached a decision he knew he might later regret.

ψ

Nick had never traveled outside the borders of the United States. To do so, he would require a passport, and just as importantly, a leave of absence from the police department. Because of the sale of his and Isabela's home, he would soon have as much cash as he needed to do what he wanted to do—what he knew he had to do.

He drove to the station. Gabriela was already at her desk and gave no indication of their previous night's activities. He, on the other hand, couldn't stop thinking about their evening together. It was one of the few times in his life he'd made love to someone who wasn't his wife, and even though his divorce was imminent, he felt somehow guilty.

At lunch, he drove to the passport office on North Stetson and picked up an application form, then had his mug shot taken at a variety store on his way back to work. He left both items in the glove compartment of his car.

He had just settled at his desk when Gabriela strolled up, leaned over his shoulder, and whispered in his ear. "Hey, partner, want to come over to my place for dinner tonight? I'm famous for my Mexican cuisine."

He looked up at her. "Is seven, okay?"

She gently touched his shoulder and gave him the thumbs up.

Their afternoon turned into a proverbial shit-show. An attempted robbery at a gas station had resulted in the murder of the lone atten- dant. Nick checked out a cruiser, and they were soon racing through the snowy, winter streets of Chicago with siren blasting. They were the first to arrive at the gas station and quickly cordoned off the crime scene. Gabriela went behind the counter to check on the victim. His hand still held the gun he hadn't had a chance to use on his assailant.

The store was a mess, but they managed to isolate half a dozen shell casings from among the litter of candy bars, cigarette packages, and broken glass scattered around on the well-worn floor.

Other officers and an ambulance had arrived, so Nick and Gabriela went into the crowd of onlookers to see if there were any witnesses.

One man came forward. He was tall, white, and well dressed in a black quilted winter coat. He looked to be in his early sixties, and his face was lined with the deep wrinkles of a man who'd done more than his share of worrying. He was accompanied by a small black dog who barked incessantly at the two officers. They took down the man's name and contact details and listened to his account of the crime.

"All I saw was a white guy, kind of tough-looking kid in his twen- ties, I think." The man tried, unsuccessfully, to quiet his excited dog. "He was wearing a black overcoat with a gray hoodie, and he ran south, towards the Loop."

"Do you think you could recognize him if we showed you some photos?"

The man stared, perhaps a little too intently, at the badge on Gabriela's breast pocket. "Yes, I'd recognize the no-good bum anywhere."

He bent down, once again, to try and stop his dog from barking.

Gabriela made an appointment for him to drop by the station to look at mug shots on her computer. She and Nick spent the balance of the afternoon at the scene, working with their colleagues from forensics. They secured video footage from the gas station's security camera, which showed a man who fit the witness's description fleeing the murder scene. Finally, they said goodbye to the officers still working at the scene and returned to the station.

ψ

At seven that evening, Nick showed up at the front door of Gabriela's apartment building. He ran into the superintendent on his way up to the fifth floor. The man smiled and winked at him. Nick ignored it and continued, finally arriving at Gabriela's door and knocking.

"C'mon in! It's open! I'm in the kitchen!"

The aroma of Mexican spices made his mouth water.

"Hope you like white bean soup and chicken enchiladas?"

Nick couldn't remember the last time he'd a had hot, home-cooked meal. Dinner in Clarendon Hills was usually cold by the time he got home. He took a deep breath, dropped a bottle of red wine on the dining-room table, and responded to her question.

"Sounds more than perfect."

Dinner was delicious and the wine surprisingly good. It was something they both desperately needed after a day that had mostly been spent outside in the freezing cold, dealing with the brutal murder of an innocent man.

They chatted about the murder, and then she asked him about Isabela and Lucy, deciding that she wanted a clearer picture of what had gone wrong.

"Nothing much to say really. You know most of the story. I wasn't around much, and she resented it. This job always had its fair share of casualties. I guess this is just another one. Tell me about your family, I bet they're nice, honest, hard-working citizens—just like their daughter."

She rolled her eyes at his oblique compliment, then smiled as she visualized her family.

"My parents immigrated to the States from Mexico City. Dad was an engineer and worked in the airline industry in Houston. Mom was a cook for a wealthy family in River Oaks. They're just regular folks who worked hard, raised a family, and went to church every Sunday."

"A cook? No wonder you're such a marvel in the kitchen."

She shook her head and laughed at his awkward compliment. "If you think all this flattery will get you somewhere, you're probably right."

She leaned over and planted a small kiss on his cheek.

They ended up talking about the gas-station case again, and then about how she'd help him move into the apartment, just a couple of floors below where they were now sitting.

Finally, Gabriela got up from the table, picked up her wine glass, took him by the hand, and led him into her bedroom. Later, as they were lying close together, Nick leaned over and whispered softly in her ear, "I'm going to be taking some time off soon."

She quickly propped herself up on an elbow. "Good. You need it."

"No, really. I'm requesting a six-month leave of absence."

She looked at him, not believing what she was hearing. "Six months?"

"Yeah, I'm going to travel."

She shot him a questioning, almost jealous look. "California?"

"No, Europe, mostly."

Then he told her about the latest apparition in his bathroom mirror.

"This all happened after I left your place?"

"It may sound crazy, but my gut is telling me I should look into why these girls keep appearing and asking me to help them."

She laid back down, and he felt her snuggle closer to him, her hand running down his naked chest. "I can't talk you out of going?"

"There's nothing more I'd like to do than stay here with you, but I've made up my mind. It'll take a while to work out the details, and jump through the hoops at the station, but I've got to go. I've just got to."

"I'll miss you, Nicholas. I'll really miss you."

"I'll miss you too," he whispered.

Nick lay there looking up at the ceiling and listening to the distant hum of traffic on Michigan Avenue. He knew the beautiful woman nestled up against him was also awake, but neither of them wanted to break the silence.

CHAPTER EIGHT

The process of getting a leave of absence from the Chicago Police Department isn't as easy as knocking on the boss's door and saying goodbye. You've got to give forty-five days' notice, have a damn good reason, and fill out innumerable, complicated forms. Nick stepped up to his supervisor's door and tentatively knocked.

Josh Nicholson was a tough, sixty-something, thirty-five-year veteran on the force. He had an unruly mop of nearly white hair, a strong jawline, and a no-nonsense attitude that was just slightly south of intimating. He also had a reputation as a decent human being, and a boss who stood squarely behind all the men and women under his command.

The man listened to Nick's story about Isabela leaving him and taking Lucy with her, about the sale of their family home, and about missing his daughter. Finally, and with great apprehension, he told the man about the apparitions he was seeing.

Nicholson listened intently, leaned back in his chair, and placed his thick muscular arms comfortably behind his head. It was as if nothing Nick had said surprised him. "Have you considered seeing a shrink, Nick? The department has people for this kind of thing, you know."

"No, sir. I think what I need is a break. Time away to get my shit together."

"How much time are you thinking?"

"Six months, sir. If that's okay?"

"Six months? That's going to leave the department pretty short-staffed." The man paused, giving Nick a searching look. Finally, he said, "If you really think you need it, I'll approve it."

Before Nick could thank him, the man put up his hand to stop Nick from saying anything else. "But, Nick, I really would recommend you see the department's shrink."

"Thank you, sir. I'll consider it."

Nick went back to his desk to fill out the necessary paperwork.

The next day, true to his word, Nick's boss approved his Leave of Absence Application and wished him good luck. Nick experienced a bittersweet feeling of relief and remorse. It was like a huge weight had been lifted from his shoulders. It felt great—and then again—it didn't.

After his shift, he went home to start packing. He had barely begun when Gabriela called.

"Hi, big boy. Do you want me to come over and help you pack?"

He was sorely tempted. He loved her company more than anything else in the world, but he declined her offer.

"Not tonight, Gabi. You're just too damn distracting." He chuckled. "But thanks for asking anyway."

She laughed. "Well then, I'll see you tomorrow. Don't get into any trouble without me."

The truth was, there were too many memories he had to pack or dispose of, and he didn't want to share his pain with anyone… especially Gabriela.

Family photographs, memories of his and Isabela's life together, and bits and pieces from when Lucy was a small baby were all carefully boxed for storage. It was a bitingly difficult task, removing the evidence of a life now passed. He tagged furnishings destined for his new apartment and others that were destined for the dump. At midnight, he finished for the day, looked at all the boxes stacked in the living room, and went to bed.

He lay there for hours, wishing Gabriela were beside him, and thinking perhaps she could help soothe his loneliness.

Maybe I really should see a shrink, he thought, before falling into a troubled sleep.

ψ

The next morning, he went into the bathroom and glanced in the mirror. The image of Susan Roberts, the girl murdered in Chicago, was looking at him, and seemed to be reading his mind.

"Thank you, Detective Palmer. You're doing the right thing. The right thing for all of us, and our families too."

The image of the girl slowly faded and vanished.

How in God's name do they know what I'm doing? Or what I'm thinking?

He stood there, unsure and bewildered, looking at his own gaunt, unshaved face.

ψ

Later that morning, he filled out his passport application and was about to add his signature to the form when Gabriela walked up to his desk.

"Rumor has it your application for a leave of absence has been approved. You sure it's Europe and not California?"

He tried his best to act nonchalant. He didn't want her knowing about the inner turmoil he was going through or the second thoughts he was having about leaving Chicago... and her.

He tried to sound as upbeat as possible. "Yup, got to follow up with my girlfriends in the mirror, and I can't do it if I'm sitting around here twiddling my thumbs."

"What you should do is see a shrink. Now, I've got to break in a brand-new partner."

He looked up at her. "Sorry. Can I make it up by taking you for dinner tonight?"

38

"You're on, partner—as long as it's steak, and it's expensive."

She smiled and strode back to her desk.

He picked Gabi up from her apartment at seven-thirty. She looked spectacular in a form-fitting black dress. They drove downtown to Smith & Wollensky. The restaurant's famous waterfront terrace was closed for the winter, but their table still had great river and city views. They both ordered the signature filet, and he selected a bottle of California cabernet sauvignon.

They were seated by an overtly attentive hostess, and Gabriela got right down to what was on her mind. "So, what's this really all about, Nicholas?"

He told her about the seeing Susan Roberts in his mirror and told her, word for word, what the murdered girl had said to him.

"There's something gnawing at my gut. It's telling me I just have to look into the murders of all these girls. I don't know if I'll discover anything, but I've got to go and see what I can find. I have to know what the hell they want from me."

"So, you're really going to Europe?"

"I am, and it seems Paris is as good a place as any to start. I've already sent feelers out to the police there."

She looked at him as if he'd totally lost his mind. "Wow, a real busman's holiday."

"Something like that, I guess."

She wanted to know every detail about his plans, and he told her everything he could.

When he drove her home, he had an uneasy feeling that he might have screwed things up between them and was thankful when she invited him up for coffee. She made their coffee and took both cups into the bedroom.

"So, what do you need? A written invitation?"

He smiled and followed her.

CHAPTER NINE

The forty-five days of pre-leave passed quickly. The house in Clarendon Hills closed on schedule, he deposited the check, and sent half of the proceeds to Isabela with a note asking how she and Lucy were. She replied, several days later, with a terse email.

"Thank you, we're fine."

Nick moved into his new apartment and was spending more and more of his spare time with Gabriela. His passport arrived, and he booked his flight to Paris. As his departure date got closer, his feelings for the beautiful police officer grew even stronger. He hoped she felt the same way he did, but he had his doubts. Sometimes, he was positive they were right for each other, but there were other times when he wasn't quite as sure. He was beginning to have second thoughts about leaving.

On the Thursday morning before his departure, he went into his bathroom and looked into the mirror. The face of Susan Roberts appeared again, looking frail and concerned, like she was on the verge of losing all hope. It was as if she could read his mind.

"Please go. You have to go... for all of us."

The image faded and vanished then, as did his reluctance to leave Chicago and Gabriela Martinez.

ψ

Nick said goodbye to his fellow officers. He relinquished his gun, badge, and other police identification material to Josh Nicholson, who quickly deposited them in his desk drawer.

"See you in six months, Detective Palmer." Then in a voice truly expressing the man's concern, he said, "Good luck, Nick. You know where I am if you need anything."

On the morning of his departure, there was no image of a young girl in his bathroom mirror; it was just him, and a tearful Gabriela looking over his shoulder. He showered, dressed, zipped up his carry-on, and took a cab to O'Hare International Airport for his American Airlines flight to Paris, departing at 1:14 p.m.

Nick settled himself into an economy-class window seat and watched his hometown slowly vanish beneath a canopy of heavy clouds. The dullness of the day matched his mood perfectly.

ψ

Detective Marcos Ruiz placed a call to the man in New York. "He's on his way to Paris."

"I suspected he would be."

"He left this afternoon, at quarter after one, on an American Airlines flight."

"Thank you, my son. You've done well."

Hector Rodriguez hung up, called the man in Paris, gave him a description of Nick and details of his flight, and conveyed terse instructions: "Locate him, and kill him."

He hung up then, knowing full well his orders would be carried out.

ψ

Nick's overnight flight to Paris's Charles de Gaulle Airport did little to relax him. He was served a passable meal of chicken and vegetables, watched a John Wick movie, and slept on and off for most of the trip.

The aircraft landed on schedule at 9:25 the following morning, and the groggy contingent of passengers disembarked into the frantic cacophony of France's busiest airport.

He passed quickly through the formalities of French customs and found a taxi at the arrivals level. Fortunately for Nick, the driver spoke passable English, and after giving the man an address in the Marais, he was on his way to the Airbnb studio apartment he'd booked three weeks earlier. The ride took the better part of an hour and cost Nick what he suspected was an exorbitant sixty euros.

He paid the driver, gave him a small tip, and was left standing in front of a charming five-story building on Rue des Bons Enfants, a tiny street in the heart of Paris. He rang the bell and was greeted by an affable young Englishman dressed in jeans and a well-worn cable-knit sweater that looked three sizes too large for his thin frame. He extended his right hand.

"Hello, I'm Jeremy Wakefield. Welcome to Paris, Mr. Palmer, and welcome to your home for the next few weeks. Glad you made it before I had to leave or you might have been left out on the street."

The man laughed. It was a loud hee-haw kind of laugh that would cause most people to cringe. "I'm off to the Cotswolds to visit Mummy and Daddy for a fortnight or so. Then it's back to the old grind at university." He faked a grimace.

Jeremy took Nick up to see the apartment. It was tiny, charming, and fully equipped. The single room had a beamed ceiling, small kitchen, writing desk, ornate French country-style wardrobe, and a pull-out sofa bed. The bathroom barely had enough room to turn around in but contained a claw-foot tub with a handheld shower.

"This is perfect, Jeremy, exactly what I was looking for."

He paid cash for his two weeks' stay, and watched the harried Englishman vanish down the stairs and into the street, pausing only to yell back over his shoulder at the Chicago cop. "Cheerio, Nicholas! Got to run! The Eurostar to London leaves in an hour." Then as an afterthought, he added, "Have fun in Paris, old boy."

Nick unpacked and settled in. He took a long look at the tub and the contraption Jeremy called a shower and thought about the twists and turns he'd need to do to get cleaned up.

That'll take some getting used to... Oh well, when in Paris.

The shrill sound of his cell phone rang through the tiny apartment.

"Hey, partner, are you safe and sound and on the ground in Paris? Have you got a cute little French pastry hanging on your arm yet? Do you miss me?"

"Yes, no, and yes. I'm here in the tiniest apartment in the world, and I miss you already. How're you doing?"

"Peachy keen. Got me a new hot-shot partner. Crazy kid from the South Side, a one-man army who's out to clean up the world."

"Sounds like a ton of fun."

"Not in my language, it doesn't."

"Let me know how it goes. I miss you."

"You already said that."

"Guess I'm waiting for you to say it too."

"Okay, okay, I miss you. I may even love you a little bit."

Nick was shocked. She'd never used the "L" word before, and he wasn't sure he was ready for it.

"Don't get too mushy; it could be dangerous."

"I live for danger. I'll call tomorrow. Okay?"

He heard a kissing sound on the other end of the line, before she hung up.

Nick was wondering if he'd made the right decision, or if he was heading on a wild goose chase created within his own imagination. Were the apparitions just figments of his fractured mind or were they real? He pushed the thought from his head and went out to explore the neighborhood.

Spring was on the verge of arriving in the French capital. The air was fresh, and the aroma of coffee and cooking reminded him that he was very hungry. He found a cozy bistro not far from his new home and ordered a café au lait and croque monsieur sandwich from the courtly, apron-clad waiter. While he was waiting for his order to arrive, he looked up at one of the restaurant's pitted, hundred-year-old mirrors. A girl's face appeared, a face he hadn't seen before.

"Please help us. Please help the ones that will follow."

The image vanished just seconds before his meal arrived at the table.

"The ones that will follow?" What the hell's that all about?

Nick's mind was reeling. None of this was normal, none of it could possibly be real, but for the sake of his own sanity, he had to see where it would lead him.

CHAPTER TEN

Nick finished his sandwich and walked to Ile de la Cité, the island in the River Seine where Notre-Dame Cathedral is located. He needed to see, for himself, the gruesome crime scene that was now over seventy years old.

He stood and looked up at the great church's stern western facade. The three magnificent gothic doorways were like nothing he'd ever seen before. Hundreds of tourists and sightseers crowded the square in front of the iconic towers, taking photographs and selfies or simply appreciating the beauty of the medieval masterpiece.

"Beautiful, is it not? But with great beauty oftentimes comes great tragedy."

Nick turned and saw an elderly man standing next to him. He guessed the man was in his early eighties. His shock of white hair was barely visible beneath a dark-blue beret, and his tweed jacket, beige chinos, and scuffed faded-red Converse sneakers would not look out of place at one of America's famous Ivy League universities. He spoke English slowly with a gentle French accent, and as he spoke, he pointed towards the venerable building standing before them.

"Our Lady of Paris has seen the best and the worst of humanity. Over the centuries, she's been raped and glorified. She's been systematically stripped of her treasures and borne witness to coronations, riots, ripping down, building up, great love, and heinous crimes."

The old man paused, pulled a bright-red handkerchief from his jacket pocket and wiped away the beginnings of a tear.

"In 1942, my beloved sister was murdered, and her body discovered on the very spot where you're now standing."

Nick was stunned. Could the man standing next to him be related to one of the girls he'd been seeing in his mirrors? *No. Too farfetched. Too crazy.* He looked down and saw a circular stone with a brass inlay showing the points of a compass. A carved inscription read: "POINT ZERO DES ROUTES DE FRANCE."

The man continued. "It is said this spot marks the center of Paris."

Nick turned and looked at the elderly gentleman. He had to ask the question. "And your sister... Was her name Margaux Deneuve?"

The old man twisted around and stared directly up at Nick. There was a startled look in his tear-reddened eyes. "Oui, monsieur. Oui. But how is it you know?"

Nick reached out his hand. "My name is Nicholas Palmer. I'm a police detective from Chicago. I would like to buy you a coffee... and tell you a story."

The old man shook Nick's hand. Then they walked slowly together through the crowds, over the busy Rue de la Cité bridge, and to the Shakespeare and Company Café.

ψ

The café was a recent addition to the world-famous book shop, which in times past had seen the likes of Ernest Hemingway, F. Scott Fitzgerald, and their coterie of literary and artistic friends, all of whom had frequented the well-stocked—some would say overstocked—little shop. The café might be a modern addition, but it still maintained much of the charming historic feel of the original. The two men settled themselves at a small table and ordered their drinks.

Nick learned that his elderly companion was a retired professor of anthropology at the Ecole du Louvre. He lived not far from where they were sitting, in an apartment overlooking the Seine on Ile Saint-Louis, a charming little island at the center of the famous river.

"The same apartment where your sister lived?" Nick asked, and then reproached himself for sounding too much like a detective.

"Oui, Monsieur Palmer. It was, and still is, our family home." The professor was staring at Nick with a quizzical look on his face, as if he were about to pose a difficult question to one of his students. "How is it, Monsieur Palmer, that you were standing in front of Notre-Dame today?"

Nick quickly countered. "And how is it, Monsieur Deneuve, that you were there too?"

Both men smiled as they enjoyed the repartee.

"Please call me Nick, or Nicholas, if you prefer."

"And you must call me Henri. Now you promised me a story."

Nick told his new friend about the murdered girl in Chicago, and the similarities between her death and the death of Henri's sister.

"And how would you know Nicholas? Margaux was murdered many, many years ago here in Paris. How do you know so much about her death, in a different time, in a different city, and on a totally different continent?"

Nick was reluctant to tell the elderly professor about the girl's faces he'd been seeing in his mirrors, but then he thought, *I've got nothing to lose, in for a dime, in for a dollar, as they say.*

"Henri, you're going to think I'm crazy, but I promised you a story... so here it is."

He told the old professor the whole thing, from the puzzle of the Susan Roberts case in Chicago, to the images of young women he'd been seeing in various mirrors, to his decision to follow up on their murders, to his arrival in Paris.

The old man listened intently, occasionally nodding, and then spoke. "Now, Nicholas, I have a story for you. A week ago, I had a dream about Margaux. In my dream, she asked me to go to Point Zero, in front of Notre-Dame, and look for an American." The man pointed towards Nick. "'And when you find him,' she said, 'tell him my story.'"

The elderly professor took a long sip of his coffee and lowered his head as if considering what to say next.

"I ignored the whole thing, but the same dream kept repeating itself, night after night, so today I went, and found you there. Now you tell me, Nicholas, who's the crazy one?"

They ordered more coffee, and Henri told Nick about his murdered sister, and about the fun they'd had growing up together in the French capital. He told Nick about their mother and father, about the family's crazy bohemian lifestyle, about dreams they'd shared, and about her untimely death. By the end of his tale, the old man was sobbing, and Nick handed him a handkerchief.

"Merci, Nicholas, merci."

The man looked up, and Nick saw his countenance change. Henri, the gentle professor, now had an expression of a man determined to help in his investigation, and Nick knew it would be near to impossible to talk him out of it.

"One more thing, Nicholas. My twin sister, Madeline, lives in Provins. It's a little town about two hours southeast of the city. She still has the items given to our parents by the gendarmes after Margaux's death, and after their investigation came to its conclusion. Perhaps something she has there might help you."

The two men exchanged their contact information, and Henri also gave Nick the phone number and address of his sister in Provins. Nick paid for the coffees, and the two men shook hands.

"Bonne chance. Good luck, my American friend."

The Chicago detective watched the old man walk slowly away until he turned the corner of one of the city's weathered stone buildings.

Nick turned and began walking down Rue Saint-Jacques in the general direction of his apartment. He had almost reached Boulevard Saint-Germain when he heard a woman scream. *"Look out, Monsieur Palmer! Look out!"*

He turned quickly and saw a black Mercedes, with blacked-out windows, swerve up onto the sidewalk behind him. He leaped out of the car's path and landed in a heap against the stone wall of a building. The car bumped back over the curb then sped off along the busy one-way street.

A small crowd had gathered, and a man helped Nick to his feet. He looked around, frantically searching for the woman who'd warned him.

"Who yelled? Who saved my life?"

The crowd of onlookers looked puzzled. Then a smartly dressed businessman, with a concerned look on his face, said in English. "Pardon, monsieur ... Are you okay?"

"I'm fine, just fine. I just want to thank the woman who yelled for me to look out."

The man looked towards the crowd, asked a question in French, then turned back to Nick and shrugged his shoulders in the off-handed way only a Frenchman could affect. "Sorry, monsieur, nobody heard anything like a warning. Shock does funny things. Can I call an ambulance for you?"

Nick assured the man he was fine, then pushed his way through the crowd of gawkers and onlookers and slowly made his way back to the tiny apartment on Rue des Bons Enfants. He'd suffered a few minor scratches from hitting the wall, so he went into the bathroom to clean them.

Margaux's Deneuve's concerned face appeared in the mirror. *"Be careful, Monsieur Palmer. Be very careful. Now they know."*

He lost his temper and screamed at the image in his mirror. "Who are they?! What the hell do they know?!"

Then he lowered his head into his hands, and the girl's image faded and disappeared. He was more confused than he could ever remember being, but deep within his heart, he knew he'd find the answers to both questions soon enough.

CHAPTER ELEVEN

Provins was pretty, postcard pretty. The medieval town where Henri Deneuve's sister lived was right out of storybook France, and now, in the early spring, every window box on every charming little weather-timbered house was bursting with colorful blooms—mostly roses, for which the town was famous.

When Nick's Uber driver dropped him at the address the professor had given him, he knocked, and the door was opened by an attractive older woman. She was slim, immaculately dressed, and had silver gray hair pulled back into a tight bun. Nick mustered his best French. "Bonne matinée, Madame Deneuve."

The elegant woman chuckled.

"And good afternoon to you also, Detective Palmer. My brother called earlier today and told me to expect you. Oh, by the way, Deneuve was my family name. Boucher is my married name. Won't you please come in?"

Her house on Place Saint-Quiriace in the old town was beautiful, centuries old, with flower boxes on each windowsill. It reminded him of the old-fashioned Christmas cards his grandmother used to send. Inside the house was equally charming and cozy. It had rough plastered walls and heavily beamed ceilings. Ancient Oriental carpets covered most of the worn oak floors, and the furnishings had the warm patina of age.

They sat opposite each other on sofas in the living room, a small cardboard box on an antique table between them. She lifted the box and silently passed it over to him. Her face revealed almost a century of grief.

"This, Detective Palmer, is all that remains of my beautiful sister. After so many years, the police finally turned everything over to the family."

Nick carefully lifted the lid and looked inside. There wasn't much to see, just a pair of shoes, some underwear, and a length of rope with faded colors. The woman winced when she saw the rope. It was obviously the murder weapon. Nick picked it up and examined it more closely. It had the remains of a thin golden thread woven into its coils. He looked back at the elderly woman. "Is this all there is?"

"Oui, monsieur. That is all there is."

Nick could tell the woman was desperately trying to hold back a flood of tears. He picked up the strangely colored rope.

"Would you mind if I borrowed this? I promise I'll return it."

The woman shook her head. "Keep it, monsieur, I no longer want that dreadful thing in my house."

ψ

The voice on the other end of the line was deep and raspy. It sounded like it had originated in the deepest recesses of hell.

"Is the detective dead?"

The man in Paris, who'd placed the call, was rightfully terrified. He knew all about the power and reach of the person he was speaking to.

"No, Holiness. He leaped out of the way of my car."

There was a long pause then... amplifying the man's terror even more.

"We do not tolerate failure, Brother Diego."

The caller wanted nothing more desperately than an end to the conversation.

"It was as if he'd been warned, Holiness—"

"Silence!"

The word seemed to shake the ground on which Brother Diego stood.

"You have just one more chance to redeem yourself, Brother Diego. Next time, do not fail me."

The man hung up, leaving the would-be executioner shaking with fear. This was a nightmare, a terror, from which he was anxious to wake.

ψ

When Nick returned to Paris, he took a closer look at the length of rope that had strangled Margaux Deneuve. During his career, he'd seen numerous murder weapons, but this one was particularly strange. He picked up his cell and called the Parisian police officer he'd reached out to before leaving Chicago. The man picked up the phone on the second ring.

"Bonjour, Lieutenant Alain Moreau parlant."

"Bonjour, Lieutenant Moreau, it's Nicholas Palmer from Chicago. We spoke earlier about a case I'm working on." "Ah oui, tu es á Paris—désolé. I will speak English. Now, what is it I can do for you, Detective Palmer? And please call me Alain."

The Chicago detective chose his words carefully.

"I have a murder weapon from 1942 Paris that I believe is connected to a case I'm working on at home. I don't want to insult or criticize your organization, but I have to believe that, in those days, the police had far more pressing issues than to fully investigate the murder of one young woman."

"I am afraid you're very right, my American friend. Back then, Paris—and indeed the whole of France—was under the thumb of the Nazis. One murder, among many, I believe could have possibly been under-investigated, and of course, they didn't have the technology and expertise we have at our disposal today."

"Alain, I realize this is a bit unusual, but is there anyone there who can give me a forensic workup on the weapon?"

"Certainly. I will call a colleague at the SDPTS; that's our subdirectory for forensics and crime-scene investigation. Let me call you back after I speak to her."

The French police officer hung up, leaving Nick holding the length of rope and wondering about its history.

His cell rang. *Wow, that was fast*, he thought.

It wasn't Alain Moreau. Instead, it was a welcome voice from Chicago.

"Hi, handsome. How's gay Paree? Miss me yet?"

"Let's just say I haven't found anyone to replace you. How're things going back home?"

If a pout could be heard, her response perfectly captured the emotion. "It's okay, just not the same without you."

"Same here, but the good news is that some of the pieces seem to be coming together. Strange coincidences rather than good detective work, though."

"Tell me."

"Not now. Say, why don't you come over for dinner?"

"Won't you ever stop being a smart-ass?"

The sound of a pout returned to her sultry voice.

Suddenly, he had a strange feeling he should end the call. It was an uneasiness in the pit of his gut that puzzled him. "Hey, Gabi, I've got to hang up, call you tomorrow."

Nick hung around his tiny apartment for an hour or so, pacing impatiently, slightly annoyed that he still hadn't heard back from his friend at the French police. When his cell phone rang, he answered it quickly.

"Hello, Alain?"

"Non, Monsieur Palmer, it is Henri Deneuve. We met at Notre-Dame."

"Yes, I remember. Please accept my apologies for not calling to thank you for arranging the meeting with your sister. What can I do for you, Professor?"

The elderly man spoke hesitatingly, as if he were embarrassed to reveal what he'd called about, obviously choosing his words very carefully.

"In my dream, Margaux told me I could help you. How, I do not know, but I am willing to offer my services whenever and wherever you may require them."

"Thank you for your very kind offer, Henri. I will definitely keep it in mind."

Saying goodbye, he hung up, wondering what other bizarre happenings he'd encounter before this was all over. His cell rang again. This time it was Alain Moreau.

"Bonjour, Monsieur Palmer. I have spoken to my colleague at the Ministry of the Interior. If you meet me at my office tomorrow morning, we'll go together to their offices at Place Beauvau. I will introduce you, and she will do everything she can to assist you."

Nick was elated. The case was moving slower than he wanted but much faster than he'd expected. He thanked the French policeman, hung up, and went into his bathroom to clean up before heading out for dinner. Margaux Deneuve's face appeared in the mirror. *"Merci, Monsieur Palmer, merci."*

Her image faded, and he took a few deep breaths, trying to calm back down. Although he'd seen these manifestations before, it still startled the hell out of him.

CHAPTER TWELVE

Brother Diego slept in the catacombs of Paris, a series of tunnels from the late 1770s that run beneath the streets of the city and hold the mortal remains of over six million people. Brother Diego felt more at ease among the dead than he did among the living and paid for this privilege by handing the security guard a handsome daily bribe. He spent the better part of the night, and most of the following day, cloistered in one of the prohibited branches of the vast network of tunnels. He slept when he could and prayed often.

Brother Diego was a viajero or traveler, one of a select group of followers of a certain Order, both men and women, chosen to scour the world for suitable sacrificial candidates. He didn't consider himself a killer, but when ordered to do so by El Cardenal, he had no choice but to acquiesce. The position he now found himself in was troubling. He was scared, not only of being arrested by the police but also of what the man he called "Holiness" was capable of.

His most treasured possession was carried in a worn velvet bag. That night he lit a candle, which released a sweet, earthy aroma into the small, dank, underground chamber he called home.

He went down on his knees and felt the rough stones of the floor dig into his flesh; then he pulled a length of brightly colored rope from the bag. He draped the rope around his neck, scarf-like, and began to chant in a strange, almost indecipherable jumble of Spanish and Nahuatl the ancient language of Mesoamerica.

ψ

The following morning, Nick and Lieutenant Alain Moreau, his new friend from the Paris police department, arrived at the front gates of the ministry.

Alain was a rotund, jolly-faced man who obviously loved the endless buffet of gourmet delights found on almost every street corner of the French city. He wasn't at all like Nick, but the Chicagoan took an immediate liking to his affable colleague, with whom he'd shared details of the Susan Roberts case.

They were joined, within minutes, by an attractive and officious young woman who introduced herself as Mademoiselle Eloise Pilon, assistante du directeur.

Mademoiselle Pilon was in her late twenties. She was wearing a dark-blue suit and a red-and-white striped shirt.

Very patriotic, Nick thought.

She spoke first, in perfect English with a sexy French inflection.

"Please follow me, gentlemen. I have reserved a boardroom where we can discuss your situation without interruption."

The policemen followed, passing the cordon of uniformed militia. They walked up two flights of an elaborately carved staircase and entered a large room dominated by a massive, ornately carved wooden table. They sat down, Mademoiselle Pilon at the end of the table with the two men flanking her.

"Now, gentlemen, how can I be of assistance?"

Nick produced the length of faded rope Madeline Boucher had given him and without mentioning the apparitions he'd been seeing, told the assistante du directeur about the unsolved 1942 murder of Margaux Deneuve.

"I acquired this piece of evidence, which I believe to be the murder weapon, from the victim's sister. I think it could be relevant to a similar case I'm working on in Chicago."

The assistante du directeur looked skeptical. Nick continued.

"I'm particularly interested in the colors of the rope. What do they represent? What's their origin? What kind of material is it made of? All things, I know, that can be determined with modern forensic technology."

He paused and looked at the woman. "Do you think you'll be able to help me?"

The woman picked up the length of rope and slowly turned it around in her fingers. "Oui, Monsieur Palmer. I do believe we can." There was a slight touch of French arrogance in her voice. "If you allow us two or three days, I will contact you with our report."

She looked at the colored coil of rope in her hands. "I will, of course, have to keep this."

Nick and his friend from the Paris police stood, shook the woman's hand, and she accompanied them back to the front gate of the ministry.

"Bonne journée, messieurs."

As she walked back towards the building, both men watched her departure with uncensored admiration.

Nick looked at his new friend and smiled. "I think she likes you, Alain."

"Non, mon ami, it is you she has eyes for."

They laughed, shook hands, and went their separate ways.

Nick now had several days with nothing to do except enjoy the sights and sounds of the beautiful French city. He decided to call Henri Deneuve and invite the elderly scholar for lunch. He pulled out his cell and dialed the number.

"Bonjour, Henri Deneuve en train de parler."

"Hello, Henri, it's Nick Palmer. I was wondering if you would have time to join me for lunch? I'd like to bring you up to date on what's been happening."

The old man switched to English. "Why yes, Nicholas. I would be delighted to."

They arranged to meet at twelve thirty the following day at a place suggested by the professor.

ψ

The ancient wood-paneled bistro the professor had recommended was small and charming. The interior and adjacent sidewalk were crowded with small round tables and wicker chairs. All the chairs were filled with chattering patrons. The servers, who scurried back and forth between the kitchen and the tables, were traditionally dressed, with white shirts, black bow ties, and long white aprons, and the menu offered a long list of French delicacies.

The two men sat opposite each other at a window table close to the front door. Neither noticed the small, pale-looking man outside, wearing a long gray overcoat and staring intently at them.

"Get down, monsieur! Get down now!"

It was Margaux Deneuve's voice, loud, urgent, and frantic.

Nick dove across the table and pushed the startled professor to the ground just seconds before a hail of bullets from a semiautomatic weapon completely obliterated the front of the small restaurant.

Screams and cries for help filled the street. There were bodies oozing blood and tables and chairs scattered everywhere. Nick shook his head and looked around. Their waiter was lying flat on his back with shards of shattered window glass protruding from his face and chest. Blood from fallen and dead victims spread across the ground like a crimson carpet. The lucky ones were dazed, wandering trance-like around the devastation. An overwhelming sense of guilt and anguish swept through his body. *It's me they're after. Why all this? Why kill all these innocent people? Why was I warned?* Nick knew the answers wouldn't come easily, but the assault on innocent people strengthened his resolve to inflict revenge on those responsible for the attack and find retribution for all the murdered girls. He looked around frantically for the professor and found the elderly man huddled under a table with a young woman who had been sitting next to them when the brutal attack occurred. When it was clear that the assault was over, Nick helped the trembling professor to his feet and brushed the debris off his jacket.

"Are you okay, Henri? Are you okay?"

The older man looked around at the devastation that surrounded them. "Oui, Nicholas, I'm fine. Qu'est-il arrive? What happened?"

"She warned me, Henri. Margaux warned me. Didn't you hear her?"

The professor looked at him quizzically.

"Your sister. She shouted out just before the attack."

This was the second time his life had been saved by the girl in the mirror. It was as if she'd become his guardian angel. Nick thought about his mother and wondered if her strange beliefs had somehow rubbed off on him.

As he led his old friend away from the smoldering scene of devastation, the sound of approaching sirens filled the air. He knew very well that he should stay and give a statement to the police but trying to explain the warning from Margaux would be more than complicated. They would think he was crazy, just like he would if the roles were reversed.

ψ

"You've failed me again, Brother Diego."

The frightened man was cowering against a wall in the far reaches of the catacombs. The reception on his cell was garbled, but there was no uncertainty as to whose voice was on the other end of the line.

The would-be assassin was shaking uncontrollably. The sweat on his hands made it almost impossible for him to hold onto the cell.

"I tried, Holiness, I tried, but he dove to the ground the instant before I fired."

"Failure is failure, Brother Diego. No excuses. No pardons. No mercy."

Then there was an ominous click, and the cell went silent.

The admonished viajero crouched down, considering his fate, the harsh reality of condemnation from El Cardenal sending more shivers through his already trembling body.

He lit a candle, knelt, and prayed, then removed his precious length of rope from its velvet bag and tied one end to an overhead beam. He made a noose at the loose end of the rope, and climbing onto a narrow ledge, pulled it over his head.

Then, with a reserve of strength pulled from somewhere deep within his inner being, he jumped.

CHAPTER THIRTEEN

Henri Deneuve led Nick back to his apartment on the Ile Saint-Louis. The professor's home was exactly as Nick expected it might be—a perfect reflection of the man. High ceilings, well-patinated antique furnishings, decorative wooden floors covered with Oriental rugs, and ornately carved molding everywhere. There were literally thousands of books and papers scattered helter-skelter throughout the rooms. The elderly man invited Nick to sit while he went into the small kitchen to make coffee. When he returned, Nick took a sip and noticed that the beverage had been fortified with a generous amount of cognac.

"Just a little something to calm the nerves, Nicholas. Now, let's talk."

Nick took another sip of the strong beverage, all the while looking around at the cornucopia of old and new treasures spread throughout the apartment. He pointed to a large painting, hanging prominently on one of the walls.

"Is that a real Picasso?"

"Oui. The artist was a great friend of my father. We have several paintings that Uncle Pablo gifted to us."

"Wow, that must be quite a story."

"It is, Nicholas, but not the story relevant to our recent close call, mon ami."

Nick looked slightly chastised. He had been trying to avoid the subject. If he didn't understand what was happening, how could he explain it to the elderly professor?

He began his story anyway.

"After we left Shakespeare's the other day, I was almost hit by a car that ran up onto the sidewalk. Someone, I'm sure it was Margaux, yelled for me to jump out of the way. No one else heard her, and if I hadn't jumped, I'm sure I wouldn't be here today."

The old professor looked at Nick over his round, wire-framed glasses. "This is the same voice you said you heard before today's shooting?"

"The very same, Henri. Saved once again by your late sister."

The professor removed his glasses, rubbed his face with his soft academic hands, and motioned to the piles of books surrounding them. "Strange. Very strange, Nicholas, but I have heard, or perhaps read, about similar occurrences before."

They sat in silence, the only sounds the tick-tock of an ancient grandfather clock and lapping waves from the wake of a riverboat passing by on the Seine.

"Are you sure you're okay, Professor?"

"Oui. I'm just very curious about your situation Nicholas. I will do some investigating and get back to you."

Nick got up to leave. "Be careful, Henri. You know what they say about curiosity."

"Oui, mon ami. It killed the cat. But don't worry; this old cat has nine lives," he said, smiling in the sly but charming manner of a mischievous old man.

ψ

Nick's time in his Paris apartment was running out, and he was anxious to hear back from the mademoiselle at the Ministry of the Interior. She must have been reading his mind, because no sooner had he closed the front door to his temporary home than his cell rang.

"Bonjour, Monsieur Palmer. It's Eloise Pilon. I have only just

62

received the report from our forensic laboratories. Would it be convenient for you to stop by tomorrow morning at ten for us to review our findings?"

"Good news, I hope. Say, would you mind if I brought a colleague along?"

"Oui, monsieur, that would be agreeable. I will meet you at the same gate where we met the other day."

The woman hung up, and Nick immediately called Henri Deneuve to see if he wanted to accompany him to the meeting.

"Oui, Nicholas. What else is there for an old man to do in Paris?"

Nick smiled at the man's obvious teasing and gave his friend directions and instructions.

ψ

The following morning, he found Mademoiselle Pilon waiting at the ministry's front gate. Professor Deneuve arrived a few minutes later. Introductions were made, and the woman led them back to the same boardroom where Nick and the Parisian police officer had met her on his first visit.

There was a large manilla envelope on the table. Mademoiselle Pilon sat between the two men and spread its contents—the rope and numerous official-looking papers—on the table between them. The woman gently picked up the rope and handed it to Nick. He fiddled with it for a moment or two, then placed it back on the table in front of him.

"What we have discovered, monsieur, is that the rope is very, very old. It was braided in the sixteenth or seventeenth century, from maguey cactus fibers, probably in South or Central America. There is also a very fine thread of twenty-four carat gold woven into the coils, which we cannot explain."

Nick and the professor looked at each other in astonishment.

The woman continued. "The colors of the rope are of a later vintage, perhaps seventeenth or eighteenth century. The pigments are made from organic and mineral materials."

She paused, as if waiting for her visitors to digest the information.

"Here's where it gets puzzling. These colored dyes originated here in Europe and were added later. We can't confirm what the colors or patterns represent."

The woman bowed her head slightly and turned towards Nick. "We also found traces of human blood. It, too, was old. By our team's estimation, from the nineteen forties."

She shuffled the papers back together and placed them, along with the rope, back into the envelope, which she handed to Nick.

"I wish there was more I could tell you, messieurs." The men stood to leave. "Pardon Monsieur Palmer, a word in private?"

Nick and the woman walked to a far corner of the room. She leaned in closer, and whispered, "Monsieur, if it's not being too presumptuous, would you be available for dinner this evening?"

Nick smiled, thinking of his earlier conversation with Alain Moreau, the Paris police officer. "I would be delighted, mademoiselle."

She discreetly handed him her card. "Eight this evening, at this address. Bien?"

Then she shook hands with both men and walked them to the front gate. They both watched her walk away. The old professor was smiling.

"I think, Mon ami, you're about to enjoy one of Paris's most pleasurable attractions."

CHAPTER FOURTEEN

News of the shooting at the Parisian bistro dominated the world press. Various groups of political no-goods and ultra-religious fanatics claimed responsibility, but the Paris police correctly determined the shooting to be the act of a lone shooter with no known ties to any terrorist or criminal organization.

ψ

Nick's cell rang. It was Gabriela, and she sounded very concerned.

"Nick, are you okay?"

Nick's heart skipped a beat; what with everything going on, he'd almost forgotten just how much he missed his beautiful partner in Chicago.

"Yeah, why?"

"You haven't called, and news about the shooting in Paris is all over the media. Aren't you living close to where it happened?"

Nick didn't remember telling her where his Paris apartment was—or had he? These days, he had a hard time being certain of what he had or hadn't said. He didn't want her to worry, so he crossed his fingers and lied.

"Not even close. How's everything in the windy city?"

Her voice suddenly changed, now sounding like the woman he

missed and wanted more than anything. "Wish you were here. I miss you."

"I'll be back soon. I promise."

She made a kissing sound and hung up. Nick stood staring at the blank screen on his phone for what seemed like an hour. In fact it was only seconds.

What in God's name am I doing here, chasing ghosts, when I could be moving ahead with my life back home?

Jeremy, his English landlord, would be returning in a day or so, and he would have to move on. He was wondering if he should tell Gabriela about his plans.

ψ

At eight that evening, Nick showed up at the address Mademoiselle Pilon had slipped him at the ministry offices. Her apartment was in an elegant 1930s Art Deco style building in the 7th Arrondissement, near the Eiffel Tower. He rang the bell and the beautiful French bureaucrat's voice responded through the speaker.

"Bonjour, Monsieur Palmer. Please come up. Apartment number six on the third floor."

When he reached her apartment, she greeted him at the front door. She was wearing a dazzling low-cut red dress that was decidedly sexier than what she had worn at his previous meetings.

"Please come in, Monsieur Palmer." She leaned in and kissed him on both cheeks.

"Please, call me Nick."

"And you should call me Eloise. Ella, if you prefer."

He followed her into the apartment. It was beautifully decorated with an eclectic mix of extreme modernism and fine French antiques.

"May I offer you an aperitif?"

She left Nick looking out the window at a stunning night view of the famous tower. When Ella returned, she was carrying a small silver tray with two martinis. She handed one to Nick and proposed a toast.

"Here's to new friends and a memorable evening."

Nick couldn't help being enamored by her looks and sexy French accent.

They clinked glasses and sat next to each other on one of the more comfortable-looking modern sofas.

"Because this is your first visit to Paris, I've taken the liberty of making a reservation at one of the city's finer dining establishments."

Nick raised an eyebrow. She noticed his misgivings.

"Our dinner is courtesy of the ministry."

He was beginning to like the way they did business in France.

They finished their drinks, and Ella called an Uber to take them to the restaurant. She gave the driver instructions, and in less than ten minutes, having driven through tumultuous traffic, they were dropped at the base of Paris's iconic tower. He was puzzled and looked at her questioningly. She just smiled.

"Le Jules Verne is one of our finest Michelin-starred restaurants. I think you'll enjoy your meal here."

They took the elevator to the second floor and stepped into the restaurant. Nick scanned the beautiful room, packed with beautiful people, and turned to his companion.

"It must take months to get a reservation here. How did you manage to get in ahead of the line?"

The charming maître d'hôtel interrupted, greeting them. "Bonsoir, Mademoiselle Pilon. Votre table vous attend."

He led them to a window table with a breathtaking view of the city.

"You haven't answered me yet."

She reached across the table and gently took his hand. "Two things, Monsieur Nick. Family connections and ministry business."

Nick leaned in towards her. "Well, mademoiselle, I am in your very capable hands."

The food, wine, and conversation flowed easily, and after the last mouthful of dessert had been consumed, they left the restaurant.

The evening was warm, and Ella asked him to walk her home. They strolled, arm-in-arm, along the Champ de Mars back to her apartment.

"It's still early, Nick. Would you like to come up for a nightcap?"

It was an invitation he knew he should have refused, but as she said, the night was still young.

ψ

Nick stood in front of the window, appreciating the view of the Eiffel Tower. It was lit up like a Christmas tree and looked like everyone's dream of what Paris should be.

Her voice came from the adjoining room. "Nick, could you please come and give me a hand?"

She was standing in her bedroom trying unsuccessfully to undo the zipper at the back of her skimpy dress.

He obliged, and as the garment pooled around her ankles, she turned, reached up, and put her arms over his shoulders.

Nick smiled and pulled back. All he could think about was Gabriela. His unspoken, unwritten, but unconditional commitment to his partner in Chicago filled his mind, and somehow, this just didn't seem right.

"I'm sorry, Ella, but I don't think this is a good idea, but I've had a wonderful evening with a beautiful woman, in a magical city, and for that, I thank you."

Ella pouted her lips slightly, then nodded and kissed him on both cheeks in the non-committal, non-personal way favored by Europeans when they greeted each other—or said goodbye.

She slipped a robe over her bare shoulders, then gently took his hand, and walked him to the door.

"Bonne nuit, Nicholas. Merci."

He left her apartment. A soft mist was drifting up from the Seine, creating warm halos of light around the streetlamps. The roads were virtually empty with just the occasional car and a couple strolling hand in hand on the opposite sidewalk. It was as if this little corner of Paris was pulling up the bed covers and saying goodnight to the day that had been.

Nick smiled, shoved his hands deep into his pockets, and walked slowly back to his tiny Airbnb apartment.

CHAPTER FIFTEEN

The following morning, Nick packed his bag, wrote Jeremy a note thanking him for the use of his apartment, and left for Charles de Gaulle International Airport. He had an 11:10 a.m. Alitalia flight to Leonardo da Vinci Airport in Rome.

$$\psi$$

In a hidden chamber beneath the ancient temple of Tenochtitlan in Mexico City, a group of twelve apostles convened in a conclave to discuss the fate of Nicholas Palmer.

These apostles, six men and six women, all dressed in black monk's habits, were known by the names of the original Doce Apóstoles de la Nueva España, the Twelve Apostles of New Spain, a group of Franciscan missionaries who'd landed on the shores of Mexico in 1524. These modern apostles, the Council of Faith, made up the ruling spiritual body of La Orden de las Serpientes de Christo. Their leader was a prominent Wall Street investment banker, known in the Order as Martin de Valencia, or to many of the Order's numerous followers, El Cardenal.

El Cardenal called the meeting to order. He had a deep, bone-chilling voice that echoed off the damp stone walls of the secret chamber.

"Brothers and sisters, it has been brought to my attention, by our followers in Chicago who initiated the recent sacrificial offering there, that a lowly Chicago police officer has come closer to the secret syllabus of our faith than any other person in the many centuries of our Order's existence."

There were hushed murmurs of consternation from those gathered in the circle.

"I ordered our faithful servant Brother Diego to deal with the man, but the American has twice eluded our wrath. He seems to possess a second sense when it comes to his own mortality."

Andrés de Córdoba, a stooped Mexican woman in her late seventies, rose to her feet. "May we inquire as to the whereabouts of Brother Diego?"

The leader addressed the woman's question, his voice softening out of obvious respect for the elderly colleague and co-conspirator. "His disposition is unknown to me at this time. I should not have ordered a viajero to do the job of a discipulo. This error of judgment has already been rectified."

Another member of the group, a dark-skinned man of undetermined age, stood and raised his arms in a sweeping arc, motioning to the group of hooded men and women surrounding him. "We look forward to being kept abreast about your solution to our unfortunate predicament."

The man's tone was slightly threatening, and it didn't go unnoticed by those in the gathering.

Martin de Valencia adjourned the meeting then, and the members filed out of the chamber, dispersing into the cool evening air of the city.

ψ

Hector Rodriguez's Gulfstream III rolled up to the terminal building at Westchester County Airport. It had been a long flight from Mexico City, and the drive to his office in lower Manhattan would take another hour.

The billionaire was digesting last night's council conclave. Among other items on the agenda, they'd given him their silent assent to eliminate Nicholas Palmer.

During the flight, he'd called his most remorseless discipula to meet him at his Fifth Avenue apartment. He hadn't heard from Brother Diego and was troubled about the man's whereabouts.

His driver dropped him at his building on Broad Street.

While most of his competitors and contemporaries favored penthouse offices, he exited the elevator at the eleventh floor. Hector worked at his day job for several hours, then called his driver to take him home. Home, in the rarefied world of this specific billionaire, was an opulent five-thousand-square-foot penthouse, overlooking Central Park, on the eleventh floor of an elegant Gothic-style building in the city's exclusive Upper East Side.

At exactly eight-thirty that evening, Hector Rodriguez's doorman rang and announced that Ms. Estella Calero had arrived for her appointment. The man was given permission to send her up to his luxurious apartment.

"Buenas noches, Sister Estella. Thank you for rearranging your plans to meet me this evening."

The woman knew she'd had no choice in the matter but smiled anyway. "It is my great pleasure, Holiness. What is it I can do for you?"

"This, Sister Estella, is somewhat different from the usual task of a discipula."

She looked at the man. Her usual assignments were to deliver the final coup-de-grace to girls selected for sacrifice. The leader placed his hands behind his back and silently prowled around the woman as if deep in thought.

"There's a man, a Chicago police officer, who is scratching at the surface of our Order. It is the opinion of the Council of Faith that he must be stopped by whatever means at our disposal."

The woman nodded. Now she understood the reason for their meeting.

"Brother Javier will fill you in on everything you'll need to know."

He rang a bell, and a large dark-haired man carrying a slim red file folder entered the room.

"You will, of course, have significant monetary assets at your disposal. *Buena suerte.* Good hunting."

Brother Javier escorted the newly anointed assassin to the apartment's private elevator.

ψ

Nick's flight landed at Rome's frenetic international airport. He quickly cleared customs and was picked up by the host of the Airbnb apartment he'd booked the week before. "Buon pomeriggio, Signor Palmer. Welcome to Rome."

Tanned and handsome, Giorgio Macri had an ear-to-ear grin on his face. In his mid-thirties, he was beautifully dressed in a soft-yellow linen shirt, faded-blue jeans, and a pair of dark-blue Tod's slip-ons. In his spare time, away from his always-demanding task of escorting wealthy female tourists, he ran a small guesthouse on the Via Boezio, near Vatican City.

The third-floor apartment they went to was only marginally larger than the one Nick had rented in Paris, but this one had a separate bedroom and a walk-in shower. The rooms were decorated in a mishmash of styles, and the kitchen, if you could call it that, consisted of a small sink, an even smaller refrigerator, and a microwave oven. However, everything was spotlessly clean. He paid Giorgio for two weeks' accommodation and walked him out. After unpacking, he went into the bathroom and looked in the mirror, seeing only his own face.

He hadn't eaten since dinner with the beautiful Eloise Pilon in the restaurant at the Eiffel Tower the night before. With the thought of a salami sandwich and a double espresso running through his mind, he went out and began walking towards Saint Peter's Basilica.

It didn't take long for him to find a bar—as cafés in Italy are called.

He ordered coffee and a sandwich and stood among a group of men engaged in a heated discussion about the previous evening's soccer game between Juventus and Torino. Quickly finishing his meal, he left for San Pietro, the huge square in front of Saint Peter's Basilica.

At the exact center of the square is a towering Egyptian obelisk said to have been erected in 1586. He stood in front of the monument and looked towards the world's most famous church—world headquarters of the Catholic religion and home to a long lineage of good, bad, mad, and sometimes disastrous popes.

"This is where they discovered my body."

The voice startled him. It was the voice of Sophia D'Angelo, the Italian girl who'd appeared to him back in Chicago. He looked around the busy square, but there wasn't anyone who matched the face of the girl he'd seen in the mirror.

"Sophia?" he asked silently.

There was no answer, just the constant hum of traffic and people, inside and surrounding the famous piazza.

He turned and retraced his steps back to his tiny apartment.

CHAPTER SIXTEEN

The following day, two flights from the U.S. landed at Leonardo da Vinci Airport in Rome, one a Lufthansa A380 from O'Hare in Chicago, the other an Alitalia Airbus A330 from JFK in New York. Each carried a passenger looking for Detective Nicholas Palmer. Both flights landed at approximately the same time.

ψ

Nick had spent the better part of the day meeting with detectives at the Via di San Vitale, near the Giardino di Sant'Andrea al Quirinale. He was trying to obtain information about the 1972 murder of Sophia D'Angelo.

"Signore Palmer, that crime occurred almost fifty years ago. It would be a miracle if any reports or evidence still exist, but I will do my best." Investigatore Silvio Bianchi shrugged his shoulders and asked Nick to call him in a couple of days.

ψ

Nick was beyond frustrated and wanted to lash out at anything that got in his way.

What in God's name am I doing, running all over hell's half acre on a wild goose chase when I could just as well be back home with Gabi?

He wandered into the small public garden by Sant'Andrea al Quirinale, found a stone bench surrounded by lush greenery, and sat down. His cell rang.

"Nicholas?" Nick recognized the voice.

"It's Henri, Henri Deneuve. I've been doing some digging and think I may have discovered something interesting."

The sound of a familiar voice was exactly what he needed. He imagined the kindly old professor sitting at his desk in his Paris apartment, poring through his piles of books and manuscripts. He smiled.

"I'm fine, Henri. How are you today?"

"Oh désolé, mon ami. I am forgetting my manners."

"No apologies necessary, my friend. Now what has you so excited?"

"Well, Nicholas, as you know, before I retired, I taught anthropology, but I don't believe I ever mentioned that I also have keen interests in archaeology and epigraphy."

Nick listened patiently. He was beginning to feel a special kinship with the old man.

"Well, after we met in Paris, something familiar clicked in my brain, so I started doing some research. You'll never guess what I've found."

Nick was enjoying the man's excitement and playfully chided him. "Go on, Professor. Please don't keep me in suspense."

The old man stopped, took a deep breath, and continued.

"In February 1593, eleven Spanish ships landed on the Yucatan Peninsula in Mexico. Among the five hundred soldiers on the ships were several devoutly religious Catholic nuns, who'd disguised themselves as soldiers."

The elderly man took another deep breath. Nick felt the best was yet to come.

"This was rare, but not unheard of in those days. These devout women believed they were part of God's chosen army, selected by angels in heaven to help in the spiritual conquest of indigenous people in this far-off land."

"Very interesting, Henri, but what has this got to do with some very puzzling murders?"

"Patience, my dear friend, patience."

Nick imagined his old friend smiling on the other end of the call.

"In pre-Hispanic times, there was a history of conquered states in Mesoamerica adding the gods of their conquerors' religion to their own pantheons. It was like... no problem, your gods are now my gods too."

Nick stifled the urge to laugh out loud. "This is quite a story, Henri, but where's it going?"

If the elderly French academic sensed Nick's amusement, it wasn't reflected in his voice. "In the ensuing months, several of the nuns lost their lives to smallpox. However, one of them, a girl named Christina de Delgado, met an Aztec high priest named Coatl, and through a native interpreter, they discussed and debated the merits and canon of their respective religions."

Henri was excited with his findings and as he continued his story, the pitch of his voice got higher and higher. "As it turned out, there were striking similarities between their religions. Quetzalcoatl's followers believed the feathered-serpent god was born to a virgin, was associated with a new star, performed miracles, and practiced a form of baptism. It is also written that he was associated with the symbol of the cross, believed in death and resurrection, and dispatched his disciples to spread the word of his beliefs. He even promised his followers that, after leaving them, he would return."

The professor stopped talking, took yet another deep breath, and then continued. "Their god predicted future events and was believed to be the creator of all things, both on earth and in the heavens."

"Slow down, Henri. You're making me very tired."

"You can joke, my dear friend, but here's the most interesting part."

The old professor took a long pause, as if he wanted to keep Nick in suspense for a little while longer and then finally went on. "The story goes that, after many meetings, the Aztec priest and the young

Catholic nun fell in love. They had a traditional, albeit secretive, wedding, and within months, the nun, Christina, became pregnant. With the birth of their baby girl also came the birth of a new religion: a combination of Christianity and the worship of Quetzalcoatl, the powerful feathered-serpent god."

This was all very interesting, but Nick was starting to get impatient, wondering how what the professor was telling him could have one iota of relevance to the murdered girls.

The old professor went on. "Their new religion needed a symbol, something like a Christian rosary. They decided on a multicolored scarf. This, too, they borrowed from the narrative of the Aztec faith. The colors of the scarf represented their four-faceted conception of the universe, where space takes the four directions of the compass."

The professor paused, and Nick was once again tempted to ask him where all of this was leading, but out of respect for his elder, he kept quiet.

"The east was called tlapcopa, represented by the color red. West was called cihuatlampa, represented by white. The north was mictlampa, represented by black, and finally, uitztlampa, south, which is blue. A golden thread, representing the hair of Jesus, was also woven into the fabric of the scarf."

The relevance of what the man was saying hit Nick right between the eyes, and he literally shouted into his cell. "Holy shit Henri! Those are the colors on the rope that strangled Margaux and all the others!"

"Bingo!" said the old professor, the sound of his excitement amplified tenfold over the cell.

"And the patterns on the rope represent the body of the snake god?"

"Double bingo, mon ami. You're not such a bad detective after all."

Now Nick was riveted by what the professor was telling him. "So why all the murders? Tell me that."

"Well, it seems Hernán Cortés, leader of the Spanish conquistadors, found out about the marriage between Christina and Coatl, and had the girl killed. She died exactly three years after she'd arrived, on

November 11, 1556. She was nineteen."

Nick's heart was pounding so hard he thought it would explode out of his chest.

The professor continued talking. "Coatl escaped with their baby daughter, never to be seen again."

"And that's it!?" Nick realized that he was almost yelling into the phone and forced himself to calm down.

"The rest, mon ami, is all speculation and rumors. It is said the high priest had a vast fortune in hidden Aztec gold, part of which he used to create a powerful and secretive 'religious' Order called La Orden de las Serpientes de Christo: in English, the Serpents of Christ. Further conjecture is that the cult still exists—overseen by a conclave of twelve apostles, and that one of its edicts is that every November eleventh, a woman born on that date must be sacrificed on her nineteenth birthday."

"Jesus Christ, Henri, if what you say is true, we've got five hundred years of murder on our hands, and that's a lot of crap to deal with."

"In France, we call it merde. Good luck, mon ami. I will continue digging."

"Merci, Henri, and good luck."

Nick hung up. His heart was pounding, and his hands were sweating, but he still didn't have the answer he wanted the most. Nothing the professor had told him explained the images of the girls in the mirrors or the voices only he could hear.

CHAPTER SEVENTEEN

"What are you doing here!?"

"Just dropped by to see my favorite cop."

Gabriela was lounging seductively on the living-room sofa of Nick's flat in Rome.

"How did you get in?"

"That cute landlord of yours couldn't resist the charms of a pretty woman. Say, aren't you glad to see me?"

Nick noticed the carry-on sitting on the floor in front of her.

"Very happy and very surprised. How'd you ever find me?"

"Give me a break, handsome. I'm a detective, and you left a trail wider than the I-95."

Nick raised an eyebrow.

"Look, it's not like you're a secret agent with hundreds of fake passports or anything. I knew you were leaving Paris, so I just checked your name against flight departures—and voilà, here I am in Rome."

"And how'd you find this place?"

"If you're a cop, investigating a murder, the Airbnb folks are more than happy to hand out confidential information."

Nick sat next to her, leaned over, and kissed her. She kissed him back, then pulled away and smiled. She seemed to be as overjoyed to see him as he was to see her.

"Now that's more like it! So, what've you been up to, Sherlock?"

Nick gave the beautiful detective a Readers Digest account of his past few weeks, leaving out, of course, his dinner with the evocative assistante du directeur in Paris.

"Wow, you've been a very busy boy."

"Yeah, but I'm not sure what my next steps should be. I only hope my old friend in Paris can dig up a little more info."

She stood, unbuttoned the front of her pretty floral sundress, and let it drop casually to the floor. "I only hope you don't have any pressing engagements for the next hour or two."

ψ

They lay in bed, her long dark hair spread over his bare chest. She leaned over and kissed him on the cheek. "Look, Nick, I've only got a week's holiday. Why don't we do the tourist thing for a few days? I've never been to Italy, and it would be fun to see the sights with you."

Nick felt a break from the case might give him a new perspective, and anyway, he was getting tired of chasing shadows. This "little holiday" Gabi was suggesting sounded like a great excuse to clear his mind.

He got out of bed, looked back at the beautiful woman splayed out under the sheets, then went into the bathroom. Sophia D'Angelo's concerned face appeared in the mirror.

"Be careful, Signor Palmer. Something dangerous is coming."

Her image faded and vanished.

"Jesus, Sophia," he murmured. "What's coming? Tell me what the hell's coming?"

He heard Gabriela's voice from the bedroom.

"Who are you talking to, Nick? Are you hiding someone prettier than me in there?"

"No, not as pretty. It's another one of my mirror girls."

He walked back, sat on the edge of the bed, and buried his head in his hands. "Damn it, why's all this shit happening to me?"

Gabriela sat up and put her arms around him. Her firm body felt good against his back.

"Let's go see Rome. You definitely need a break."

She touched up her makeup and pulled a pretty, almost indecently short, pale-blue dress from her bag. He gave her a wolf thistle and tried to coax her back into bed, but after a second unsuccessful attempt, he gave up, and they left the little apartment to enjoy the afternoon sunshine of the Eternal City.

They found a charming trattoria with outdoor seating in a secluded piazza near the Pantheon and sat down for an early dinner.

Gabriela ordered first. "I'll have the spaghetti Bolognese, please, and a glass of your best red wine."

The waiter was on the verge of being overly attentive to the beautiful American woman, smiling warmly at his attractive customer, then turning to Nick.

"Make that two, if you don't mind."

The meal was simple and sensational, and as dusk arrived, families started entering the square—mothers and fathers, nonni and nonne, and kids running around kicking soccer balls. It was a scene plucked right from a romantic Italian movie.

They strolled across the square to a gelato vendor and walked slowly back to the apartment savoring their icy treats.

They were about to go inside when Nick heard an urgent voice.

"Run away! Run away, now!"

He grabbed Gabriela by the arm and dragged her forcibly down the street. Moments later, a horrific explosion engulfed the building where Nick's rental apartment had been.

The blast flattened them. Then all Nick could hear was a loud ringing noise. Glass, stone, wood, and other debris rained down over them. The street was covered in a cloud of fine dust, and bodies of dead and injured people seemed to be everywhere. He reached over and touched Gabriela, but she didn't move. Struggling to his knees, he took her arm and felt for her pulse. She was still alive but unconscious.

The ringing in his ears began to subside, only to be replaced by the sound of approaching sirens.

Gabriela slowly pushed herself up and shook her head. "Did the earth move for you too?"

Nick didn't know whether to laugh or cry. He wrapped his arms around her and pressed her against his chest. That was close, too close, and the thought of what might have happened, the thought of losing her, sent cold shivers down his spine. If Gabriela had died in the explosion, a hole would have been ripped into his heart—a hole bigger than the Grand Canyon.

When he was confident that she was okay, he raised his head and looked around at the death, destruction, and devastation surrounding them. It was like a scene from a war movie.

Police cars and ambulances had arrived quickly at the scene, the area was cordoned off, and paramedics now faced the daunting task of sorting through the many casualties. Two of the paramedics, a man and a woman, came over to where they were sitting. They gently pried the American couple apart, checked their vital signs, examined their injuries, and loaded them into one of the waiting ambulances.

As the vehicle sped through traffic in Italy's biggest city, Nick closed his eyes and quietly whispered, "Thank you!" to Sophia D'Angelo, the dead girl, the ghost of an angel, who had warned him to run away.

The woman from New York saw them being loaded into the ambulance and driven away. She swore silently under her breath, terrified of what her failure to kill the detective would mean for her future.

CHAPTER EIGHTEEN

Nick and Gabriela were checked, treated, and discharged from the hospital. Their general prognosis was good—severe headaches, minor cuts, and bruises—but they would recover. The young American intern who treated them in the frenzied emergency room signed their discharge papers and gave them one last word of advice before scurrying off to help other victims of the devastating explosion: "Go home, get some rest, and you should both be fine in a couple of days."

Unfortunately, their home in Rome was now a pile of rubble, and their other ones were several thousand miles away in Chicago. Gabriela looked at Nick's dust-covered face.

"What now?"

"A hotel, I guess."

They were both exhausted, dirty, and sore.

Most of their belongings had been lost in the explosion, but thankfully, they'd both been carrying their passports, wallets, and cell phones.

"First thing tomorrow," he said, "we'll go shopping, but all I want right now is a hot shower and about a hundred hours of sleep."

Gabriela looked up at him and gave him the come-hither look. "Nothing else?"

Nick rolled his eyes and smiled at her. "You're a goddamned sex maniac."

"Yup," was her demure reply.

They hailed a taxi and asked the driver to recommend a place where they could stay. The taxi dropped them in front of a charming little hotel on Via Vittoria Colonna, and as luck would have it, a junior suite was available. After they explained the reason for their disheveled appearance, the man at the front desk became graciously sympathetic, registered them, and handed them two keys.

They dragged themselves up the stairs to their second-floor room and collapsed on the bed.

ψ

Hector Rodriguez was at his desk in his sumptuous eleventh-floor office in downtown Manhattan. Priceless gold Aztec masks and other invaluable artifacts and antiquities held places of honor in the room. He looked lovingly at the objects. Besides their incomparable splendor and obvious connection to his ancestry, their inherent value had been a significant factor in financing his life of luxury and power.

Hector Rodriguez was the direct descendant of Coatl, the Aztec high priest who'd founded the ancient religious order that he now headed. For more than five hundred years, his predecessors had dealt with nonbelievers and charlatans who wanted to destroy his birthright. Now it was his turn. That Chicago detective who was scratching at the surface of his organization had to be permanently dealt with. He picked up his phone and called a number in Rome. The obvious fear in the voice of the woman who answered amplified his sarcasm. "Buenos dias, Sister Calero. I do hope you have good news for me."

The discípula's normally confident voice quavered. "I failed, Holiness, but I promise, on the spirit of the great god Quetzalcoatl, I'll fulfill your orders next time."

The man's fist clenched in rage, and his face turned a violent shade of red.

"So, I've heard. You've virtually destroyed a whole city block, killed or maimed numerous innocent people, and yet you were still unsuccessful in your mission?"

The vitriol of his words sprayed through the line like white-hot lightning.

The woman stammered. She knew her failure to kill the Chicago cop would result in dire consequences and so she tried, unsuccessfully, to defuse the wrath of her superior.

"It was as if he was warned."

Hector paused. This was the third time he'd heard this excuse, and it troubled him greatly.

"One more chance, my discípula, just one more chance is all I'm giving you."

He slammed the phone down into its cradle. He knew Estella Calero was terrified. He only hoped her terror would give her the resolve she needed to complete her task.

ψ

The ring of his cell woke Nick and Gabriela from a deep, much-needed sleep. Nick fumbled for the phone.

"Bonjour, Nicholas."

Nick shook the cobwebs from his brain. It was Alain Moreau, his friend in the Paris police.

"Good morning, Alain. You certainly don't believe in letting a guy sleep in. What time is it, anyway?" He pushed himself up and sat on the edge of the bed, his muscles still aching and his ears still ringing slightly from the previous day's close call. "So, what's up?"

The French police officer was all business. "We've discovered a dead body in the catacombs."

"Just one? I thought the place was crawling with millions of them." Nick was smiling at his little joke.

"Get serious, my American friend. This one may be of particular interest to you."

Nick had no idea what the police officer was talking about. "Go on."

"We've identified the body as one Diego Lopez, a Mexican citizen who's been living, illegally, in Paris for the past year or so."

"And what makes you think this is something that'll interest me?"

"It looks like he committed suicide—hanged himself with a multicolored rope."

Nick jumped to his feet, suddenly wide awake. Gabriela looked at him as if he'd lost his mind, then threw her arms apart, indicating she wanted to know what was going on.

"Jesus, Alain, what else?"

"We found a gun, a Heckler & Koch semiautomatic. We believe it may be the same gun fired at you, and your friend the professor, at the café."

Nick was pacing the room, frantically trying to put the pieces together.

"How did you find him? There's got to be a thousand miles of tunnels down there."

"The smell, and the rats, Nicholas, neither of which are very pleasant. I'll call you back when we have more information."

The French policeman hung up.

Nick sat on the edge of the bed, then flopped back down on the pillow. He had no idea what was happening, or what he should do next. Gabriela snuggled up from behind and wrapped her arms around him.

"C'mon, tough guy," she said, after he explained what the call was about, "let's get some breakfast and go shopping. We both need a change of clothes and a change of perspective."

ψ

The restaurant in their hotel was intimate and oozed with Tuscan charm. The breakfast buffet, spread out along a rough-hewn wooden table, was laden with all kinds of deliciousness: cornettos, crostatas, biscotti, a generous selection of salami, ham, cheese, fruit, and a variety of juices. They ate like they'd never eaten before and finished their meal with double espressos.

The hotel's friendly concierge recommended a department store, close by on Piazzale Appio, and by lunchtime, they'd replaced most of what they'd lost in the explosion. As they were leaving the store, Nick's cell rang.

"Bonjour, Nicholas. It's Alain again. Forensics just confirmed that the bullets found at the café came from the gun we found in the catacombs."

Nick thanked him, hung up, and turned to Gabriela. "You know, I seriously think someone's trying to kill me."

After a few minutes, he called the Parisian police officer back.

"Say, Alain, do you know anyone with the Rome police? I think I might need a gun."

"Getting cautious, eh Nicholas? An excellent idea. I don't like funerals, especially the funerals of friends." Nick thought he heard the man stifle a laugh. "I have a detective friend, Silvio Bianchi. He's with the polizia in Rome, and I'm sure, with your Chicago credentials, you'll have no problem getting a license and a firearm."

Nick remembered the investigatore from his previous visit to the police.

Alain Moreau gave him Silvio's number, and Nick made the call. After two rings, the man answered, and Nick reintroduced himself.

"Ah, Signor Palmer, I remember. We're still looking into the unfortunate murder of Miss D'Angelo. As a matter of fact, the file is on my desk right now."

"I'm calling on a different matter this time. My friend Alain Moreau in Paris said you could possibly expedite an Italian firearms license for me."

"Ah, Alain. I was speaking to him just last week about your old cold-case murder in front of the Notre-Dame. Drop by tomorrow morning, fill out the forms, and I'll get you a license in about an hour. Cop-to-cop benefits, eh signore?"

Nick thanked his new friend; then he and Gabriela wandered, hand in hand, through the charming streets of the Eternal City. If it weren't for the ominous cloak of danger hanging like an all-enveloping cloud over their heads, they could have easily been mistaken for a couple on their honeymoon.

ψ

The following morning, Nick picked up an Italian firearms license, which allowed him to carry a concealed weapon; then he and Gabriela walked to the Beretta Gun Shop on Largo del Nazareno.

The shop was beautiful and well stocked with all manner of firepower, from spectacular hand-engraved shotguns to the latest in high-tech handguns. He selected a lethal-looking APX, a holster, and ammunition. With his new firearm nestled snugly beneath his shoulder, they made their way back to the hotel. They needed to figure out their next move, but mostly they desperately wanted to rest their aching bodies.

CHAPTER NINETEEN

"The only way to end this is to cut off the head the serpent."

Sophia D'Angelo's unsmiling image faded from the mirror in the hotel's tiny bathroom.

Nick got the message and had done the math. If what Henri Deneuve had told him was true, over the years, the Serpents of Christ had committed close to five hundred sacrificial murders. The numbers were staggering. This level of evil, sanctified by a divinity without moral standards, was abhorrent and dangerous.

Gabriela was packing. Her one week's vacation, if you could call it that, was over and she had to return to Chicago and her job with the police force. She faced Nick with her hands placed firmly on her hips and gave him an ultimatum.

"Promise me you'll be careful—very, very careful. I don't want to see your body in tiny pieces spread all over Rome."

"I promise I'll do my very best to stay in one piece."

They shared a long, lingering goodbye kiss. There was a smattering of tears, and then she left for Leonardo da Vinci Airport and her flight to Chicago.

Nick waved at her cab until it rounded the corner; then he kept walking. He still had a headache that felt like his brain was about to explode, and his muscles still ached from the aftermath of the bombing. He found a bar near the Trevi Fountain, sat at a small sidewalk table, and ordered a double espresso.

He was unaware that the woman from New York—the woman sent by Hector Rodriguez—was watching his every move.

ψ

Henri Deneuve hadn't left his computer for what seemed like days. He was engrossed, still trying to find any relevant documentation about Nick's mysterious mirror girls. Occasionally, he lifted his head and stared at the ceiling, his analytical mind sorting through a myriad of unfamiliar scenarios. *Are there such things as ghosts? Is my new friend channeling the dead? In which case, is he a kind of medium?*

The elderly professor was entering a world he knew little, or nothing, about. Then he heard a woman's voice. She was pleading to him, almost crying out to be listened to.

"Please, monsieur, your friend is in mortal danger!"

He spun around in his chair and scanned the cluttered room. No one was there.

"My name is Sophia D'Angelo. Call him! Call him and warn him!"

The professor was at odds with himself. He was a man of science and lived in a world of facts, figures, and proven hypotheses, but he had a gut feeling he should do what the voice pleaded with him to do. He picked up his cell and called Nick.

"It's me, Henri Deneuve. We met—"

"Yes, Henri, I remember. What's up?"

The elderly man told Nick what he'd just experienced, and what the woman's voice had instructed him to do.

Nick scanned the area around him, just in time to see an attractive woman pull a gun from her purse. He flipped the table, dove forward, and tackled her to the ground. Her gun went off, a bullet sped harmlessly into the air, and the gun slipped from her grasp.

Nick pinned the woman on the pavement as a small crowd gathered around them. She was writhing, kicking, and screaming like a banshee.

Nick yelled out. "Quick, someone call the police! Hurry!"

Within minutes, he heard sirens reverberating off the centuries-old stone walls of buildings surrounding the small piazza.

Italian exuberance filled the air. Shouts, whistles, and cheers of encouragement followed them as both Nick and the woman were loaded into blue-and-white police cars and taken away. Eyewitness accounts of the incident cleared Nick of any wrongdoing, and he was released, while the woman was placed in a holding cell, pending charges.

Investigatore Silvio Bianchi caught up with Nick as he was leaving the station. "Hey, paisano now I know why you wanted a gun. What the hell was that all about?" He gestured back towards where the woman was being held in custody.

"Not sure, Silvio, but what I do know for sure is that someone desperately wants me dead."

"Then I'd better not stand too close to you." The Roman police officer laughed and walked back into the station. Nick followed him.

"Have you been able to identify her yet?"

The Italian lifted a blue file from off his desk and flipped it open.

"We have her passport." He opened a small blue book with a gold-embossed American eagle on its cover. "Her name is Estella Calero. Born November 12, 1987. She went through customs at Fiumicino just last week. Her passport was issued in New York."

He paused and looked at Nick. "The only unique identifying mark is a tattoo of a snake running up her backbone."

"Did you take any photographs of it?"

The detective lifted a printout from the file and handed it to Nick.

Nick felt the hair on the back of his neck stand up. The tattoo must have been at least twenty-four inches long. A red, black, blue, and white viper appeared to be crawling up the woman's back, ready to deposit its deadly venom into her slim neck. The image of the snake tattoo sent a tremor through his whole body. He handed the photo back to the Italian detective.

Nick found an empty desk and called the professor in Paris to thank him for the warning and to tell the elderly man what had happened earlier in the day. "Mon dieu, Nicholas, it sounds like the Serpents of Christ are alive and well… and are afraid you're getting too close to their secrets. Please be vigilant, mon ami."

After hanging up, Nick went back to find his police officer friend.

"Ciao, Silvio. Can I be there when you interrogate the woman?"

"Poliziotto to poliziotto? Why not? Come down at nine tomorrow morning; that's when I plan to start questioning her."

Nick was confused. *Why did Sophia tell the professor to warn me? Why didn't she warn me herself, like she did before?* He made a mental note to ask her—if, and when she next appeared.

ψ

Hector Rodriguez was at his vast country estate in Bedford, an affluent suburb of New York City. When the call came in, he was stretched out in his private spa, enjoying a massage by a beautiful Asian woman wearing nothing but an enigmatic smile.

When he heard the news from Paris, he catapulted off the table.

"Jesus fucking Christ! What the hell's happening?"

The naked woman quickly scurried from the room.

"What do you mean, she's in police custody?"

El Cardenal threw his cell phone against the wall, where it shattered into a million shards of glass and plastic.

ψ

At nine the following morning, Nick showed up at the police station. Silvio Bianchi was waiting for him on the front steps. He had a serious, almost despondent look about him.

"She's dead. We found her body last night. Forensics believe she may have been poisoned."

Nick felt deeply sympathetic for the officer. He understood the man's gloomy frame of mind but said the first thing that entered his head—which he thought, in retrospect, may have sounded insensitive.

"Do you think it was a snake bite?"

CHAPTER TWENTY

Sophia D'Angelo's parents were in their early nineties and looked it.

He'd called earlier to ask if they would see him. They told him he'd be welcome, so he drove south to Italy's famed Amalfi Coast. He wanted to find out more about the dead girl—her life, her death, anything that could help him make sense of what was happening. Besides, he had a hunch, a gnawing feeling deep within his gut that this was what he was supposed to do. What he had to do.

The D'Angelo villa was perched on a rocky outcrop high above a town, with spectacular vistas of the craggy coastline and sparkling azure waters of the Mediterranean. He walked up to the front door and pulled on a cord attached to an ancient bell. There was a shuffling sound from within the house, and then the door was opened by a middle-aged, gray-haired housekeeper, dressed head to toe in black. She silently motioned him to come inside.

Elvio and Aurora D'Angelo welcomed him and led him out onto the terrace. A large, pale-blue-and-white-striped canvas awning shaded them from the bright midday sun. He was offered lemonade made from fruit hand-picked that morning from a tree occupying a corner of their small, sun-drenched garden. He readily accepted the drink, and the housekeeper was sent scurrying to get it.

"Grazie per avermi…"

The elderly couple smiled at his dismal attempt to speak the Italian language. "We both understand and speak English, Signor Palmer."

Nick blushed. It was a possibility he should have considered. In a tone of voice that conveyed the real sympathy he was feeling, he then began questioning the distraught couple.

"Could you please tell me about Sophia?"

Aurora's eyes clouded over, and a lonely tear rolled down her deeply lined, sun-tanned cheek.

"She was beautiful and smart. She was an honors student at the university."

Elvio smiled, gently patted her hand, and looked over towards Nick. "She had many suitors."

His wife shot him a reprimanding glance, but he continued.

"She could dance like an angel, and her smile would light up a city. She's still with us, even though she's no longer here."

Nick was puzzled by the man's remark.

As Elvio continued to speak, the tone of his voice softened. "It's the flowers on her grave. They're always fresh. More than forty years have passed, and they still look like they were planted yesterday."

His wife interjected, her voice quavering as if what she was about to say would be misconstrued by the man from America. "They never die. They're just like her: a beautiful everlasting angel."

Nick asked if they'd mind if he visited her grave.

Elvio pointed in the direction of a nearby church. "It's at the Cimitero de Positano, not far from here."

With directions in hand, Nick left the still grieving couple in their sad but idyllic seaside retreat.

ψ

The cemetery was sheltered from the burning Mediterranean sun by the ancient yellow tower of the Church of Santa Maria Assunta. Nick strolled quietly among the aging headstones until he found her name: Sophia Maria D'Angelo. 1953–1972.

A colorful patch of flowers looked as if they'd just been planted, and a soft, warm breeze wafted through the solemn, wall-enclosed space. It carried the voice of an angel.

"Buona giornata, Signor Palmer. Welcome to where my mortal body lies."

Nick was, by now, no longer surprised by the voices that only he, and apparently Henri Deneuve, could hear. He whispered a question then—a question nobody would ever hear, a question to which he desperately needed the answer: "Why me?"

The air suddenly went still, as if a downy-soft blanket had descended over the cemetery; then Sophia's voice, as clear and beautiful as the alluring pale-blue sky above him, spoke.

"There are five hundred of us, perhaps more, all murdered, in the name of the unholy god of a duplicitous church. We are neither dead nor alive. Our souls are destined to be entombed in a realm of nothingness until the evil deity is crushed."

The girl's voice trailed off, and when it returned, it conveyed a plaintive passion the likes of which he'd never heard.

"The only way to end it is to sever the head of the serpent, and you, Signor Palmer, because of your extraordinary connection to our world, are the man we have chosen to do it."

The acrimony in her voice, as she mentioned the serpent, shocked him. There followed a silence so deep and despairing that it crushed the sounds of traffic, birdsong, and music wafting upward from the town below. The revelation surprised him.

"What can I do?"

"We are no longer flesh and blood. We are shadows, ghosts of our former selves. We no longer have the capability to dispose of this malignant cult and the man who heads it. We need your help."

Sophia's voice began to falter and fade with the gentle breeze that had now returned.

"We will do our best to guide and protect you. Please help us, Signor Palmer. Please help us find the peace we all desire."

He looked down and watched in amazement as the tiny patch of flowers on her grave wilted and collapsed into a small pile of dying leaves and petals. Then, as if by magic, new pale-green shoots began to sprout from the mound of decay.

"Why did you tell Henri Deneuve to warn me? Why not warn me yourself?"

"He must also know. He must also believe."

A suspension of disbelief washed over him. What he'd heard, and seen, finally convinced him that he wasn't crazy—wasn't on a wild flight of fancy ignited by his anguished imagination. He reached for his cell and called Henri Deneuve in Paris.

ψ

Hector Rodriguez had always managed to conceal his personal and business activities behind a veil of respectability, but now the layers of secrecy he'd worked so hard to weave were in danger of being unraveled by a lone police detective from Chicago.

The Serpents of Christ Order that he headed was just the tip of the iceberg. He had numerous other ventures. His primary source of income came from drug and human trafficking from Mexico into the U.S., but there was also a veritable arsenal of other equally heinous enterprises that, for obvious reasons, he didn't want exposed. The detective from Chicago had to be dealt with and dealt with quickly. He retrieved a second cell phone and punched in a number he'd memorized years earlier. The call was forwarded to voicemail. Hector swore under his breath. The last thing he needed right now was another goddamn annoyance in an already annoying day.

"Call me. I've got something demanding your immediate attention."

The man on the receiving end of the call was in bed with a young Mexican girl he'd recently smuggled across the border. After checking the message, he turned to the crying girl and kicked her to the floor. "Adios, baby. Gotta go. I've got work to do."

CHAPTER TWENTY-ONE

Henri Deneuve was scouring through ancient documents in the Sorbonne University library. More specifically, he was in the Special Collections Reading Room, a magnificent fourteenth-century space with a soaring vaulted ceiling, pale, highly decorated green walls, and row upon row of severe wooden tables worn to a warm patina from use and age. The room was unworldly quiet... until the shrill ring of the professor's cell shattered the silence.

"Bonjour, Henri Deneuve parle."

"Henri, it's me, Nick. Can we talk?"

"Ah Nicholas, good to hear from you! Good to hear you're still actually alive."

He was quietly chuckling and spoke in a voice barely above a whisper. An elderly librarian shot him a harsh look and placed her index finger against her pursed lips.

"Can I call you back in a little while? I'm in the Sorbonne Library and being severely chastised for talking." The old man stifled a giggle, then hung up.

Nick sat down on the edge of a huge sarcophagus, one of many in the crowded Italian graveyard. Several elderly women, all dressed in black, were praying or placing flowers on the graves of loved ones. If it weren't for the turmoil raging in his head, it would have been a peaceful, albeit bizarre, way to spend an hour or two. His cell rang and he frowned. *That was quick.*

"Hello, Henri?"

It wasn't his French friend. It was Isabela, his ex-wife.

"Where the hell are you?"

"Nice speaking to you too, Isabela. What can I do for you?"

Her voice softened ever so slightly.

"Lucy misses you and wants to speak to you."

A tidal wave of remorse engulfed his entire body. He missed his little girl more than words could ever say and wished he could be with her, hug her, and tell her just how much he really loved her.

"Is she there? Can I speak to her?"

Nick could feel the cold blast of indifference coursing through the cell.

"Call her in the morning, after she's had breakfast."

Isabela slammed down the phone.

In that one moment, Nick connected with the grief felt by the D'Angelo's. He thought about how he'd feel if his beloved Lucy had met the same fate as Sophia. His cell rang again, and the ladies in black stared at him in annoyance.

"Hello, Henri?"

"Oui, my friend. Now we can talk."

Nick recounted the events that had transpired since he'd last spoken to the elderly professor, including Sophia's passionate declaration that he'd been chosen by the martyred girls to track down and rid the earth of the Serpents of Christ cult. The professor listened intently and then spoke. He sounded more disappointed than optimistic.

"I've been searching, and I've found no reasonable or scientifically proven evidence regarding either the voices you hear or the images you see."

Nick quickly interjected. "But you've heard the voices yourself and witnessed the evidence. You, of all people, must believe these things are really happening."

There was an extended silence on the other end of the line. Nick could almost hear the gears clicking in his friend's head. Then, finally, the old man replied, "Come back to Paris, Nicholas. I will join you in your mission."

Nick now understood exactly why Sophia had chosen to include the elderly professor in the deadly game he was playing.

ψ

An hour after Hector had left the message, the call he'd been waiting for came through.

"G'day, mate. What can I do fer yer t'day?"

Nigel Thomas, an alumnus of the Black Bandits motorcycle gang, had earned his criminal doctorate in robbery and murder. He'd managed to narrowly escape authorities in his native Australia and now considered himself a citizen of the world. The thirty-something killer was six-foot-four, taut, tanned, and tough. He boasted that he'd killed far too many men to count and frequently bragged that he'd killed two large male crocodiles with his bare hands. Nigel Thomas now worked exclusively for the man he was talking to and was paid handsomely for services rendered.

"There's a Chicago detective, Nicholas Palmer. He's getting too close to our business enterprise, and I need your magic touch to deal with him."

The killer could almost hear his boss smiling on the other end of the call. "I go to Chicago then?"

"No. Last I heard, he's in Rome. Staying at a small hotel near the Vatican."

Nigel wondered how the man had acquired the information but quickly brushed it aside as Hector Rodriguez kept talking.

"I don't have the name of the hotel, but there can't be too many places where he can hide. Where are you now?"

"I'm in Houston. Send me photos of the bloke an' his description, and I'll be on the next flight t'Italy."

El Cardenal hung up. He was smugly confident that he'd heard the last of the meddlesome Chicago cop.

ψ

The three-hour-and-thirty-minute drive from the Amalfi Coast back to Rome took Nick through some of Italy's most beautiful countryside, but he was too preoccupied to enjoy the scenery. Too much was happening. Too much, too fast. His investigation in Italy wasn't finished. He needed to speak to Silvio, his police contact in Rome, about the woman who'd tried to kill him. He needed to consider Henri's request that the elderly man join him in the case. But most of all, he needed to call Lucy in California.

The time difference between Italy and California is nine hours. He'd call her at five in the afternoon, after he got back to his hotel. It would be eight in the morning in Sacramento, and Lucy would be having her breakfast.

ψ

As Nick sat on the edge of his bed, he swore he could still detect the alluring scent of Gabriela's perfume lingering throughout the rooms.

His heart was pounding. So much had happened since he'd last spoken to his daughter. He held the cell in his hand and looked at the small screen for what seemed like an eternity. Finally, he dialed the number. Isabela must have been looking at call display, seen who was calling, and passed the phone directly to his daughter.

"Hi, Daddy! It's me."

At the sound of his daughter's voice, Nick's heart melted, and he struggled to hold back the torrent of tears beginning to well up in his eyes.

"Hi, sweetheart. It's me! It's your daddy."

CHAPTER TWENTY-TWO

The call with Lucy had left Nick's heart pounding. He was emotionally drained, and it took a tremendous amount of restraint for him not to immediately book a flight to California.

He took a deep breath to calm his frayed nerves and made his next call. He needed to speak to Silvio Bianchi at the police department.

"Ciao, Silvio. Do you still have the body of the woman who tried to kill me?"

The Roman investigatore sounded happy to hear from him. It was almost as if he were also relieved to hear Nick was still alive.

"Sí, Nicholas. She's downstairs. They're about to conduct an autopsy to determine the cause of death. Why do you ask?"

"I want to take a closer look at her tattoo. Something in my gut tells me there's a lot more to it than meets the eye."

The Roman police officer was puzzled by Nick's remark.

"Come on down. It'll be good to see you again."

Nick grabbed a quick shower, dressed, and took a taxi to the police station, where Silvio met him at the door and took him downstairs to an antiseptic-looking white basement room filled with medical equipment. The facility was state-of-the-art and more up to date than most similar places he'd seen back home in the States. Silvio introduced him to the forensic pathologist who was preparing the woman's body for autopsy.

The would-be assassin was lying face up on a stainless-steel table. Nick thought she looked pretty in a perverse kind of way. He shook the thought from his mind. This was, after all, the body of the woman who'd tried to kill him and Gabi.

"Do you think we can we flip her over?"

The doctor, who spoke no English, looked questioningly at the investigatore. Silvio translated the request, and the doctor and his assistant did as they were asked.

This was the first time Nick had seen the snake tattoo in person. He was dazzled by the colors and detail of the artist's work. He turned to Silvio with an undisguised look of admiration.

"Whew! That must have taken someone hours, even days, to do."

The two men stepped in for a closer look at the image. Although it was grotesque, it was clear the artist was a master in his field.

The tattoo was symmetrical. If the woman's backbone was a center line, the writhing coils of the snake, on opposing sides of her spine, were mirror images. The vile creature's head pointed towards her left shoulder and the tail to her lower right thigh—in perfect uniformity. Silvio handed him a magnifying glass, and Nick leaned in. Starting with the reptile's head, he methodically scanned down the image, taking a full ten minutes to reach the tail.

"Silvio, take a look at this."

He handed the magnifying glass to the Roman cop.

"Can you see that tiny red square tucked in next to the last coil?"

"Sì, I see it. It looks like something's written on it."

Nick smiled at the sound of the man's astonishment. He took out his cell and snapped a picture of the hideous creature, then called Alain Moreau in Paris.

"Bonjour, Alain. It's Nick Palmer. Sorry to bother you, but I've a quick question. Were there any tattoos on the body of the guy you found in the catacombs?"

"Oui, my friend, I remember it well. He had a tattoo of a snake on his back."

Nick felt a prickling sensation on the back of his neck. It was a familiar feeling he always seemed to get when he believed pieces of a case were beginning to fall into place. He was thinking, hoping even, that perhaps this was the connection that would help get him on the right track to what he was looking for.

"Don't do anything to the body. I'm on my way."

Hanging up, Nick turned back to the investigatore. "Thanks, Silvio. I've got to get back to Paris to check out a body with a similar tattoo."

Waving, he quickly left the antiseptic basement room, with its inventory of violent death.

He rushed back to his hotel, packed his bag, checked out, and took a taxi to Roma Ostiense and the high-speed train back to the French capital.

ψ

The Australian assassin arrived at Rome's airport at approximately the same time as Nick was boarding the train to Paris. The man carried a small carry-on and a fake British passport. The friendly immigration officer in Rome welcomed him to Italy and wished him a pleasant visit.

ψ

Nick called Henri from the comfort of his first-class seat on the Intercity Express, rocketing through the picturesque Italian countryside.

"Bonjour, Henri. It's Nick. I'm on my way back to Paris. Can I impose on your good graces to let me stay at your apartment for a few days?"

The elderly professor sounded more than happy to hear from his American friend.

"Oui, yes, it would be my great pleasure. I have plenty of room, and your company would be a welcome respite for an old man with very little to do."

105

Nick smiled at his friend's obvious understatement and settled back to enjoy the balance of his twelve-hour trip.

ψ

The Australian found a cheap hotel near the Trevi Fountain and made two calls. One to Hector Rodriguez, his patron in New York, telling him he'd arrived in the Italian capital, and the second to a contact who traded in illegal, unregistered firearms. Then he began the arduous task of calling hotels in the vicinity of the Vatican.

He discarded the large expensive hotels and the ones listed as being exclusive boutiques, and then began working his way through his culled list. He ostensibly wanted to speak to one of their guests, a man named Nicholas Palmer. Several hours and many calls later, he hit pay dirt, a small hotel on the Via Vittoria Colonna. A pleasant-sounding woman with an alluring Italian accent answered almost immediately, stating the name of the hotel and inquiring as to how she could be of service.

"Hello, would you please put me through to Mr. Nicholas Palmer's room."

"Sorry, signore. Signor Palmer checked out several hours ago."

The Australian hung up and swore at his bad luck—and bad timing.

"Fuck! Where's the bastard gone now?"

He slumped back onto the bed, thinking about what he should do next.

Where the fuck do I go from here? I'd better call the boss.

ψ

Nick's train pulled into Paris's frantically busy Gare de Lyon station. Once he was out on the platform, he pushed his way through crowds of travelers, locals, porters, lost tourists, and people looking to meet family and friends, finally leaving the melee and finding a taxi to take him to Henri's apartment on the Ile Saint-Louis.

The professor answered the door, pulled Nick in, and gave him a huge hug.

"Bonjour, mon ami! It's so good to see you're still alive. Now tell me everything."

Nick didn't think the reference to his well-being was entirely appropriate but smiled at the kindly academic anyway.

Once comfortably settled and given a large glass of wine from Henri's well-stocked cellar, the two men sat and examined images of the snake tattoo on Nick's screen. There seemed to be some type of Asian calligraphy at the center of the tiny rectangle. He pointed it out to the professor.

"Désolé, mon ami. I'm not familiar with either Chinese or Japanese symbols. Let me consult with one of my colleagues at the university, but first let me show you to your room."

Nick thanked his host, and once he was in the comfort of his room, he placed a call to his friend Alain Moreau, on the police officer's private line.

CHAPTER TWENTY-THREE

Nick was disappointed to learn Alain Moreau wouldn't be available until the following morning and sighed. *It is what it is.*

He hung up and went into the bathroom to clean up from his trip. As he looked in the mirror, the shadowy face of Margaux Deneuve appeared. He'd almost forgotten that this was how the investigation into the multiple murders had started, way back in Chicago.

"Bonjour, Monsieur Palmer. Merci. Thank you from all of us."

She smiled and slowly moved her head from left to right, surveying the surroundings.

"You're staying in my room. That is good. Perhaps it will bring you good fortune."

The image of the pretty French girl faded away, and then, in its place, his own face appeared. He was tired and unshaven, but his look was one of dogged determination—a stony-faced reflection that laid bare his resolve to bring to justice those responsible for the horrific murders of so many young women.

His thoughts were interrupted by a loud knock on the door.

"Nicholas, there's a young man, a student of one of my colleagues at the university, who's apparently an expert on tattoos. He's agreed to meet us for coffee."

The excited old man stopped talking and took a deep breath. His voice, from the other side of the bathroom door, sounded urgent.

"He may be able to assist us in uncovering the meaning of the calligraphy on the tattoo."

"Be right with you, Henri."

Nick slapped water on his face, smoothed out his hair, and walked out of the room.

The elderly professor was obviously excited; his face had turned a bright shade of red, and he was pacing up and down the hallway.

"We're to meet him, in ten minutes, at a bistro not far from here. Hurry, mon ami. Hurry."

ψ

The small café was quintessentially Parisian, with perhaps a dozen small, round, marble-topped tables inside, and an equal number crowded outside on the sidewalk.

The young man was waiting for them. He was in his early twenties, wearing a worn black AC/DC T-shirt, torn jeans, and black combat boots. His muscled arms and the visible part of his neck were covered in the most beautiful, albeit bizarre, tattoos. Introductions were made and coffee ordered.

Jules Boulanger was not as intimidating as he looked. In fact, he a was pleasant and intelligent young man. Nick showed him the photograph of the tattoo on the woman's back. "Ouf, c'est sensationnel. This is the work of a master."

He leaned in closer to examine the image, his nose almost touching the screen of Nick's cell. He pointed to the small red box tucked into the last coil of the snake and enlarged the image.

"Look, it's even signed."

Nick, who was contemplating what kind of tattoos Jules might have on the covered parts of his body, looked up at the man.

"Is that significant?"

"Sure is. Most inkers don't sign their work. This was done by irezumi."

Nick shot him a questioning look, and the man continued. "It's a style, not a person. Irezumi is done by hand, not by machine. The process originated hundreds of years ago in Japan. It's time-consuming and very painful. Only after many years of apprenticeship are you allowed to practice this kind of art."

Jules took a long sip of his coffee, then continued.

"This one's unique. Typically, only large-scale, full-back art is signed, usually by Japanese masters, but this looks Mexican, more specifically Aztec inspired. Very unusual."

The professor interjected, "Can you read the signature?"

Jules held the cell to within an inch of his nose.

"It's not Japanese or Chinese." He kept staring at it. "I'd say it looks like it's a Mesoamerican symbol. They didn't have an alphabet like we have, so it either represents a god or some other kind of deity."

He laughed and handed the cell back to Nick. "Your tattoo was done by a god. That doesn't mean they weren't a very talented tattoo artist, though."

Nick thought about what Jules had said. "How would we go about finding such a master artist?"

"Well, if it was me, there's two people I would speak to: Paul Novare and Ms. Ing Ink. Both are masters, and both are of Mexican descent. They also both live in California, as far as I know."

The mention of California made Nick think about his daughter.

"Also, perhaps Dr. Delvine. I believe he works in Mexico City."

The affable young man had to leave for classes and rose from the table. "I hope I was able to be of assistance. Thank you for the coffee."

They watched him walk away. The crowds of people on the sidewalk, intimidated by the man's bulk and appearance, parted to let him pass.

Nick and the professor looked at each other.

"Well, my young American friend, what now?"

ψ

Gabriela was worried; she hadn't heard from Nick for several days, and she missed him. Her new partner was a nice enough guy, but he was nothing like Nick. Paired with the fact that everyone, from the mayor down, was bitching about the seemingly endless crime wave in the city, made her job almost untenable.

She was off duty, sitting at home alone in her Gold Coast apartment, watching some lame excuse of a cop show on television, when her cell rang.

"Hi, honey. It's me. Nick."

A warm wave of relief washed over her entire body. This was the call she needed.

"Hi, cowboy. What's new? I've been really worried about you."

Nick brought her up to date on what had been happening, up to and including his and Henri's meeting with the tattooed student.

"So, is there anything I can help you with?"

"Sure is! I need you to find some info on tattoo artists for me."

"I didn't know you were into that kinky stuff."

He laughed and gave her the names of the tattoo artists given to him by Jules.

"Anything else?"

He tried, unsuccessfully, to sound nonchalant. "I really miss you—a lot."

They talked for about thirty minutes more, mostly about her replacement partner, her increased workload, and finally what could best be described as phone sex. He promised he'd take a break very soon and come home to see her.

ψ

The professor left Nick to go to his office at the university. He wanted to do more research on the information imparted by their tattooed friend. Nick went back to Henri's apartment, sat down on one of the well-worn leather chairs in the living room, and promptly fell asleep.

111

He woke up when he heard Henri come through the front door.

"Any luck?"

"Not yet, mon ami. It's very easy to get confused with the machinations of Mesoamerican religions and cultures. There's so many gods, so many incarnations, so many variables." The old man scratched his head with an exaggerated, confused look. "Why don't we take a break and go out for dinner?"

Nick hadn't eaten since the bite of croissant he'd devoured earlier at the bistro.

"Sounds great. Give me a minute to freshen up."

He went into the bathroom and looked in the mirror.

"Buenas noches, Señor Palmer."

It was the face of Juanita Diaz, the young woman who'd been murdered in Madrid. Her pretty features had a serious, almost solemn look. She spoke slowly and clearly, obviously wanting Nick to take in everything she was saying.

"In the early 1500s, the sisters of Charity founded a convent in Madrid. Christina de Delgado, one of the young novices who lived there, was devoutly Catholic and had a burning desire to spread the word of God's gospel throughout the world. It was she who stowed away on a ship to Mexico with the conquistadores."

Her image began to fade, but then added, in a slightly tentative voice. *"Perhaps, Señor Palmer, you'll discover something important in Madrid."*

Her reflection waned and vanished. Nick just stood there transfixed, staring at himself in the mirror for what seemed like an eternity. The voice of Henri interrupted his reverie.

"Are you ready for dinner, my dear friend?"

"Yes, I'm starving. Say, Henri, have you ever been to Madrid?"

CHAPTER TWENTY-FOUR

Nick tried calling his friend at the Paris police again. This time he was lucky.

"Bonsoir. C'est Alain Moreau."

"Hi Alain, it's Nick Palmer. I have a quick question I need answered."

"Ah, Nicholas, what is it you require?"

Nick wasn't sure if the man could still help him. The body of the man who'd tried to kill him was probably long gone from the basement room in the police station.

"Do you remember if there was a small red box, which looked like part of the snake tattoo, on the man whose body you found in the catacombs?"

"To tell you the truth, my friend, I don't, but I can check on it. His body is still downstairs. The last time I checked, the pathologists hadn't gotten around to doing the autopsy. Their workload is extreme."

Nick thanked the detective and went out to the living room where the professor was waiting. He'd tell the elderly scholar about his conversation with the detective later, over dinner.

ψ

Nigel Thomas, the Australian killer, called his employer at his country home.

"He's left Rome. Any idea where he'd go?"

"Fuck!" Hector Rodriguez said through clenched teeth. "I'd think he'd go to Paris. He's befriended a retired professor there and may be on his way to see him."

He purposely didn't tell the Australian about the unfortunate demise of Estella Calero, the woman who'd seemingly committed suicide in her prison cell in Rome.

ψ

Gabriela was at her desk in the South Wentworth Avenue station, deeply engrossed in whatever was on her computer screen. Her boss, Josh Nicholson, peered over her shoulder.

"Hey, Gabi, what are you working on? Looking to get yourself a tattoo?"

He'd startled her, and she hadn't had time to clear her screen. He saw images of the colorful and grotesque tattooed men and women she was looking at. She tried to sound nonchalant.

"Oh, hi boss, just following up on some leads on the Susan Roberts's case." Her face was as red as the bright lipstick she was wearing.

"For Nick, I assume?"

Gabriela smiled. The man had better instincts than people gave him credit for.

She cleared the images on her screen and brought her boss up to speed on the conversation she'd recently had with Nick, including the visions and warnings he'd told her about. Josh Nicholson looked skeptical. He still believed Nick should've seen a shrink, but the close calls on his detective's life were beginning to make a believer out of him.

"Do you really think all this 'woman in the mirror' crap is for real?"

She nodded. "The names have turned out to be legit. A couple so far, anyway."

Her boss's brow furrowed, as if he were deep in thought.

"Well, the Roberts case is still an open file, and God knows we still need something closed. Tell you what, I'll give you the time off, but travel and all that shit is on your nickel."

She leaped up from her desk and hugged the man. "Thanks, boss. I know I can help Nick with the case."

He quickly brushed her off. He didn't want the other officers in his department thinking he was becoming a softie. "Okay, get the hell out of here. Oh, hold on a minute. Let me get you Nick's police ID. It sounds like he may need it sometime soon."

She followed the man into his office, picked up Nick's badge and police identification card, then went back to her desk, grabbing her coat and heading for the exit. Josh Nicholson yelled after her. "And, for Christ's sake, Gabi, keep me informed!"

His words followed the departing woman as she rushed out onto the street.

ψ

Gabriela had managed to get the contact information of the tattoo artists Nick had wanted and called him to give him the news that she was booking a flight to California.

Nick, both surprised and delighted, and wondered just how she'd convinced their boss to let her go.

"You know, when you get to California, find out what you can from the tattoo artists, then join me here—and don't worry; I'll pick up the tab for you."

CHAPTER TWENTY-FIVE

Claire Rodriguez, Hector's wife of seventeen years, lived in Paris. Theirs was a loveless union of convenience. Her job—and she considered her marriage, to a man she hated a job—consisted of being available to accompany him on important social and business events throughout the world and spreading her legs when ordered to do so. For this she was paid a substantial salary. The one part of her job she cherished was being a mother to their two children, Philippe and Angelina, both of whom attended university in England.

In her previous life, Claire had been a highly sought-after model who'd graced the runways for top fashion designers throughout Europe and America. She was still stunningly beautiful and entertained a steady stream of lovers at the sumptuous apartment she and Hector owned in the city's fashionable 8th Arrondissement. She was getting dressed for a long, lingering lunch with one such paramour when she heard the phone ring. It was answered by Jacqueline, her longtime maid and confidante.

"Madame, that was Monsieur Hector. He told me to tell you to expect him tomorrow. He has business here and will be staying for two days."

"Shit, shit, shit! Jacqueline, cancel my lunch with Pierre and get Jonathan's things out of the apartment. I don't want any fights this time around."

The maid scurried away, and her mistress slipped out of her new Armani suit, replacing it with a tight-fitting pair of Versace jeans, a bright-orange Hermès sweater, and Chanel ballet slippers. She checked herself out in the ornate full-length mirror in her closet, and silently complimented herself on her still-stunning good looks.

ψ

Hector Rodriguez arrived in Paris. The driver who picked him up from the airport took him directly to the quai d'Anjou on Ile Saint-Louis, where he'd arranged to meet the Australian assassin. They faced each other on the sidewalk opposite Henri Deneuve's apartment building.

"Do you think they're here?"

The Australian sneered. "If they are, it makes my job a whole lot easier."

The killer walked across the avenue and rang a bell on the massive front door of the professor's building. There was no answer. He was about to turn away when the door opened, and he was greeted by an elderly woman in a loose-fitting housecoat that would have looked garish if it weren't so faded. Her long gray hair was piled high on her head with occasional wisps of truant locks falling across her face. She wore thick tortoiseshell eyeglasses that magnified her already bulbous pale-blue eyes, and her countenance looked anything but friendly.

"Pardon Madame, do you know if Professor Deneuve is at home?"

Her response to the Australian's question was delivered defensively. "Non, monsieur, he's not. May I ask who's calling, and I will pass on the message when he returns."

"My name is Nigel Thomas. I'm a colleague of Henri's at the university."

The woman didn't like the look of the man. He didn't look like an academic, but he obviously knew her elderly neighbor, so she passed on information she probably shouldn't have.

"The professor and his friend left about thirty minutes ago."

A wave of anger swept across the assassin's face; this was news he didn't want to hear.

"When are they expected to return?"

"Je ne sais pas, monsieur. They're going to the airport."

The woman sensed immediately that she had inadvertently put her elderly neighbor and his companion in danger and hated herself for being so thoughtless.

"Merci, madame."

The assassin turned and strode purposefully across the street to where Hector Rodriguez was waiting.

The woman peeked through her blinds at the two men, who were deep in conversation. Something about their manner sent a chill down her spine. It was a deep-seated fusion of fear and anguish she hadn't felt since the Nazis had pushed their way into her parents' home in 1942. Even though she had been just an infant, the horrible memory of the event remained. She picked up her cell and called the professor. He answered on the first ring.

"Bonjour, Denise. Is something wrong?"

The worried woman quickly told him what had just happened, and he passed the information on to Nick.

"Ask her to lock all the doors and stay put. I'm calling Alain."

The police officer was just walking into the station when his cell rang. He looked at the screen to see who was calling.

"Bonjour, Nicholas. What can I do for you on this beautiful morning?"

Upon hearing the story, his jovial demeanor vanished.

"I'm on it. Tell madame we're on our way and not to be alarmed."

ψ

Hector whispered instructions to the Australian killer.

"Get in, and if necessary, kill the woman; then search the fucking place. Perhaps they left a clue about where they're going."

The sounds of sirens suddenly broke through the early morning hubbub of a city in the throes of waking up. The two men waited for the armored police van to pass by and continue on its way. It didn't. Instead, it pulled up in front of Henri's building and four heavily armed gendarmes spilled out, taking up defensive positions at the front door. Hector turned to his accomplice.

"Let's get the hell out of here."

The Australian didn't need any encouragement. They walked towards Pont Marie, and once across the bridge and safely out of sight, they stopped. Hector was seething. His face had turned an ugly shade of purple, and his heart was pounding out of his chest. The Australian was much cooler. He'd been in many similar situations before and had always managed to get away scot-free.

Hector turned to his accomplice. "The old bitch must have called the cops." He almost spit out the words.

"Don't worry; I'll get 'em. I'll check the airports. Passenger info's always easy to get if you know how to pull the right strings."

"Stupid prick. What if she saw me? What if she could identify me? That kind of publicity could destroy me and everything I've ever worked for."

"Don't worry, boss. She's old and probably couldn't see her hand if it was in front of her face. Didn't you see the thick fucking eyeglasses she was wearing?"

The Australian's line of thinking did little to comfort him.

"Fuck you. Go and find out where they're going." He turned then and strode away. He wanted as little as possible to do with the man he'd hired.

The Australian killer flipped his middle finger towards the back of the departing man and smiled.

ψ

Nick and the professor were standing in the Air France line at Charles de Gaulle, waiting to purchase tickets for their flight to Madrid. Nick's gut was telling him something—something he couldn't put his finger on—but it was worrying him.

"You know, Henri, I've got a hunch this is a big mistake."

The old professor shot him a quizzical look.

"They'll think of checking airports. Perhaps we should take a train instead. That way there's no record of us leaving Paris."

"Whatever you say, my young friend. You're the detective. I'm new to this world of yours, but quite frankly, I'm enjoying every second of it. I've never had this much excitement. Being an academic is quite boring compared to this."

Nick smiled at the decency and naivete of his friend.

ψ

Hector was on his way back to Paris-Le Bourget, Europe's busiest private airport. He'd had his fill of the city and was anxious to return to his life in New York. He dialed his wife at their plush Paris apartment.

"Good news, darling. I'm not coming to see you this trip."

The sarcasm was dripping from his voice like venom from a rattlesnake. Claire Rodriguez tried not to sound happy.

"Oh, I'm sorry, my darling. Perhaps next time."

She hung up then, happily yelled and pumped her fist in the air.

CHAPTER TWENTY-SIX

Gabriela had an idea. Before booking her flight to the West Coast, she'd check in with the LAPD to see if they could help her with the investigation and save her the long trip. She found the number she wanted on a secure police website and dialed it.

A man answered. "Detective John Fraser."

"Good morning, this is Detective Gabriela Martinez of the Chicago Police Department. We're working on a homicide case and were wondering if you guys in LA could do a little leg work for us?" She gave the officer her badge number and contact information.

"Happy to oblige, Detective. How can we help you?"

Gabriela told the officer about the Susan Roberts murder in Chicago, and about the unusual circumstances of her death.

"The person we believe to be the perp has a unique tattoo of a snake on his back. I'll send you images of the tattoo, which we think may have been done by an expert inker, quite possibly in LA."

"Do you have any names?"

"Just a couple. I'll send those along too."

"Thanks, Martinez, that'll be a great help."

Gabriela had one more request from her West-Coast colleague. "Also, there's a small red square with a marking we're curious about. It could be the signature of the artist."

"Great, we'll take a close look at that too."

"If you need my assistance, or my department's, I can hop on a plane."

"Thanks. Send me all the info, and I'll get back to you as soon as I can."

Gabriela hung up and began the process of sending the relevant information to the detective in California.

ψ

Nick and the professor stepped out of the lineup at the airline counter, pushed their way through the seething mass of humanity crowding the departures level, and made their way to the line of waiting taxis outside the arrival doors at Charles de Gaulle. The train they were hoping to catch was scheduled to depart from the Gare de Lyon in a couple of hours.

It was a fast trip through the city. When they arrived at the train station, it was busy but nowhere near as crowded as the airport they'd just left. Nick was directed to the appropriate counter by an attractive blonde attendant at the information kiosk and was soon purchasing two premier-class tickets on the TGV high-speed train. Their trip would take them to Barcelona, then on to Madrid's Atocha train station. It would take them roughly twelve hours to reach their destination.

They moved easily through passport control and security. Thankfully, Alain Moreau had called the border authorities ahead of time and assured them that the Chicago police officer, who was legally carrying a concealed weapon, would not constitute a security threat to either the train or its passengers.

Nick and the professor found their seats and got comfortably settled. A steward brought them coffee, gave them directions to the buffet car, and explained the other benefits of their premier class travel accommodations. When the steward left, Nick excused himself and went to the washroom. He closed the door and turned to face the mirror, not knowing what to expect. Would it be just the reflection of himself looking back or one of his "mirror girls" (as he had begun to think of them)? This time the girl who faced him was someone totally new. She had dark-blonde hair done up in pigtails, dark expressive eyes, and millions of freckles on her well-tanned face.

Of all the girls, this one looked the most mischievous.

"Buenos días, Detective Palmer. My name is Adriana Diaz."

"We haven't met before."

"No, señor, me han pedido que lo ayude en España."

The girl smiled at his obvious discomfort.

"Sorry, Adriana. My Spanish is next to nonexistent. Do you speak English?"

"Lo siento, sorry. I said I have been chosen to be your angel in Spain."

"Are you an angel? Or a ghost?"

"Both. We are the ghosts of angels, señor."

Nick smiled at the contradiction. The pretty face of Adriana Diaz began to fade.

"Adiós lo Palmer."

When he returned to his seat, he found the professor deeply engrossed in a book on pseudoscience. Obviously, the old academic was trying to find a scientific rationale for the apparitions Nick was seeing, and the voices both he and Nick had heard.

"Penny for your thoughts, Henri."

The old man recoiled. Nick had surprised him, causing him to lose his concentration. He looked up and glared at the detective.

"No thoughts yet, my annoying young friend. Scientifically speaking, what's been happening to us is impossible."

He buried his head back into the book, oblivious to the beautiful countryside they were speeding through at 220 kilometers per hour.

ψ

Nigel Thomas, the Australian assassin, had one core belief: anyone or anything could be bought if the price were right. His viewpoint was, once again, proven valid in a grungy, unkept apartment in Goutte d'Or, an unpleasant and often dangerous, suburb of Paris—a district purposely overlooked on travel sites and in tourist books that tout the glamor and joie de vivre of the French capital.

The apartment in question was rented by an illegal immigrant from Nigeria, a woman in her mid-twenties with an uncanny skill for hacking into classified information on some of the world's most top-secret sites.

Efetobo Adebayo, known to her friends as Tobo, had a room filled with the latest computer gadgetry and technology, most of it stolen, purchased by her for a fraction of the retail cost. The woman spent most of her time crouched over an array of terminals. Today's uniform was tight, well-worn jeans and a black T-shirt with a graffiti image of a skull covering most of its front. She turned and looked up at the Australian.

"This one's easy, arabinrin."

She spoke with an appealing accent, part Yoruba, part French, and part English. Her voice was as soft as the constant hum of machines that filled the air of the confined space.

"Then get on with it. I didn't pay ya t' sit round gabbing."

The woman went to work and was soon deep into the secure passenger list files of all flights leaving that day from both Charles de Gaulle and Orly airports. Soon—very soon—lists of names began to scroll down her screens. She scanned the screens with a practiced eye of a professional, then turned to her guest.

"Sorry, monsieur. Nobody by the name of Nicholas Palmer or Henri Deneuve has taken a flight out of Paris today."

The man went white with anger, pulling out a gun and pointing it at the terrified woman's head.

"Gimme my money back, bitch. I didn't pay ya t' get sweet-fuck-all."

Efetobo quickly reached into the back pocket of her jeans and handed the cash back to the man. She muttered something under her breath and watched him leave. As soon as the door to her apartment closed behind the exiting Australian, she picked up her cell and dialed a number.

"James, it's Tobo. Some prick stiffed me for my fee. He just left my crib. Can you get the money back for me? I'll split it with you."

Efetobo went back to her computers. Leaning forward, she felt a slight breeze against her face, but it wasn't a breeze, really. It felt more like someone had gently caressed her cheek with a down feather. She wrote it off to the morning's excitement.

Margaux Deneuve smiled and vanished silently, and invisibly, into the ethereal world that she (and the others like her) inhabited.

ψ

The Australian killer didn't make it to the building's front door. He was met in the grungy stairwell by four well-armed Nigerian gangsters. He was no match for the men called upon by the diminutive Tobo, and he was left broken, bleeding, and very much dead in a vacant lot three blocks away from the scene of the fight and ensuing murder.

Nick and Henri had no inkling that the man Hector Rodriguez had hired to kill them was now himself dead.

CHAPTER TWENTY-SEVEN

Hector Rodriguez was enraged and uncharacteristically disconcerted. Everything in his carefully orchestrated life was systematically unraveling, and it had all begun with the girl in Chicago, sacrificed to Quetzalcoatl.

His company, IGI (Inca Gold Investments), was seriously under-performing, and the firm's shareholders and investors were beginning to question his leadership and authority. There were similar rumblings and rumors of discontent from the twelve apostles who made up the inner council of La Orden de las Serpientes de Cristo. To top it off, the goddamned cop from Chicago seemed to be shatterproof. Rodriguez slammed his fist down on his desk so hard that the silver-framed photographs of his two children fell facedown.

"Where the fuck is the Australian? Why the hell hasn't he called?"

The angry spittle that spewed from between his thin dry lips sprayed out like a virus-laden sneeze. He paced angrily back and forth, finally stopping at the massive floor-to-ceiling window occupy-ing one whole wall of his office. Looking down, he saw the throngs of people crowding the lower Manhattan sidewalks. Going to work, going to lunch, going about their business, trying desperately to carve out a small niche of happiness and success from the dog-eat-dog life in America's biggest city.

Fucking lemmings, followers going nowhere until they jump off the cliff to their deaths.

He turned, strode back to his desk, and picked up the photographs of his children. He stared at one, and then the other, for what seemed like an hour but was, in reality just a few seconds.

Angelina's the one. She's the only one strong enough to take over from me one day.

ψ

The phone on Gabriela's desk rang. It was the detective from California.

"Good afternoon, Detective Martinez. It's Fraser at the LAPD. What do you want first, the good news or the bad news?"

"Always the good news. Somehow it makes the bad news easier to take."

The man on the other end of the call laughed.

"Well, it seems like the community of tattoo artists here are a very close-knit group. They all seem to know each other and each other's work—at least, masters of the art do."

Gabriela was beginning to get impatient. She wasn't one for long preambles. "Is that the good news, or the bad news?"

"Well, it seems like the person you're looking for is Mexican, but here's the bad news. It's not any of the people whose names you gave us. Everyone we've spoken to acknowledges the artist is a master inker, but none of them knows who it is. Also, none of them has ever seen an image of a snake like the one you sent me."

"So where do you think this leaves us?"

"Quite frankly, I don't know, but if it was my operation, I'd head to Mexico City and start looking around there."

She thanked the officer and hung up. Her next call was to Nick, who was hurtling south on the train to Madrid. He checked the call display and answered on the first ring.

"Hi. Still miss me?"

"Oh, shut up! You know I do. Say, what's that loud noise?"

"It's either the train or Henri's snoring."

Nick's traveling companion had been sleeping, his face scrunched up against the window, for the better part of an hour. The book he'd been reading was lying at his feet, open to a chapter on paranormal activities.

"Train? Where are you going now?"

"Madrid."

Nick told Gabriela what had recently transpired, including his latest encounter with the girl in the train's washroom mirror.

"Well, thank God someone's looking out for you two babies, even if she is a ghost. Do you want to hear my news?"

"Absolutely. Anything to keep you on the line."

"Oh, shut up. It's important."

Nick laughed at her feigned annoyance. In truth, he just loved the sound of her voice and wished he could be with her.

Gabriela told him about her conversation with the LAPD detective, including his suggestion she go to Mexico City.

"What do you think? Should I go?"

"No, I'd rather you came to Spain. We can go to Mexico City together, after we finish up in Madrid."

In all his time as a cop, he'd seen some rough-looking tattoo parlors, and he somehow knew the ones in Mexico City would be the same—or very possibly worse. He didn't want her getting into any dangerous situations without the backup of a partner—and that partner, for sure, was going to be him.

"Great idea. I speak Spanish, and I know neither of you two conquistadores do. Let me know when you get there, and I'll make the arrangements to fly over." He heard a kissing sound over the phone. "Love you." Then she was gone.

Nick was left alone with his thoughts but in the company of an old academic who somehow felt like the father he'd never known.

ψ

The professor woke with a start. He looked out the window, then reached down for his book. Randomly flipping through several pages of the tome, he turned to face Nick.

"It's an interesting fact that over forty percent of Americans, your fellow countrymen, believe in ghosts, and over fifty percent believe in life after death, but... my young friend, general acceptance still doesn't make it real."

He referred to his book, and when he lifted his head again, his face showed a look of total skepticism. Henri continued, as if he were lecturing to a room full of attentive students.

"However, some science points to paranormal activities that are actually seen as being illusions caused by overactive minds or perhaps an affliction brought on by schizophrenia. The good news, Nicholas, is that I don't believe you suffer from either condition."

Henri turned his attention back to his book. Nick was sure he glimpsed a mischievous smile on the old man's face.

"Let's go and grab a bite to eat, Professor."

"Merveilleuse idée, Nicholas. Just let me clean up first."

ψ

When Henri got to the washroom, he bent over the sink to splash some water on his face. He was about to reach for the hand towel when an image of a girl appeared in the mirror before him.

"Hola, Professor Deneuve, un placer conocerte."

The elderly professor almost leapt out of his skin. He dropped the towel and jumped away from the image in the mirror, backing up until he hit the wall behind him, still not taking his eyes of the apparition that was facing him.

"Qui es-to? w-w-who and what are you?"

The apparition was laughing so hard at the professor's amazement that tears were running down her beautiful face.

"If you could only see your face, señor."

She took a deep breath and regained her composure.

"My name is Adriana Diaz. I am one of Detective Palmer's guardian angels. Because you're beginning to consider our actuality, and because our detective friend likes and trusts you, I've been asked by the others to appear, to speak to you in person, and hopefully alleviate any doubts you may have about our existence."

The professor reached down, picked up the towel, and wiped his face. He was hoping that with this simple act, the apparition in the mirror would also be wiped away.

But the face of Adriana Diaz was still there, looking directly at him. She lifted her hand and placed her palm against the back of the mirror. Henri tentatively reached forward and placed his palm against hers. The mirror didn't feel like cold, hard glass; it was soft and warm like a young woman's touch. He quickly pulled back his hand.

"Now do you believe, señor? Now do you believe?"

She paused, looking straight into the old professor's eyes and slowly starting to fade away.

"Start your quest at the Convent of Las Descalzas Reales in Madrid."

There was a loud knocking on the washroom door, which snapped him out of his trance, breaking his eye contact with the girl.

"Henri? Henri? Are you okay in there?"

The professor returned his gaze to the mirror and spoke to it in a barely discernible whisper.

"Sí, señorita. I believe. Now I believe."

CHAPTER TWENTY-EIGHT

Angelina Rodriguez was twenty-three. She'd inherited all her mother's good looks, had a brilliant mind, and excelled academically. She was also a relentlessly tough competitor and ranked first in most scholastic and sporting competitions. What she'd inherited from her father was a mean streak and a win-at-all-costs mentality that often set her at odds with her classmates and teachers. Even though she was beautiful and intelligent, she had few friends and no suitors.

Like her father, she didn't give a damn. She was in it for herself and herself alone.

Her brother, Philippe, on the other hand, was personable and well-liked. He was a handsome young man who also did exceptionally well at school. He knew that, when the time came to take over their father's business, it was very likely that his older sister would be his boss, and it didn't bother him one iota. He knew that, whatever happened, he'd be well taken care of financially.

They were both aware that their father ran a successful financial management company on Wall Street, but because they had scant understanding of their Mexican lineage and heritage, neither of them knew about La Orden de las Serpientes de Cristo or Hector's exalted position within it.

Angelina was studying economics and business. She had almost completed the thesis for her master's degree and was putting the final touches on the document when her cell rang. The voice on the other end of the call was deep and portentous.

"Hello, Angelina, it's your father."

She was excited to hear from the man she both admired and feared. He didn't call often, only when he felt it necessary to congratulate her on one of her numerous achievements.

"I want you to come to New York. I believe the time has come for me to begin mentoring you about our business—just like my father did for me, and his father did for him. I must prepare you for the eventuality of taking control."

She hadn't expected this line of conversation and was uncharacteristically worried about his well-being.

"Daddy, are you okay?"

"I'm fine, Angelina, but it's never too early to be prepared. You'll stay with me at the apartment in Manhattan. Just let me know when you'll be able to come."

Hector Rodriguez hung up, walked over to the bar in his office, and poured himself a tall glass of La Ley Del Diamante, the world's most expensive tequila. He looked impatiently at his watch, as if it would somehow answer the question he was obsessing over: *Why in Christ's name hasn't the Australian checked in?*

His second call of the evening was to the Paris bureau chief of the New York Times, who he had met socially at one of the tedious galas his wife, Claire, had dragged him to.

The man answered on the first ring. "Bryan Evans here."

"Mr. Evans, this is Hector Rodriguez calling. We met—"

"Yes, I remember. What can I do for you, Mr. Rodriguez? An interview perhaps?"

It was a long shot for the newsman. Hector Rodriguez was famous for zealously guarding both his business and private life. He'd never given interviews and shunned the press as much as was possible for a man of such great wealth.

"Sorry, Mr. Evans, not yet, but if you could assist me with a little problem, we could perhaps discuss the possibility at a later date."

The New York financier paused, as if he were considering the wisdom of his call. Finally, deciding his options were limited, he pressed on. "What I am requesting is strictly off the record. Total discretion and confidentiality are important, and necessary. Do we understand each other?"

The man at the Times was intrigued. Why would a man like Rodriguez need anything from him? But the possibility of an exclusive interview with the elusive businessman appealed to his journalistic soul.

"What can I do for you, Mr. Rodriguez?"

"There's a man, an associate of mine in Paris, who seems to have gone missing. I don't want to call the police directly, because of the publicity it may cause. I just need you to make some discreet enquiries as to where he is, or what might have happened to him."

Rodriguez gave the newsman the assumed name of the Australian he'd hired to deal with the detective from Chicago and his description.

"I'll do what I can, Mr. Rodriguez. Can I reach you at this number?"

Rodriguez agreed and hung up.

Bryan Evans looked at the recorded number on his cell phone. This felt like it could be the beginnings of an interesting story… conversely, it could be a complete waste of time. He dialed the number of an old friend in the Paris police department.

"Bonjour, Alain. It's Bryan Evans. I've just received an interesting call."

The detective lieutenant listened intently as his friend told him about the call from Rodriguez.

"Please keep in mind that this is all totally off-the-record stuff. I don't want the wrath of Rodriguez coming down on me if he finds out I called you."

"Don't worry, my friend. I'll make some discreet enquiries. If there's something illegal going on, I'll call you. If there's something immoral going on, I'll call you about that, too."

The Paris police officer laughed at his own little joke and hung up. The man from the New York Times just rolled his eyes.

ψ

"It's not plausible. It's not possible. It's not real… but I saw her with my own eyes and heard her with my own ears."

Henri stood staring at Nick. He looked like he'd just seen a ghost, which of course he had, his face almost as pale as the white shirt he wore beneath his gray cardigan. His voice had a slight tremor. Nick reached out and took the elderly man by the arm.

"Henri, are you okay?"

"I just met your friend Adriana. She was right there in the mirror, just like you've been telling me, but it's impossible; ghosts just don't exist. They just don't, but there she was."

The professor regained his composure and shook off Nick's hand. "Let's go and get something to eat. I hope what they have is delicious, because now I'm really famished."

He marched ahead of Nick to the dining car. Everything he'd ever believed in was now in question. Every scientific theory, every rational thought, everything needed to be re-examined and reviewed. Regardless, he believed that what he saw in the mirror was real, and everything he'd heard and discussed with Nicholas was true. He decided he wouldn't be searching anymore for the scientific evidence he needed to prove that his friend was losing his mind. He felt relieved and slightly remorseful about his previous doubts.

ψ

Alain Moreau didn't like the way things were going. The bloody body his people had found in Goutte d'Or matched exactly the description his friend at the New York Times had given him, though the name didn't match.

Forensics had identified the body as Nigel Thomas, an Australian and escaped murderer, whose name occupied one of the top spots on the most-wanted lists of law-enforcement jurisdictions throughout the world. What a man like Hector Rodriguez was doing with scum like Nigel Thomas was uncertain, but troubling. He dialed his friend at the Times.

"Bryan, it's Alain. I've got some interesting news about the friend of your friend Monsieur Rodriguez."

The detective lieutenant recounted the conversations he'd had with fellow officers regarding the murdered man, including the victim's criminal history.

"I think, Bryan, we'd like to have a conversation with your Monsieur Rodriguez. Do you know where I can reach him?"

Bryan Evans paused; he'd promised the New York businessman that whatever he learned would be off the record, but now it looked like it could be front-page news. He crossed his fingers and lied to the police officer.

"No, Alain, he said he'd be in touch in a couple of days. I'll call as soon as I hear from him."

He hung up and buried his head in his hands. He'd never lied to the authorities before, and now he was getting himself into a situation that could be construed as obstructing justice, or even aiding and abetting a criminal. He had no doubt he would be fired for his indiscretion if discovered, though he knew the police could quickly track down Rodriguez without his help. It was just a matter of time. He felt the clammy sweat from his hands sticking to his cheeks. He didn't know what he should do next, but he'd better think of something fast, because both his reputation and his career were now at risk.

CHAPTER TWENTY-NINE

Their high-speed train pulled into Madrid's Atocha Railway Station on schedule. Nick and Henri picked up their bags and detrained.

Atocha is one of Europe's most beautiful train stations. The original 1892 train shed has been transformed into a passenger-friendly oasis with a soothing turtle pool surrounded by several bars and restaurants. The exit to a waiting line of taxis is located off this cavernous, garden-like haven. Nick and the professor decided to sit and have coffee before continuing on to their hotel.

Nick had booked two rooms at the Hotel Mexico. The budget accommodation was near the Convent of Las Descalzas Reales, home to the order of cloistered Franciscan nuns where Adriana Diaz had said they should start their investigation.

Nick sipped his drink and watched as his friend tried to process the events of the past several hours.

"Nicholas, we're being guided and guarded by apparitions—apparitions for which there is absolutely no logic or scientific rationale or explanation. Now, both you and I have seen and heard them."

The old man paused, sipping his coffee, and then continued. "They've given us directions and are leading us to God knows where, and it's very possible where they're directing us could lead to some dire and very dangerous consequences."

He reached up and scratched his head, leaving his shock of virtually white hair in disarray.

Nick couldn't help smiling at his friend. He'd often had similar thoughts himself, but the specter of all those murdered girls was something he couldn't walk away from.

They finished their coffees, found a taxi, and were soon racing through the busy streets of the Spanish capital. The endless array of colorful shops and restaurants they passed on route were a pleasant distraction from their dark thoughts. As their car was careening around another busy corner, Nick's cell rang. It was Gabriela, and she sounded very happy.

"Hi, handsome. Want company?"

"Well, it's a lot hotter here than it is in Chicago."

"Trust me, I can make it even hotter. Where are you?"

"Henri and I are on our way to the hotel. I've booked a double room for us."

"Isn't that a little presumptuous of you? How'd you know I'd be coming?"

"Let's just say I had a hunch. When do you get in?"

"I'm at O'Hare waiting to board shortly. Should be there in the morning. Try to stay out of trouble until I get there. Oh, and give Henri a big hug for me."

He laughed. "You can do that yourself when you get here."

"Love you."

The line went dead, and he slipped the device back into his jacket pocket.

The Hotel Mexico was much nicer than he'd anticipated. They received a warm welcome from the accommodating front-desk attendant and were shown to their rooms by an equally friendly bellman. The accommodation was anything but luxurious, but it was clean, well appointed, and had everything they needed in the way of toiletries. Nick fell back onto the bed, bounced up and down, and thought about the imminent arrival of his partner from Chicago.

The plan for the evening was to have an early dinner of paella

Valencia and a good night's sleep. Unfortunately, neither of them had considered the eating habits of Madrilenians: work, lunch, siesta, work again, tapas, and dinner at about ten or eleven. They found a neighborhood tapas bar and filled up on the delicious selection of small dishes laid out on the counter.

After finishing their meal, they walked back to the hotel and said goodnight. Nick went into the small bathroom, flipped on the lights, and looked in the mirror.

"Buenas noches, Detective Palmer."

The young woman facing him was not Adriana Diaz but instead Juanita Diaz, one of the first "mirror girls" he had encountered. He was well beyond being shocked by what he was seeing.

"You're Adriana's twin sister?'

"Sí, we are sisters. It was the only time two were sacrificed to that unholy god—on one horrific night."

Her face portrayed a look of unbearable anguish and a powerful resolve to get retribution for the years of lonely nothingness she, her sister, and all the others had suffered.

Nick tried to imagine the brutality, the absolute terror, and unspeakable agony the two beautiful young sisters had suffered through during that cold November night in 1962. It sent a frigid shiver through his entire body.

"Your sister told us she'd be our guardian angel here in Spain."

"She and I will share those duties. With three of you to guide and protect now, one of us is not enough."

"How do you know Detective Martinez will be joining us?" He looked directly into the girl's eyes, offering a cheeky half smile. "And do you think just the two of you is enough?"

Juanita smiled back. *"Only if you behave yourselves, señor."*

The image of Juanita Diaz slowly faded. Nick splashed cold water on his face, took off his clothes, and fell into bed. He was asleep in seconds.

ψ

Gabriela's eight-hour Iberia flight from Chicago's O'Hare airport arrived at 7:45 the following morning. Nick had managed to drag himself out of bed and was waiting for her in front of the international arrivals gate at Madrid's airport. It seemed like an eternity since he'd last seen her. So much had happened. His previous life, as a Chicago police officer, seemed dull by comparison.

When she came striding through the double glass doors, every man in the crowd wished he were the one she'd be looking for. Gabi spotted Nick, flashed a smile that could light the whole Empire State Building, and wrapped her arms around him in an embrace that virtually took his breath away.

"Jesus, Nick, I've really missed you."

Nick felt his shoulders drop and his worries melt away like ice cream on a slice of hot apple pie.

"Me too! Let's get out of here. We're supposed to meet Henri back at the hotel for breakfast."

He took her by the arm, picked up her carry-on, and marched her to the line of taxis waiting at the front door of the terminal. He didn't know it, but he wore the smile of a man who was very much in love.

ψ

Alain Moreau called off the security detail he'd stationed at Henri Deneuve's apartment building, but he still needed to question Denise Faucher, the professor's neighbor, about the men who'd been enquiring into the whereabouts of the elderly academic. He rang the bell to the woman's apartment and waited. He caught a glimpse of her face peeking through the slightly opened curtains before she came to the door.

"Bonjour, Madame Faucher. I'm Detective Lieutenant Alain Moreau of la PP. I'd like to ask you a few questions about the man who came here looking for Professor Deneuve."

The woman invited the officer into her apartment. The room was stuffy and musty, filled with worn furnishings, threadbare carpets, and the smell of what seemed like hundreds of cats. The detective tried to stifle a sneeze but was unsuccessful.

"Pardon Madame. I must be getting a cold."

He took out a photograph of the Australian killer that had been taken in the morgue and passed it to her. Even with all the cuts and bruises on his face, the likeness was unmistakable.

"Oui, monsieur. That is one of the men. The one who came to the door."

The officer showed the woman a photograph of Hector Rodriguez. "Is this the other man?"

The woman took the photograph and stared at it for about thirty seconds before shrugging and handing it back to the officer.

"I am not sure, monsieur. He was across the street, and most of the time all I saw was his back. My eyesight isn't what it used to be." She pointed to the thick lenses in her glasses.

Alain Moreau thanked the woman and saw himself out of the dingy apartment. As soon as he got into the hallway, he let out another huge sneeze. The woman looked out through a crack in the closing door and shouted to the departing police officer.

"Brandy and honey, monsieur, brandy and honey. It will cure your cold by tomorrow."

The officer smiled, waved back at her, and walked out into the fresh air.

ψ

When Nick and Gabriela arrived at the hotel, Henri was waiting for them in the lobby.

"Bonjour, Mademoiselle Gabriela. It's wonderful to see you again."

The elderly professor scooped her up in his arms and kissed her on both cheeks. Then he released her from his grip but still held her, at arm's length, by the shoulders.

"I've become really attached to this companion of yours." He looked over towards Nick, who had a grin on his face that was as wide as the grill of a '49 Cadillac. "He's taught me more about life in the short time I've known him than anything I've learned from all the books I've ever read. Make sure you take good care of him. Promise me."

"Don't worry, Henri. You know I will."

The three friends went to find a café where they could have breakfast and plan their visit to the Convent of Las Descalzas Reales—the place where Adriana Diaz had suggested they begin their search.

CHAPTER THIRTY

The Convent of Las Descalzas Reales was founded in 1559 by Joanna of Austria. Since its inception, it has been home to an order of cloistered nuns, and it was from this convent that the novice nun Christina de Delgado had left to go to Mexico with the conquistadors.

Nick, Gabriela, and Henri entered the magnificent seventeenth-century neoclassical Renaissance building that fronted the Plaza de las Descalzas in downtown Madrid. The historic convent also served as a museum, run by the Patrimonio Nacional, Spain's functionary overseer of National Heritage sites, though it was still home to a few cloistered nuns.

Gabriela asked the man attending the reception desk if it would be possible to have a few words with the Mother Superior of the Order. There followed a long, wildly animated conversation, in Spanish, until finally the man reluctantly agreed to see if the elderly nun would be agreeable to meeting them.

He sent a guide scurrying off to carry the message to the Mother Superior.

Gabriela turned to Nick and the professor. She had a look on her face that could best be described as falteringly hopeful.

"Problem is… 'cloistered' means exactly that. These nuns have shut themselves off from the outside world. They generally don't meet or see anyone who isn't in the order. I've told him it's a police investigation, hoping that might work."

They waited for what seemed like an eternity, watching the comings and goings of tourists from all over the world, anxious to see the priceless treasures held within the walls of the convent.

Eventually the guide returned, followed slowly by an elderly woman dressed head to toe in an ominous, black nun's habit. She motioned them to follow her to a private room off one of the building's main galleries. She faced them and spoke quietly to Gabriela. Her quavering voice had a decidedly hostile tone. Then she faced the men and spoke in almost fluent English.

"What is it you require from me?"

Nick was taken aback by the woman's directness. He was not expecting this kind of response from the old woman.

"We are investigating the murders of numerous young women, instigated by a religious cult called La Orden de las Serpientes de Cristo. We believe one of the cult's founders was a novice from this convent, who left for Mexico in the early fifteen-hundreds."

The old woman's deeply lined face showed no sign of shock, nor any knowledge of the cult or the young nun who was supposedly instrumental in founding the offshoot religion. It was as if the Mother Superior's features were carved in stone, like the cold, hard walls of the room in which they were standing. She turned her gaze to Nick and then to the others. The disdain in her eyes was bone-chilling.

"You're wasting my time."

She left the room in a swirl of coarse black fabric, moving much more quickly than would be expected of a woman of her advanced years. The three of them were left staring at each other. They couldn't believe they'd come so far for so little.

"She's not Spanish. She's Mexican. I could tell by her accent."

Nick and Henri looked at Gabriela as if wanting more information. She shrugged and suggested they find someplace nearby where they could get a cup of coffee and discuss their options.

Henri declined. He wanted instead to look at the stunning art and rare antiquities proudly displayed on the museum's ancient walls and in its many display cases.

"They have a magnificent collection of priceless masterpieces and tapestries, and if I don't see them now, I'm sure I won't be getting another opportunity anytime soon."

As the old professor wandered off towards the museum's interior, he glanced back, over his shoulder, and smiled at them.

"Au revoir, mes amis." Call me on my cell and let me know where I can meet you."

ψ

Henri strolled quietly through the museum, stopping occasionally to marvel at some of the museum's numerous masterpieces, most of which were hundreds of years old.

One of the main galleries was eerily quiet, with just an American couple in their early thirties, plugged into audio guides supplied at the reception desk, looking intently at something on display on the far side of the room. Henri guessed, by their body language, that they might be on their honeymoon. Their affection for each other fondly reminded him of his two friends, Nicholas and Gabriela.

The Mother Superior entered the far end of the gallery. She was stooped over, looking down towards her feet. As she shuffled along the stone floor, she fiddled with a rosary held loosely in her gnarled fingers. She bumped into the surprised professor, and the rosary she held dropped to the floor.

"Disculpe, señor."

The professor kindly accepted her apology and bent down to pick up the rosary. As he was bent over, the old nun pulled a hypodermic from where it was hidden in the sleeve of her voluminous habit and plunged it into the neck of the unsuspecting academic.

Henri collapsed onto the floor and was dead within seconds. The nun then walked swiftly away from the man's crumpled body and vanished through a doorway in the gallery. A few minutes after the nun had left the scene, the young American couple found the elderly man's body and sounded the alarm.

Henri's cell rang, and the young American pulled it from the dead man's pocket. He looked at the instrument, then tentatively answered.

"H-h-hello."

"Who am I speaking to? Is this Henri Deneuve's phone?"

The young American tried to explain what had happened. He didn't finish the story.

"Stay right there! Don't move or touch anything. I'm on my way."

Nick grabbed Gabriela by the arm, threw some cash on the table to cover their drinks, and rushed out of the café back towards the convent.

"Something's happened to Henri."

He didn't have to say anything more. The anguish in his voice said it all.

ψ

When Nick and Gabriela entered the gallery, they found ten or twelve people gathered around the professor's body. Nick pushed his way through and knelt beside his friend. He felt the man's wrist for any sign of a pulse. There was none.

Nick fell onto his friend's body, his desolation quickly giving way to uncontrollable sobbing. His pain was excruciating, the most he'd experienced since the death of his mother. In the short time he'd known the man, they'd become close—very close. Henri was more like a father to him than the biological father he'd never known. The wretchedness in his heart was searing, the anguish overpowering, and the guilt he felt about bringing the kindly old man into danger tore at his soul. This wasn't the way it was supposed to end. This wasn't how he imagined his friend would die, far away from his beloved Paris, his books, and his quiet life. Nick's grief was beyond comprehension, and he struck out in anger.

"Get out of here! All of you, get the hell out of here!"

He started pushing out at the small gathering until Gabriela pulled him into her arms. His head collapsed on her shoulder, and he cried the tears of a man who felt he'd lost everything—everything except his love for the woman who now gently held and comforted him.

ψ

The old nun's room at the convent was cold and spare. There was an iron-strung single bed with a thin, lumpy mattress, a well-worn wooden desk with a small drawer, and a hard wooden chair. Across from the bed was an ancient armoire where the woman kept her meager belongings.

She sat down on the bed and breathed a sigh of relief. She had completed the task she'd set herself to do, killing one of the evil ones who were attempting to unravel the religion to which she'd devoted her whole life. Then she opened the desk drawer and dropped her rosary next to a coil of multicolored rope.

She lifted the rope, ran it through her fingers, and bowed her head in prayer—not to Jesus Christ, or to the Virgin Mary, but to Quetzalcoatl, the serpent god. Next, she retrieved a cell phone from a drawer in her armoire. It was against the rules of the order to have such a device, but as a member of the twelve apostles of La Orden de las Serpientes de Cristo, she was obligated to have one. She pressed 1-1 on the cell's dial pad.

"Buenas noches, Cardinal. Henri Deneuve is dead."

Hector Rodriguez couldn't believe what he was hearing. "How? When? Give me the details."

Mother Christina de Delgado told the man about the Chicago detective and his friends visiting her at the convent, and about how, when the professor was alone, she had managed to kill him.

"I heard people at the scene say the old man must have had a heart attack."

"Excellent work, Christina, excellent work. You will be rewarded twice in the afterlife."

The man was exuberant, amazed the old hag had it in her to do this.

The old woman, who'd taken the name of the original innocent girl who'd gone to Mexico to spread the word of God—the old woman, who'd refused her share of the treasures due her as a member of the twelve apostles (the old woman, whom he disliked intensely)—had rid him one of his greatest adversaries.

Hector leaned back in his chair, poured himself a tall glass of tequila, and raised a toast to the old hag in Madrid.

ψ

Mother Christina de Delgado readied herself for bed. She carefully removed her habit and hung it in the armoire, then slipped a coarse linen nightgown over her frail body. She hadn't seen the serpent tattoo on her back for more years than she could remember, but now, in the darkened room, she felt again the sting of the needle as it made a thousand jabs into her much younger flesh.

CHAPTER THIRTY-ONE

"Heart attack? What do you mean, heart attack?"

Nick was on the line to the hospital where they'd taken his old friend. He couldn't believe what he was hearing. This wasn't in their plans. This wasn't the way his friend was supposed to die—all alone in a strange place far from home. Gabriela sat silently, her heart aching for her lover, and for the old professor she'd only recently met.

Nick slammed down the phone and shuffled into the bathroom. He was despondent and angry. *"Where were the guardian angels who were supposed to be watching over them? How could they let the gentle professor die like that?"*

He slammed his fist into the wall.

The reflected image of two young women appeared in the mirror, their faces showing the same anguish Nick felt in his heart. He struck out at them.

"Why? Why did you let him die like that? Why a fucking heart attack?"

The twin sisters, Adriana and Juanita Diaz, looked back at him, tears trickling down their cheeks from reddened eyes. Juanita stepped back behind her sister and her image faded, like the ghost she was.

Adriana spoke, her voice tenuous and infinitely sad. *"It was not a heart attack, Señor Palmer. Henri Deneuve was murdered."*

The news hit him hard, so hard he felt like he was going to throw up, but the bile in his throat was nothing compared to the anger he was feeling towards the girls in the mirrors—the girls he'd trusted and believed in. It was this anger that flowed out from between his clenched teeth now, aimed directly towards Adriana Diaz.

"Who killed him? Why didn't you warn him? What the fuck are you? Why are you doing this to me? What good are you?!"

He leaned over the sink and cried like a man condemned to eternal damnation.

Then Adriana explained. Her voice was a whisper—so soft, so empathetic, and so heartfelt that it felt as if it were being spoken by a soft cloud in a clear blue sky.

"Henri Deneuve had a bad heart, a very bad heart. Even if he hadn't been murdered, he would have died today anyway. We cannot warn you about natural events: we can only protect you from danger. His body will provide you with a clue that will lead you to retribution. Retribution for you, for the professor, and for all of us."

The girl's image faded and vanished, and Nick was left looking at his own pale, disheveled image. He splashed water on his face, pushed his hair back, and went out to face Gabriela.

"It wasn't a heart attack. Henri was murdered."

She looked at him as if he'd lost his mind. "The doctors said it was his heart. Why are you doing this? Can't you just let it be? Why do you think evil about everything? Let's just go home."

She slumped back into the chair, staring at him, her mouth tightly pursed. Then she dropped her head down into her hands and began to cry. Nick walked over and sat beside her, putting his arm around her shoulder and doing his best to comfort the stricken woman. After several moments, she raised her head, now with a look of steely determination—a look he'd seen many times before when they'd worked on tough cases back in Chicago.

"Let's go and get the bastards."

Nick smiled. This tough cop persona was one of the things he loved about the woman.

ψ

"I'll call Alain Moreau and tell him to expect Henri's body. I need the forensic guys in Paris to confirm the cause of his death. If it's murder, as Adriana said it was, we'll find a clue, but first I have to call Henri's sister and break the bad news to her."

"Adriana? I'm assuming that's one of your mirror girls?"

Nick nodded and picked up the phone to make the kind of call he'd always hated. It was answered on the second ring.

"Bonjour! Madeline Boucher parle."

"Bonjour, Madame Boucher. It's Nicholas Palmer. I'm afraid that I have some very bad news for you."

He paused, not quite knowing how he should proceed, then just got right to the point of the call. "Henri is dead. The doctors, here in Madrid, believe he suffered a massive heart attack."

"Mon dieu! My poor brother!" There was a long pause. Finally, the woman in Provins spoke again. "Do you believe it was a heart attack, Detective Palmer?"

Nick was caught off guard by the woman's uncanny perception and directness. He was expecting tears... or at least some indication of grief and loss.

Madeline Boucher explained. "I am, of course, heartbroken, as I'm certain you are. Henri had a great love and respect for you, the kind of love and respect I'm sure you had for him, but he also had a very serious heart condition. Since meeting you, he became his old self once more, full of energy and enthusiasm. You, Detective Palmer, extended his life far beyond what was expected, and for that, I am eternally grateful. But I can tell, by the tone of your voice, that you suspect foul play."

The Frenchwoman paused, took a deep breath, and resumed

speaking. "Because of what you meant to my brother, I will support you in any way and down any avenue you wish to travel to discover the truth."

Nick thanked the elderly Frenchwoman and told her he'd be in touch as soon as they got back to Paris. Then he called his friend Alain Moreau.

ψ

Henri's body arrived at the police morgue in Paris and their forensic team began the slow, and often arduous, task of performing the autopsy.

It didn't take long for the doctors to discover the tiny puncture in Henri's neck. Blood analysis soon determined the cause of death to be poison, injected by a hypodermic needle into the old academic's external jugular. This information was passed on to the detective lieutenant, Nick, and the Madrid police.

ψ

Nick had arranged to meet Madeline Boucher at her brother's apartment on the Ile Saint-Louis.

The place hadn't changed since he was last there. The presence of his old friend permeated every nook and cranny of the cluttered rooms, the countless books, extraordinary art, well-worn furnishings, and his computers. It felt as if the man had just left to take a stroll along the Seine, perhaps to get a coffee at one of the island's charming cafés, or lunch at one of the city's much-loved bistros.

Madeline Boucher knocked and entered the apartment. As before, she was impeccably dressed in vintage couturier French fashion. She looked around at the organized shambles of books and papers that defined her brother, then sat and faced Nick and Gabriela.

"My brother gave me a letter before you left for Spain. It was his wish that you, Nicholas, be his sole heir. This apartment, its contents, his cash, and his investments... are all to be yours."

Nick was dumbfounded, and for a moment, he didn't know what to say.

The woman continued. "As I told you, although he hadn't known you for long, he felt you were like a son. It was his wish to leave everything to you... and I am in total agreement."

"But—"

"But nothing, young man. I'm old and neither he nor I have any other family. Once I'm gone, it will be the end of the Deneuve's. Like Henri, I feel it's better to leave what we have to a loved and trusted friend rather than to the government."

Nick didn't know what to say to the kindly old woman. "But I... we don't even live here."

"I'm sure you soon will, and soon will come to love Paris and France as Henri did, and I do. There's nothing more to be said but to arrange for dear Henri's funeral, and of course, find the persons who perpetrated his murder. I hope you won't mind if I stay here until after the funeral?"

She stood, smiled at the incredulous couple, picked up her bag, and strode purposefully into the guest bedroom. "A plus tard!"

Nick and Gabriela just stared at each other, neither one knowing quite what to say. Then, almost in unison, they both turned and looked at the door which the elegant Frenchwoman had departed through. Nick turned to face Gabriela.

"So, how do you feel about living in Paris?"

Her response was immediate. She jumped into the arms of the startled detective and smothered him with excited kisses.

"It's a dream—a dream I've had ever since I was a little girl."

ψ

Henri's funeral was a modest affair attended by a couple of friends, a few faculty members, and several dozen students from the university where he'd taught. Alain Moreau was there, as were Madeline Boucher, Nick, and Gabriela. The service was held at the Saint-Louis-en-l'Ile Catholic Church, a beautiful Baroque edifice built between 1664 and 1726. Nick and Gabriela hosted a small reception at the apartment following the service and subsequent interment.

It was a difficult day for Madeline, and equally so for Nick and Gabriela, and when the final guests had said their condolences and goodnights, all three retired to their bedrooms.

ψ

The aroma of fresh croissants and coffee woke Nick from a deep but troubled sleep. He staggered out of bed, pulled on a robe, and wandered into the kitchen, where he found Madeline washed, dressed, and smiling.

"Bonjour, Nicholas, Puis-je faire pour aider."

It didn't take a genius to understand that the woman wanted to take over where her brother had left off.

CHAPTER THIRTY-TWO

Gabriela came out of their bedroom and joined them at the breakfast table. Even without makeup, she was stunningly beautiful. She picked a croissant from the plate, smothered it with butter and strawberry jam, and was about to take a first bite when Henri's cell rang. All three of them looked at the device as if it were possessed. Nick pushed the speaker icon for them all to hear.

"Hello, this is Nick Palmer."

"Bonjour, is this the detective I met with Professor Deneuve about the tattoos?"

Nick recognized the voice. It was Jules, the tattooed student he and Henri had met earlier at the café.

"I'm very sorry to hear about the professor's passing," he continued. "I was hoping to give him information about the snake tattoo you were enquiring about."

"Go ahead, Jules, my associates and I are still trying to figure that one out."

"Well, I did some digging. You know the tattoo community has strong bonds, almost like family, and I'm as interested as you are in finding the artist that does such amazing work."

The man paused as if trying to determine if what he had to say next would be relevant.

"I don't have a name, but apparently there's a woman in Mexico

City who's been trained by a master artist to do work such as this. Again, no proof, but supposedly, she's allowed to execute one design only, and only on people connected to a kind of religious order. It's a design that's been passed down from generation to generation for what I hear is hundreds of years. Hope that helps. I'll keep looking and will call if I hear anything else."

Nick thanked the man and pressed the end-call button.

"I guess our next step is to return to Madrid and speak to Mother Superior again."

Madeline put her cup down firmly on the table and stared at Nick and Gabriela.

"Non, mon ami. The next step is to visit our family avocat. I want all of Henri's wishes to be legalized. We need to transfer title to the apartment and issue procuration so that you have access to all of Henri's assets." She paused and looked sternly at them. "Our grandfather was an extremely successful businessman and left a considerable fortune to my parents. They in turn bequeathed their estate to my brother and I. Henri was an extremely wealthy man, and because of the confusing French inheritance laws, some of the legal work may be quite complicated."

Nick spoke for both him and Gabriela. "Are you sure you want to do this? All of it is really yours."

"I have plenty and need nothing more than I already have, so there will be no more discussions about it. C'est tout."

Madeline crossed her arms in front of her chest and assumed a seriously stubborn look.

Obviously, the discussion regarding the disposition of Henri's estate had closed. With nothing further planned, Nick began going through the papers and files piled high on the old professor's desk. Surprisingly, everything was meticulously organized. He found a file titled "La Orden de las Serpientes de Cristo," the words written with bright blue ink in Henri's neat, almost perfect handwriting. Nick opened the file and read the first few pages, then stopped and reread the account of the novice nun and her association with the high priest in ancient Mexico.

He turned to the others.

"Say, what was the name of the old nun at Las Descalzas Reales?"

Gabriela looked up from a large leather-bound book on the history of Paris she was leafing through.

"Mother Christina de Delgado. Why?"

"Because that's the same name as the novice nun who stowed away on a ship to Mexico in the fifteen-hundreds. The same nun who colluded to create the snake cult. Henri mentioned it to me before, but I'd forgotten the specifics."

Madeline was listening intently to what Nick was saying and interjected her thoughts into the conversation. "It isn't unusual for a novice, when entering holy service, to change their birth name. Usually it's Mary, Marie, or the name of a saint they admire. It's a way of showing respect."

"Then we can assume the old nun in Madrid is somehow involved with the snake cult?"

"Didn't I tell you she was Mexican and not Spanish?"

Gabriela had an *"I told you so"* look on her face as she went back to reading her book.

Madeline picked up the cell, called the avocat, and made an appointment to see the woman later in the afternoon. Then she literally ordered Nick to book three business-class tickets on a flight to Madrid for the following day.

ψ

Mother Christina de Delgado had a sleepless night. Over the past five years, her rheumatoid arthritis had advanced to the point of being almost unbearable. Her cold, dank room did little to help her condition, and the frightening dreams of countless girls, sacrificed to appease the serpent god, were becoming more and more frequent.

Last night had been the worst of all. The anguished screams and distorted faces of once-beautiful young girls seemed somehow real. She had murdered a kindly old gentleman for no other reason than to protect the secrecy and sanctity of her faith. She knew the American detective and his lady friend would soon discover her complicity in the man's death, and they'd soon return to question her further, and perhaps even have her arrested.

She slipped into her heavy black habit, left her dismal room, walked down the long stone hallway, and gently tapped on a door that was much like her own.

"Hermana Agnes, so yo."

The door was opened by a young nun, who upon seeing Mother Superior, bowed deeply in respect.

"Por favour entra, Madre."

The elderly nun entered the room and handed her cell phone to the young novice. Then, in halting English, she explained her visit.

"Take this phone, and if anything should happen to me, you must press one, and one again. It's a programmed number. Then, when you have told the person who answers what has occurred, you must immediately destroy the device and scatter the pieces where nobody will ever find them."

The young woman looked down at the cell phone she was holding in her trembling hand and nodded her understanding.

"Our Lord Quetzalcoatl will bless you."

The old nun kissed the forehead of the girl and left the room as silently as she had entered.

Christina de Delgado retraced her steps, entered her own sparse room, and sat down on the edge of her bed. Bowing her head in silent reflection, she then opened the creaky wooden drawer of her desk. Lying next to the rope and her rosary was the hypodermic she'd used to kill the old professor. She went down on her knees and prayed, like a child saying prayers before bedtime. Then she took the needle and pushed it gently into her forearm.

ψ

Madeline and Henri's avocat, Madame Delphine Agard, was a sixty-something Frenchwoman with a pugnacious attitude. She questioned the wisdom of Henri's last wishes and advised his sister that moving ahead on the dead professor's requests would be, at the very least, foolhardy. She also added that the very convoluted French laws regarding such things would be difficult to maneuver and the taxes involved would be astronomical.

She stopped her tirade and looked at each of them, one by one.

Madame Agard underestimated the strong-willed Frenchwoman she was facing, and after much polite, and sometimes forceful, discussion between the two, the lawyer agreed to proceed with preparing the necessary documents. They shook hands, and when the three of them were safely out of hearing range, Madeline broke into laughter.

"Oh, mon dieu! That woman can be very stubborn, but I've known her for many years, and she's always had Henri's and my best interests at heart."

ψ

The Iberia flight to Madrid that Nick had booked was scheduled to depart at 12:20 p.m. the following day. The two-hour flight would get them into the Spanish capital by midafternoon, and they had decided they would go directly to the convent from the airport. For now, they were happily ensconced in the Paris apartment that would soon belong to Nick.

"I'm beyond starving. Where should we go for dinner?"

Gabi's question was pointed directly at Madeline, knowing full well that her elegant French friend would know some charming little bistro serving wonderful food. Her suspicion proved to be correct, and they were soon seated in a bustling, oak-paneled room in Saint-Germain-des-Prés.

"La spécialité is boeuf bourguignon, and I heartily recommend it. I promise you will not find anything like it in America."

They had walked to the restaurant and were seated at a window table. The dish was as good as Madeline had said it would be. They mopped up the last remains of the delicious stew with big chunks of baguette, then strolled back to the apartment through the lively early-evening streets of Paris.

ψ

"The old nun is dead!"

This proclamation came to Nick, from Adriana Diaz, while he was in the bathroom cleaning up before going to bed. The young woman appeared in the mirror, just as she had on several occasions before, to deliver the news.

"She committed suicide, using the same poison and same needle that killed your friend."

Nick looked directly into the woman's eyes. He was no longer surprised by these apparitions. More and more, they were becoming a normal occurrence in his life.

"We were planning to go and see her tomorrow."

"Still go. There are important clues to discover there."

The image of the young Spanish martyr faded, and Nick was left wondering just exactly what kind of clues they'd find at the convent in Madrid. He went into the room where the two women were sitting and didn't hold back.

"The old nun is dead."

The two women spun around and looked at him. They'd been chatting about French food, Paris's best restaurants, and designer fashion that Gabriela wouldn't find anywhere except in the city's charming boutiques. Nick's startling announcement caught them off guard.

Gabriela spoke first. "How do you know? Was it a girl in the mirror?"

Madeline was confused. She looked first at Nick and then at Gabriela. It felt as though they were keeping a secret from her—a secret they should absolutely share.

"Qu'est-ce que tu racontes? What are you talking about?"

Nick pulled up a chair and faced her, then began telling her about the apparitions appearing to him, and on one occasion, to her late brother. He told her about how he'd seen her dead sister in his mirror and had heard her heartbreaking story. He told her about how he'd spoken to many of the other young women who'd been brutally killed and sacrificed by the evil cult of murderers he was trying to bring to justice. He told her about Henri's initial disbelief, and eventual faith that what Nick was telling him was all true.

The elderly Frenchwoman looked skeptical, but then her countenance brightened. It looked as if she'd just awakened from a long, dark nightmare, a horrific dream that had haunted her since the disappearance of her older sister so many long years before.

"Mon dieu. Now I understand why Henri wanted to be a part of your great adventure. Do you think that Margaux will appear and speak to me? Do you think that Henri is with her? Do—"

Nick gently cut her off. "I think that we should all go to bed. Tomorrow's going to be another long day."

CHAPTER THIRTY-THREE

News about the death of the old nun reached Hector Rodriguez in Manhattan. It came from another believer, a novice who'd been converted to the order several years earlier by the now deceased Mother Superior. The woman on the phone was in tears, sobbing and inconsolable as she explained her discovery of the elderly nun's body.

"Did you remove the sacred rope and the needle from her room?"

"Sí, señor. I have them safely hidden."

"Did the sister give you instructions about destroying the cell phone you are using?"

"Sí, señor."

"Excellent, make sure you adhere to all her wishes. Do this my faithful child, and you will be greatly rewarded in the afterlife."

After he hung up, Hector leaned back in his chair and closed his eyes. His thoughts were scattered. Too much was happening—too much he couldn't explain. It was a feeling he'd never experienced before: vulnerability. He stood and began pacing the room, trying to rationalize the events—events which all seemed connected to the detective from Chicago.

ψ

Nick's cell rang. It was his friend Alain Moreau, at the Paris police department. The man sounded perplexed.

"Nicholas, mon ami, I've just received a call from the police in Madrid. A second body, an old nun, has just been discovered in the Convent of Las Descalzas Reales."

Nick feigned ignorance and surprise. He didn't want his friend to know the information he'd just reported was old news. He especially didn't want the man to know how he'd heard it.

"What? I'm flying to Madrid tomorrow and wanted to speak to her again about Henri's death. I guess I'll have to speak to the police instead. Hopefully, they'll let me see the scene, and perhaps her body."

"I will call Javier Ruiz, my police contact there, and try to arrange it. Let me know right away if you find out anything new."

Gabi and Madeline came into the kitchen. They both had small carry-on bags for their flight to Madrid, and both were stylishly dressed for their first-class flight. Gabriela looked over at Nick, who was casually dressed in jeans and a Cubs T-shirt. She asked him two pointed questions: "Really, is that what you're going to wear? … Who called?"

Nick ignored the comment about his wardrobe and told them about the conversation he'd had with the lieutenant detective. Then he called a limo, at the women's insistence, to take them to Orly airport.

ψ

Madeline had selected a charming little boutique hotel within walking distance of the convent. The accommodations were over-the-top. Their suite was colorfully decorated in a modern interpretation of traditional Spanish style. It exceeded Nick's expectations, and pay scale, but when he saw the look on Gabriela's face—the way her countenance lit up when she entered the room—he decided that whatever the price, it was well worth it.

While Gabi was exploring every nook and cranny of the luxurious suite, Nick sat on the edge of the plush king-sized bed and called Inspector Javier Ruiz. He arranged to meet the police officer and his partner in the hotel lobby the following morning. They planned to visit the convent together, simply because Nick felt an official police presence would make the institution's custodians more likely to cooperate with their investigation.

That evening, Nick and his two women companions enjoyed a meal of delicious tapas in the hotel's small restaurant, then retired to their rooms for what they hoped would be a good night's sleep.

ψ

A small group of cloistered nuns were gathered in a windowless room not far from the spot where Henri had been murdered. A few of the older ones were indignant at being called from their duties and prayers. The others just stood quietly with their eyes looking down from beneath their hoods. This interruption in their normally routine life was anathema to them, and their discomfort was tangible.

The slim, well-groomed Spanish police inspector informed the assembled group that it would be necessary for his officers to inspect each of their rooms. Nick and the Spaniard had discussed this strategy earlier, not necessarily to fulfill the threat but rather to gauge the reaction of each nun to the possibility. The scheme paid off. Most of the group displayed outright hostility, but one of them, a novice known to be favored by the late Christina de Delgado, became extremely nervous. The police inspector walked towards the frightened girl, gently lifted her head with his hand, and saw the look of panic in her pretty face.

"Tu eres primera, hermana."

Upon being told hers would be the first room to be searched, the young nun fell to her knees and broke down in tears. She felt suddenly very alone and very vulnerable. Her mentor the Mother Superior was dead, and El Cardenal was in a country far removed from Spain. One of the older nuns, who'd knelt to try and comfort the young woman, was quickly ushered aside by the officer's partner.

"Hice lo que me indicaron," the girl said.

Gabriela turned to Nick and Madeline and translated the woman's tearful confession.

"She says she did what they told her to do."

The police inspector helped the young woman to her feet and escorted her through the eerily quiet corridors to her room. All the other nuns were kept back by the inspector's partner.

Sister Agnes's room was an exact duplicate of the dead Mother Superior's in that it held only the bare necessities of life: a hard bed with a wall-hung crucifix above it, a small side table, a wooden chair, and an old armoire. It was cold and inhospitable, a stark contrast to the deluxe hotel suite Nick and Gabi had left earlier that morning.

The young nun stood quietly sobbing in the corner of the room as the two detectives began their search. It felt to Nick like they were playing a game of hot and cold. The closer they got to what they were looking for, the louder the girl cried. It didn't take long. Hidden in a small opening at the base of the armoire they found what they were looking for: a hypodermic half filled with a pale-amber liquid, and a length of multicolored rope that Nick turned around in his fingers, thinking about the damnation it represented.

"Hermana, debo llevarte a interrogarte."

The police inspector handcuffed the frightened young woman, led her back through the confusing complex of corridors, past the gathering of sisters they'd recently left, and into his waiting car. Nick, Gabriela, and Madeline followed them to the station.

ψ

Hector Rodriguez made two calls that morning. The first was to Jacques Bisset, one of the twelve apostles of La Orden de las Serpientes de Cristo. As well as his duties with the Order, Monsieur Bisset ran

Franco Pharma Corporation, a successful pharmaceutical company based in Paris. Like Hector, he was a billionaire, and Hector's Inca Gold Investments was one of his company's major shareholders and financiers. They were also close friends, sharing their strong belief in Quetzalcoatl and the ruthless indulgences that come with having amassed vast personal fortunes.

"Bonjour, Hector. To what do I owe the pleasure of this call? Business or business?" The pharmaceutical tycoon laughed at his own little joke.

"Bonjour, Jacques. Business, I'm afraid. Business that concerns Las Serpientes."

The man in New York told his Parisian friend about what'd been happening since the Chicago detective had entered the scene, including the most recent developments in Madrid.

"I don't know the fucking detective, wouldn't know him if I ran into him, but he and his friends seem to have a hotline to everything we do and think. The poison that you concocted has already cost us the lives of several of our most devoted believers."

This last piece of information worried the man in Paris. He was concerned that somehow the trail of the special toxin he'd developed in his lab would lead the authorities right to his front door, and he expressed this concern to the man on the other end of the call.

"Hector, I'm very worried. If the police discover what we've been doing, I could end up in prison for a very long time."

"Don't worry, my old friend. Together, we can rid our world of these inconveniences. I'm flying to Paris tomorrow. Perhaps we can have dinner and discuss any solutions to our problem you may be able to think of."

Hector's second call was to his wife, Claire, to let her know he'd be seeing her the following day. As always, she was lovingly cordial on the phone, but as soon as he hung up, she turned to the man who was sharing her bed: a young Italian artist she'd met at a club the night before.

"The party's over, my beautiful amour. You'd better get up and get out of here before my husband arrives."

She didn't need to ask a second time. The terrified man got dressed and ran from her bedroom like an Olympic sprinter.

Claire smiled, pulled on a robe, and called Jacqueline to run her a bath.

CHAPTER THIRTY-FOUR

Sister Agnes Annunciata was being held in a cell at the National Police district Madrid-Centro station on Calle de Leganitos in the city's downtown. The young nun was terrified, virtually paralyzed with fear about what was going to happen to her. When she had taken her vows to God, and again, at the Mother Superior's encouragement, to Quetzalcoatl, she'd had no idea she'd end up in prison as an accomplice to murder.

She was on her knees praying for forgiveness from God. She was deeply ashamed that she'd been convinced to stray from her original path by the Mother Superior, and she was frightened about what her parents would say and think.

Sister Agnes's parents were devout Catholics, poor farmers, scraping out a life in Galicia, in the furthermost area of northwestern Spain. When their only daughter had become a postulant and entered the service of God, it was one of the family's most joyful moments. These feelings weighed heavily on Sister Agnes's soul, to a point where she wished she were dead, like the old woman who'd led her down this unholy path.

"Get up, Sister Agnes. You have visitors."

The arrogant guard spoke to her in English, a language she knew the frightened girl had limited understanding of. Her sadistic little joke to make the girl even more uncomfortable got the desired effect.

The young woman raised her head. Her face was crimson red and stained with the many tears she'd shed since being incarcerated. She stood and nervously fingered the large wooden cross that hung from her neck. The cross, a gift from her parents, was held by a string of marble-sized wooden beads on a heavy strip of well-worn leather.

Nick, Gabriela, Madeline, and Police Inspector Ruiz were ushered into the station's holding area by the sadistic guard. The anomaly of seeing a nun in such place was bizarre, as all the other cells were crowded with the normal retinue of petty thieves, vagrants, prostitutes, drug addicts, and repentant drivers coming down from an alcohol- or drug-induced high.

Javier Ruiz stepped up to the nun's cell. "Disculpas hermana Agnes pero necesito preguntar en inglés."

Gabriela translated for her two friends, telling them the questioning would be conducted in English, which she would translate for the unfortunate young girl, and then relay her response. The Spanish police inspector continued. His discomfort at interrogating a nun was apparent in the gentle tone of his voice.

"First, Sister Agnes, I must advise you that you are not being charged with any crime. For the time being, you are only being held for questioning about the mysterious death of Mother Superior Christina de Delgado."

Gabriela translated the officer's words, and the young nun broke down. Tears rolled down her reddened cheeks, and she once again fell to her knees. The inspector looked to the three people standing behind him, shrugged, and turned back to the distraught young woman.

"Please tell me, in your own words, what happened on the day the body of the Mother Superior was discovered."

Once again, Gabriela translated the officer's questioning.

The nun's voice was low, trembling, and often interspersed with an outpouring of tears.

She told them about Christina de Delgado's uncharacteristic visit to her room, about her request that she hide the needle and the sacred rope, and her instructions that she destroy the cell phone following her making a call to a man she did not know.

News about the phone was a surprise to all of them.

"This phone, did you destroy it as Mother Christina requested? Did you make the call? Do you know who you spoke to?"

The girl looked confused and was alarmed by the barrage of questions being thrown at her. She slowly moved away from the police officer's verbal onslaught until her back was pressed firmly against the cell's stone wall.

"I broke it to pieces and deposited the bits into trash bins throughout the museum and the kitchen. Men from the city pick the trash up every day and take it to be burned."

The police officer repeated his question.

"Did you make the call? Do you remember the number?"

"I called and told the man who answered about Mother Christina's death. I don't know the number, because I just had to push the number-one button two times."

The young nun began crying again, and Gabriela stepped up to the bars of her cell to try to comfort her. The girl was inconsolable, and in a quavering voice, between her sobs, proclaimed how sorry she was for what she'd done, for her actions and sinfulness, and very sorry she'd followed the path suggested by the late Mother Superior.

"Please don't tell my parents. It will kill them."

Nick motioned for Gabriela to join the group. He had a question he needed answered and believed that Gabriela would be the best person to ask it.

"Do you have any tattoos? A tattoo of a serpent along your backbone?"

The question brought another flood of tears from the visibly shaken girl.

"N-no, I was supposed to travel to Mexico City with Mother Christina in the new year to be ordained with the mark."

She turned her back on the assembled group and crouched down into the corner of her cell with her hood pulled tightly down over her face. Obviously, there'd be no more answers that day.

"Well, what do you think?"

The police inspector rolled his eyes upwards towards the ceiling, a sign that he knew what he had to do—even though he had serious reservations about doing it.

"I don't know what I can charge her with, so I guess I'm going to have to release her."

He called the guard and gave the heartless woman orders to release the frightened young nun.

Sister Agnes left the confines of her cell and walked, head down, through the station without looking at or saying a word to anyone she passed. The driver of a large delivery truck didn't see the woman dressed in a nun's habit step off the curb in front of him until it was too late. There was a loud screech of brakes and the heart-wrenching sound of steel hitting flesh and bones.

Nick, the inspector, and their two women companions rushed out of the station and pushed their way through the crowds already gathered at the scene.

The lifeless body of the young nun lay on the road, her hand tightly holding the now-bloody wooden cross she wore around her twisted neck.

ψ

Hector Rodriguez kissed his wife on both cheeks, took the glass of tequila she handed him, and downed it in one quick gulp. There were no other pleasantries.

"I'm only here for two days. I hope you can keep your long string of boyfriends away for that length of time."

"You know, darling, there's only you." The sarcasm dripped from her beautiful lips like honey from a hot spoon.

Hector laughed out loud. He loved the woman's smug confidence. If only he could say the same about loving her.

"I have dinner this evening, with the president of a firm we hold a major position in, and a morning meeting at the plant. You'll be happy to know I'll be out of your hair by late afternoon tomorrow—God willing."

Claire shrugged and followed her husband into the bedroom. She knew, from prior experience, that the only other meeting he'd be having in Paris was with her, on her back, with his large hairy body pumping up and down against her naked torso.

ψ

Hector got up, showered, and dressed for his dinner appointment. He left Claire lying in bed.

"Goodbye, darling. See you later."

She chose not to respond.

Hector's car was waiting at the curb, and when the driver saw his boss leave the building, he jumped out, ran around to the car's right-side passenger door, and opened it with a flourish worthy of royalty. Hector didn't notice, didn't acknowledge, and didn't really care about the man's enthusiastic efforts.

Dinner was a formal affair at one of the city's exquisite Michelin-starred restaurants. Hector and Jacques Bisset sat at a secluded corner table, a table especially reserved for men of great wealth and great influence—men who often escorted their thought-to-be-secret mistresses to the restaurant for an excellent pre-coitus dinner.

The French billionaire was the first to speak.

"I'm very concerned, Hector. The police in Madrid now have a sample of the poison I developed in my lab. Soon they'll discover it's the same poison Christina used to kill the professor and end her own life—the same poison that killed Estella Calero in Rome."

Hector smiled at the mention of the Italian discípula's name. He alone had recruited a prison guard to inject the sleeping assassin. It had cost him a small fortune, but the man had performed his assignment

171

perfectly by committing the task, then retrieving and destroying the evidence following the woman's apparent suicide.

"There's no need to worry, my dear friend; you concocted it yourself in your own private lab. The authorities will never know the truth. It's not as if you're mixing up a batch of pathogens to create havoc throughout the world."

Hector laughed. Jacques' expression was doubtful, but Hector didn't really care if his assurances eased the Frenchman's concern.

"Now, for our other business, I will be at the plant at ten tomorrow morning. Nothing serious, just a quick visit so I can inform our investors that I've seen it, and still heartily endorse our investment in your company."

Hector left the restaurant and returned to his apartment. He threw his coat over a magnificent antique French bergère chair and called out to his wife, "Bonsoir, Claire, my darling. Are you ready for round two?"

ψ

Jacques Bisset and his wife were lounging in their sumptuous living room watching television when they heard the latch on the room's only outside door click shut. The television turned itself off, and a low murmur of ethereal screams filled the room. The anguished cries of long-dead women got louder and louder—a barrage of reverberating misery that was unbearable to hear. The couple covered their ears with their hands, but the horrific howling only got louder. The nightmarish screams were coming from inside their heads, heard by only themselves. They writhed on the floor, their agony beyond endurance. Blood began to seep from their ears, noses, and eyes.

"Stop it, stop it, stop it, please…"

"Only your death will stop it, only your death."

The voices seemed to come directly from the burning fire pits of hell.

"Only your death can stop it, only your death."
"Only your death can stop it, only your death."
"Only your death can stop it, only your death."

The stricken chemist crawled to his secret lab and pulled a vial of pale-amber liquid off a shelf. He somehow managed to fill a hypodermic with the deadly mixture, then dragged himself back to where his wife was twisted in agonizing torment. Jacques's brain felt as if it had imploded. The tortured screams of haunted girls were ricocheting off the bones inside his empty skull. He showed his wife the needle, and she nodded. He plunged it into her arm, and then into his own. The frenzied screaming stopped.

CHAPTER THIRTY-FIVE

When Nick, Gabriela, and Madeline arrived back at their hotel, they stepped into the lobby bar to decompress from the day's intense events. The contorted body of the young nun, lying dead in the street, was a brutal sight none of them would soon forget. Nick slouched in an armchair while the two women sat opposite him on a small two-seater lounge. There was a chic acrylic cocktail table between them with an assortment of nuts and olives in small blue ceramic bowls.

"Buenas tardes, que puedo traerte para beber?"

Nick looked at Gabi.

"The young man wants to know what we'd like to drink."

"Double scotch, no ice. It doesn't matter what brand."

Madeline nodded her agreement.

Gabriela ordered for the three of them, and within minutes, the server returned with three large glasses filled with the smoky amber liquid. Gabriela, whose preference had always been red wine, steeled herself, took a sip, and felt the scorching heat of the drink as it flowed down her throat and into her gut. Her eyes began to water, and her face turned a bright shade of red.

"Whew! That's nasty. And you guys really like this stuff?"

Madeline smiled at the woman's discomfort, and Nick began laughing out loud. It was a small moment, but it instantly relieved the overwhelming tension.

"C'mon, drink up! I'm starving. Where to tonight, Madeline?"

"It's a surprise, Nicholas, but I'm sure you'll enjoy it. Have you ever had Moroccan food?"

Nick finished his drink. Gabi, still feeling the effects of her first taste, left her almost-full glass on the table.

They stepped into the elevator. Its four mirrored walls polished to dazzling perfection. The perception of endlessly reflected images of the three friends was disquieting and slightly disorienting as they slowly ascended. Then they jolted to a sudden stop. The digital level indicator placed them somewhere between the fourth and fifth floors. The lights flickered out then, and they were left in total blackness. They groped around, searching for each other, and were soon huddled together in the center of the cramped, pitch-dark space.

As if lit from within, a face appeared in the mirror in front of them. It was the image of Juanita Diaz, the martyred girl from Madrid. Another face appeared behind them: Sophia D'Angelo, the girl who was murdered in Rome. Juliana Cortez, the girl from Mexico City, appeared on the wall beside them next, and then opposite them, on the fourth wall, was the image of Madeline's deceased sister, Margaux Deneuve.

Madeline let out a cry. She sounded like a person who'd been mortally wounded. It was a combination of utter surprise, infinite pain, and total disbelief. It was as if she'd woken from a bad dream only to find herself locked in a nightmare. She gripped Nick's arm, her fingers digging deeply into his bicep. She looked at the image of her long-dead sister and began to weep. Margaux spoke softly to Madeline. Her voice sounded like a distant angel, conveying feelings of sadness, joy, hope, and expectation.

"Bonsoir, Madeline. I have missed you."

This simple message, spoken from the innermost soul of the dead girl, propelled Madeline into another fit of crying.

Gabriela was sitting on the floor, wide eyed, her mouth opened in shock. This was her first exposure to the girls in the mirror, and she was beyond awestruck. All her doubts and all her beliefs in the man she loved had just collided into one thunderbolt of faith. Every thought of being rescued from the elevator vanished from her mind as she looked to each of the girls in turn. Just seeing their beautiful, heart-wrenchingly despairing faces made her angry and hardened her resolve to get the bastards still perpetrating the depraved and disgusting human sacrifices.

"Ciao, my name is Sophia D'Angelo. We four, and the hundreds of others like us, have decided that all three of you, not just Detective Palmer, should know of our presence."

"I'm Juliana Cortez. We do not seek revenge. Only that the heinous sacrificial killings stop."

"And to do that you must sever the head of the serpent." With these final words, from Margaux Deneuve, Madeline reached up and placed her hand gently on the cheek of her long-dead sister. Then the fourth girl spoke.

"My name is Juanita Diaz. Follow the path shown you by the good professor. His papers will guide you."

The images slowly faded away to nothing. Then the lights came on; the elevator trembled to a start and proceeded up to their floor. They got off and looked at each other, the women's faces showing amazement, bewilderment, and resolve. Nick broke the tension with just three words.

"Moroccan sounds great."

ψ

Hector Rodriguez leaned back in a plush, black-leather seat aboard his private jet and contemplated his trip to the French capital. He hadn't bothered to visit the pharmaceutical factory and had no doubt that, by now, Claire had lured another lover to her bedroom. He smiled. It didn't matter. She meant no more to him than a casual, albeit pleasurable, distraction. What worried him most was his friend

Jacques Bisset. The pharmaceutical tycoon might do something stupid to protect his company and his reputation—even though there was no way the customized concoction of deadly poison could ever lead the authorities to him. He would have to assure the man that he had nothing in the world to worry about, or conversely, have him killed.

His beautiful flight attendant stopped by his seat and asked if there was anything she could do for him. He thought about the obvious and declined.

"Nothing right now, Anna. Perhaps later, before we land."

He pulled a blood-red cashmere blanket up around his neck and, lulled by the sound of the aircraft's powerful jet engines, fell into a fitful sleep.

ψ

He felt a soft hand touch his shoulder, and the intoxicating scent of his flight attendant's perfume filled the air around him.

"Wheels down in an hour, Mr. Rodriguez. Are you sure I can't do anything for you?"

He smiled and once again declined her transparent offer. "Perhaps the next flight, Anna. Perhaps the next flight."

The aircraft pulled up to the terminal building, and two Homeland Security officers boarded the jet, asking the usual questions. In this type of facility, it was nothing more than a cursory inspection, one he'd been through countless times before.

Hector deplaned, climbed into his waiting limo, and instructed his driver to take him to his home in Bedford. He needed a massage, and the talented hands of his Asian masseuse would soon offer him welcome relief from at least some of his tensions.

ψ

The crowded Moroccan restaurant Madeline suggested was just outside Madrid's busy downtown area. The aroma of slowly cooked lamb, mixed with an exotic blend of herbs and spices, reminded them of just how hungry they all were. The maître d' who seated them on low, multipatterned cushions wore a brightly colored djellaba, the traditional garment of Morocco. Small plates of savory salads soon appeared, followed quickly by a steaming-hot lamb tagine. Dessert was a plate of briouat, delicious little pastries with a distinctive orange-blossom taste. Neither Nick nor Gabi had tasted anything quite like them. Following dinner, they lingered for about thirty minutes more, enjoying small glasses of Maghrebi mint tea. It was Madeline who spoke first.

"I think we should return to Paris and do what Juanita told us to do: go through Henri's papers. Perhaps we'll find something that'll lead us to the people we're looking for."

Nick interjected. "And I can touch base with Alain to see if the police have gotten any further with the autopsy on the girl that they found dead in her cell."

ψ

They got back to the hotel, picked up their room keys, and found themselves somewhat hesitant to enter the small elevator. Madeline broke the silence.

"Do you think that the girls will appear again?"

The two women looked at Nick, as if he'd have the answers to everything.

"I very much doubt it, but if they do, you'll have a second chance to see your sister."

Madeline nodded sadly, a tear trickling down the old woman's face.

They stepped into the elevator, pressed the button, and when it stopped at the fifth floor, they got out. This time, no images had appeared and nothing out of the ordinary had happened.

"Bonne nuit, Gabi, bonne nuit Nicholas."

She hugged them both, then turned towards Nick.

"And thank you, Nicholas. Thank you for giving me the opportunity to see my sister."

She turned and walked silently into her room.

CHAPTER THIRTY-SIX

Nick was lounging against the bed's headboard, sipping a cup of strong black Spanish coffee that he'd ordered from the hotel's room-service menu. Gabriela was facing him, legs crossed in a lotus-like position. She was wearing one of his T-shirts, which perfectly accentuated the firm contours of her breasts.

They were discussing the previous day's appearances in the elevator when Nick's cell rang. He checked the screen and didn't recognize the number, but the area code appearing before the next seven numbers indicated the call was from Sacramento.

"Hello, it's Nick Palmer."

He recognized the voice on the other end of the call. It was his ex-father-in-law. The man was not his usual prickly, self-centered self. His speech was broken and raspy, like he'd been crying.

"There's been an accident. A gravel truck ran a red light. Isabela's dead and her mother died on the way to the hospital."

Nick jumped off the bed, spilling the remains of his coffee all over the sheets. He felt like he was the one who'd been hit by the truck. A gut-wrenching tremor shot up from his stomach, and it felt like he was going to throw up.

"Lucy? Is Lucy, okay?"

"She's okay, she's here with me. The funeral is the day after tomorrow. You should come."

Nick sat on the edge of the bed and buried his head in his hands. "Fuck, fuck, fuck!"

Gabriela hadn't the slightest idea of what was wrong, but she knew something terrible must have happened. She tried to comfort the distraught man. He lifted his head and turned to her.

"I've got to go to California. Isabela's been killed in an accident, and her mother's dead too."

"Jesus Christ, what happened? Do you want me to go with you?"

"No, you go back to Paris with Madeline. Start going through Henri's papers. I'll be back in a day or two."

There was a knock on their door. They hurriedly put on the plush cotton bathrobes they'd flung aside the previous evening and opened the door. Madeline came into the room. She looked at the coffee-stained bed, and then at their strained faces.

"Mon dieu! What's happening? Is everything all right?"

Gabriela pulled the elderly woman aside and explained what had happened in California.

"C'est terrible!" Madeline went over to where Nick was standing and hugged him.

ψ

Nick's British Airways flight departed from Madrid-Barajas at twelve thirty p.m. the following day, and after a short layover at Heathrow, he was scheduled to land at San Francisco's International Airport at 6:20 p.m. Pacific Standard Time. It was a long, almost fourteen-hour flight, which would give him plenty of time to put his thoughts together. In the forefront of his mind was Lucy. What was he was going to do about Lucy? He hadn't ever considered something like this happening and worried about his young daughter's state of mind. How would she cope following the loss of both her mother and grandmother so suddenly and so violently?

Then he thought about the murdered girls guiding and protecting him, appearing in mirrors, and from time to time, speaking to him in his mind.

Why in God's name did they pick me, when just about anyone else would do?

Then he thought about something his mother had said to him when he'd told her he wanted to be a cop like his father.

"You'll be a really good cop, Nicky. You'll make your father proud, and I won't have to worry, because the angels will be sitting on your shoulders looking after you and protecting you."

He'd always known his mother was eccentric, believing in the paranormal and all that crazy stuff, but now it seemed that she'd maybe been right after all.

ψ

The flight was uneventful: no crying children, no snoring old men, and no bumpy bad weather. He passed through Homeland Security, headed down to the rental-car desks, and picked out a Ford Focus, which turned out to be dark blue, the exact same color as his mood. The two-hour drive on I-80 from the airport to Sacramento's outskirts took him over the spectacular Bay Bridge, the equally impressive Carquinez Bridge, past Napa Valley, and on to the house where his late wife had lived with Lucy and her parents.

The front door was opened by an old man. He was much frailer than Nick remembered and looked as if he hadn't slept in weeks. He didn't say anything, just motioned for Nick to step inside. Nick looked around the darkened interior. It had the stench of filth, ingrained urine, mothballs, and old people who didn't care about anything except the eventuality of dying.

This is no place for a seven-year-old girl, he thought.

"Where's Lucy?"

"She's two doors down, staying with Caroline, her friend from school."

Nick rushed out and ran down the street to the house where his daughter was staying.

The girl who answered the door wasn't Lucy but her best friend. She screamed into the house behind her. "Lucy, I think it's your dad."

Nick heard his little girl running down the stairs. She stopped before him, broke into tears, jumped into his waiting arms, and hugged him like she would never let go. Tears began to streak down his cheeks. Lucy had suffered more than anyone should: first the move, then the divorce, and now the untimely death of her mother and grandmother. They held each other tightly for what seemed like an eternity, neither of them wanting to break the bond, which at that moment was all that was holding them together.

"I love you, Daddy."

The tears came again, but this time it was for the pure joy of being there with her. Nick hated himself for not having been there for her, for being too busy when they lived in Chicago, for not calling more often after her mother had moved them to California, and for ever getting angry with her for what now seemed like petty little things. He promised himself that, from this moment on, he'd be the perfect father to her.

"And I love you too, baby."

They both finally released their grip. Nick was still on his knees, holding his little girl by the shoulders and looking at her lovingly.

"Wow, you've really grown up... and so beautiful too. Let's go to your grandfather's house and get to know each other again."

"I don't want to go back there, Daddy. I want to stay with you."

Nick understood why she didn't want to return to that house, reeking as it did of death and dirt.

"Okay, I'll get us a hotel room. Stay here, and I'll be back before you can count to a hundred."

He strode down the street and went into his ex-father-in-law's house. The old man was sitting in the living room staring into space; he turned his head slightly when he heard Nick come through the door.

"I'm taking Lucy to a hotel. She'll stay with me until after the funeral."

The old man looked like he, too, was waiting to die.

"I think you should take her full time. I'm too old to look after a little girl by myself. She'd be much better off living with her father."

Nick looked around the darkened space. It somehow felt as if evil lived there.

No shit she'd be better off living with me, he thought.

The old man went back to his memories, staring at nothing but the lifeless room. Nick went into his daughter's room and crammed her backpack with things she might need for the funeral, and for a few days' stay in the hotel. He called the Embassy Suites and booked a room for the two of them, then went back to Caroline's house.

"Okay, honey, let's go. I've got us a nice room in a hotel with a swimming pool, and I've packed your swimsuit in case we want to try it out."

Lucy said goodbye to her friend. Caroline's mother was there and offered her condolences to both Nick and Lucy. Then father and daughter climbed into the Ford rental.

Nick drove to the hotel. Lucy said nothing but held tightly onto her father's arm as he maneuvered the car through the city's evening traffic.

"Daddy, can I live with you forever?"

"Forever, honey. Forever. I promise."

The room at the hotel was perfect for them. A small living room with a large-screen television, pull-out couch, a tiny kitchenette, and a bedroom. Nick ordered pizza from a nearby restaurant, and after it arrived, they settled in for the evening.

They watched an animated movie about an African princess who befriends a giraffe with superpowers. About halfway through the film, Lucy fell asleep snuggled up to her father's side. The utter joy and love Nick felt, as he looked down at the little girl, was overpowering and almost bought him to tears again. He gently lifted her, carried her into the bedroom, covered her, and kissed her forehead. Then he tiptoed out of the room, took a moment to regain his composure, and called Gabriela.

"Hi, honey, do you miss me? Do you still love me?"

Gabriela noticed the palpable exhaustion in her lover's voice and softly answered. "I do miss you, and I do love you. How's it going?"

Nick gave her all the details of his trip and finally worked up the courage to ask her a question that would, perhaps, change everything between them.

"Say, how do you feel about having a little seven-year-old come to live with us?"

There was a long pause on the other end of the line. Then he heard a voice that alleviated all his fears—a voice that could hardly contain all the excitement it held.

"That would be fantastic! Amazing. I can hardly wait to meet her, and I can hardly wait to tell Madeline."

Then her voice changed to one of real concern. "How's she doing?"

"As well as can be expected. Tomorrow's the funeral. I'll let you know as soon as we get through that. Good night, I love you."

He hung up and thought about his new life as a full-time father.

CHAPTER THIRTY-SEVEN

The funeral service for both Isabela and her mother was held at Saint Francis of Assisi Catholic Church, in the city's Midtown district. There weren't a lot of people in attendance, just a few friends, and a small group of Mexican Americans who stuck together near the back of the church. Nick and Lucy sat next to the bereaved husband and father of the deceased women.

The service was given in Spanish, the mother tongue of both Isabela's parents, and following the service, the congregation moved to the cemetery of the same name for the interment. The whole ceremony lasted just two hours. At the small gathering that followed, one man in the group of Mexican Americans, Hector Rodriguez, came over to Lucy's grandfather to pass on his condolences.

"Señor Lopez, lament tu gran Perdida."

The distraught man bowed his head to Hector, took his right hand, and kissed it. The recipient of this strange adulation turned and followed by a retinue of the men and women he'd sat with during the service, he left the room. Nick and Lucy followed shortly thereafter and returned to their hotel.

"Lucy, honey, I need to talk to you."

The girl looked up from the book she was reading. Her face was still stained from almost two days of continual tears.

"We won't be going back to Chicago. Your mom and I sold the

house when you moved to California, so there's nothing there to go home to."

The little girl looked apprehensive, uncertain of what the future held for her. "Where will we live then?"

Nick had been racking his brain trying to figure out the best way to break the news about Gabriela, Paris, and their new home on Ile Saint-Louis. He finally concluded that the best way was just to be direct.

He sat down next to her on the sofa and told her the whole story—except for the part about the apparitions he was seeing.

"Okay, Daddy. When are we going to go?"

She listened to his answer, then snuggled up to him and calmly went back to reading her book.

ψ

Nick's priority was to get a passport for Lucy. After a few calls, he found out that, if he wanted it quickly, he'd need to go to the Western Passport Center in Tucson, Arizona. That would be his and Lucy's first flight together—the first of several more to come before they got to France.

Nick returned to Lucy's grandfather's house. Lucy didn't come. She didn't want to say goodbye to the man she and her mother had lived with. Nick packed her belongings into a small suitcase, picked up her social security card, birth certificate, and other documents, and left the old man still sitting in the darkened living room staring into space.

Nick said goodbye to the man and got no response in return. Nick's thoughts were sympathetic. No matter what his true feelings were about the man, this wasn't how anyone should live, let alone Lucy's grandfather. Nick said goodbye again, and there was still no acknowledgement from the sad old man sitting alone with his thoughts in the dirty darkened room.

No wonder Lucy didn't want to come, he thought, as he left the house.

ψ

The Delta flight from San Francisco to Tucson was scheduled to leave at 11:19 the following morning, and after a short stop, arrive in Tucson at 4:53 p.m. He'd booked them into a small hotel near the Passport Center, where he had booked an early appointment to get an emergency passport for his daughter.

Lucy and Nick settled into a hotel room that was much like the one they'd left back in Sacramento. Then the questions came tumbling out of the young girl's mouth.

"Daddy, I don't know French. Where will I go to school?"

"Daddy, will I meet new friends?"

"Daddy, will I have my own room?"

"Daddy, do you think that Gabriela will like me?"

The forty-five-minute interrogation felt like hours. He tried to answer all her questions truthfully, including those he had no answer for. Finally, she went to bed, and he called Gabriela in Paris.

"Hi, honey, we're in Tucson getting a passport for Lucy."

"Tucson? Why Tucson?"

Nick explained that this was where he could fast-track her passport, and with any luck, have it within twenty-four hours.

"Then we'll grab a flight to Paris. I can hardly wait to see you, and I really hope you'll like Lucy."

"Madeline and I are both really excited to meet her, and you know I can hardly wait to see you too."

Her last few words were spoken with her sexy Spanish inflection, which he found irresistible.

ψ

"Bonsoir, Detective Palmer."

Nick had stepped into the hotel bathroom to shower before turning in for the night.

"It looks like everything is going according to plan."

Margaux Deneuve smiled. It was the first time he'd seen a look of contentment on the young Frenchwoman's face.

"What plan are you talking about? I don't have a plan."

"Our plan, your happiness."

"Isn't the plan to find the people who murdered you and all the others?"

The image in the mirror faded and vanished, leaving Nick more confused than ever. He didn't notice Lucy enter the bathroom.

"Daddy, why are you talking to yourself?"

The sudden appearance of his daughter startled him. He wasn't used to having her around, and he absolutely wasn't going to tell her about the women appearing in his mirrors, at least not yet. He knelt and put his arms around her.

"Sorry, honey, I guess I'm just a little tired."

She looked up at him and smiled, then before turning to go back to bed, she rolled her eyes back in a way that only an adorable seven-year-old could do.

"You're so weird, Daddy."

ψ

Their appointment at the Western Passport Center went smoothly, and the friendly official promised they'd be able to pick up Lucy's passport later that afternoon. That was a lot sooner than Nick had anticipated, so he immediately phoned the airline to arrange their flight to Paris.

He booked two economy-class tickets on a Delta flight leaving Tucson at one p.m. the following day, with a ninety-minute layover in Los Angeles. Their almost fifteen-hour flight was scheduled to land at Charles de Gaulle Airport at 11:15 a.m. Paris time. Now they had almost the entire day together to explore Tucson before they could pick up the passport.

"So, what do you want to do today, honey?"

Lucy had noticed an ad for the Tucson Children's Museum in their room's Tourist Guide, so that was her choice for the day's activities.

"After, can we have dinner at McDonald's?"

Wow, this is really going to be a deep dive into fatherhood, he thought.

He nodded, taking hold of her hand and leading her to the car for the drive to the museum.

ψ

Nick and Lucy arrived at Tucson International Airport two hours before their scheduled departure time. He returned the rental car, and they took the shuttle bus through the cactus-strewn desert landscape to the terminal building. One of the surprise advantages of being a single father, traveling alone with a pretty, seven-year-old girl, is that the level of service and attention you receive from airline staff is heightened tenfold. Nick wasn't about to complain about this unexpected perk.

Their trans-country, trans-Atlantic flights were faultless, and between eating, watching movies, and sleeping, the time passed quickly. An hour before their arrival, Lucy became taciturn and reserved. Nick had told her about Gabriela, Madeline, and all about her new home on the island in the middle of the Seine.

"I hope they'll like me."

Nick put his arm around her small shoulders and kissed her gently on the top of her head.

"They'll love you, sweetheart. They'll love you."

CHAPTER THIRTY-EIGHT

News of the apparent double suicide of Jacques Bisset and Claudette, his wife of twenty-one years, was the lead news story in media throughout the world. The pharmaceutical billionaire was a business legend, a brilliant chemist from a small town in Burgundy who'd hit the jackpot by cleverly misappropriating formulas from other industry giants—a much disliked and frequently litigated individual with many enemies. Nick's friend Alain Moreau, the lieutenant detective on Paris's police force, was assigned to the case.

The bodies were discovered, by a maid, in the living room of their palatial apartment in one of the city's poshest neighborhoods. She'd tried her best not to vomit, but the stench of death and the sight of dried blood, caked hard on the faces of her employers, overcame her. An almost-empty vial and a hypodermic needle were found near the couple's bodies.

The police were summoned, the area cordoned off, and soon the street in front of their building was crowded with journalists, news vehicles, and numerous men with shoulder-held cameras pointed towards earnest-looking on-air reporters from both the local and national media.

A preliminary search of the premises resulted in the discovery of a small laboratory, hidden behind a secret door, off the apartment's huge living room.

The tiny, windowless room contained shelves filled, jar after jar, with various powders and liquids. There was a marble wall-mounted table, loaded with lab equipment, and the array of computers found in the room would be the envy of the Direction Générale de la Sécurité Extérieure (DGSE), France's equivalent of America's CIA. There was also one small vial, partially filled with a clear pale-amber liquid. The lieutenant detective, whose hands were protected with tissue-thin rubber gloves, picked up the vial, looked closely at the contents, and dropped it into a plastic evidence bag.

"Marcel, emméne ça au laboratoire et fais-le analyser."

As instructed, the police officer's young subordinate took the bag and rushed to deliver the vial to the police lab to be analyzed. If it matched the poison that they'd found in the woman who'd died in her cell, as the lieutenant detective suspected it might, he'd call his friend Nicholas Palmer.

ψ

Hector Rodriguez was sitting in his office when he heard the news about the double suicides in Paris. It was all over CNN and just about every other news station he scrolled through on his massive wall-mounted television. He felt the pressure rise in his chest; his pulse was racing, and his head was pounding. He jumped up and started pacing the room and screaming at the television.

"Fucking idiot! Why did the fucking idiot kill himself? I need this like I need another goddamned hole in the head!"

Now three of his apostles were dead. This wasn't random or coincidental; it was a carefully planned and executed scheme to get to him. He didn't know why or how this was possible, but he somehow knew the Chicago detective was behind it all. He vowed, one way or the other, that it would stop, and that meant killing the meddlesome cop.

ψ

Written testaments of the Order's decree stipulated that there must always be twelve apostles, and over the hundreds of years they'd been in existence, this edict had been closely followed. As members died, or become disabled, they had been effectively replaced by other followers deemed deserving of the honor. Now it was his job to replace Jacques Bisset, the old nun in Madrid, and the elderly American woman who'd just recently died in the unfortunate automobile accident in California.

He picked up his cell and made the first of nine calls he was going to make that day. All were to the remaining apostles, requesting that they each put forward names to be considered to replace their departed conspirators. Once he'd received names of potential candidates, he would assemble the council to vote. He already knew who his suggested candidate would be. He placed a call to England. It was answered by Angelina, his daughter.

"Daddy?"

"Good morning, Angelina. I need you to come to New York. It's time to start your education."

ψ

The scene in the apartment on Ile Saint-Louis was one of quiet apprehension and guarded happiness. Lucy was strangely ambivalent about the loss of her mother and grandmother. It was as if they were now a fragment of her life that she'd soon like to forget. She looked around the charming apartment. It was a far cry from her home in Chicago and about a million miles different from her grandparents' house in California. She liked what she saw.

Nick introduced the little girl to Gabriela and Madeline.

"Are you Daddy's new girlfriend?"

Gabriela nodded, and her face turned a brilliant shade of red. She felt the heat rising in the back of her neck, and her heart was beating out of her chest.

The little girl looked at her as if she were examining a painting in a gallery.

"You're very pretty."

Gabriela didn't know what to do next. Thank her? Shake her hand? Hug her? This was new territory for the Chicago cop.

Madeline suffered no such trepidation. She rushed up to Lucy, hugged her, and buried the girl's head in her bosom. She'd never had children of her own, and you could tell by her actions that this child would soon become her adopted granddaughter. Lucy managed to wiggle herself away from the grinning Frenchwoman's grip and turned her attention back to Gabriela.

"Can I call you Gabi?"

Whereupon the enraptured Madeline quickly staked her claim on the little girl's affections. "And you can call me Grand-mère."

The two women couldn't contain their excitement. What they'd thought would be a difficult adjustment just didn't happen. Instead, Lucy seemed to readily accept them as part of her family.

"Laisse-moi te montrer ta chambre, ma petite princesse."

Madeline scooped up the girl's luggage and led her into the smallest bedroom. The draperies had been pulled back and the view across the Seine, towards the charming neoclassical buildings of the 4th Arrondissement, was pure Paris.

Lucy stared out the window. The activity on the street and the tour boats chugging along the river were a far cry from anything she'd ever seen in her short life.

Madeline walked up behind her and put her hands on the girl's small shoulders.

"This used to be my sister's room and mine when we were little girls like you. We had many happy times here."

Tears welled up in the old woman's eyes. Was it the memory of her dead sister that triggered them or the happiness at seeing the wonder in the little girl's eyes? She quickly wiped away the tears and turned to Lucy.

"Mon dieu, you must be hungry and tired after such a long trip. Let's see what we have in the kitchen."

Gabriela had already prepared their lunch: a fresh baguette, cheeses, newly churned butter, pâtés, pickles, and a selection of fruit and jams, all deliciously displayed on the century-old wooden table.

Nick's cell rang. It was Alain Moreau. He excused himself and went to the old professor's study.

"Bonjour, Nicholas, are you still in Spain?"

"No, Alain, I'm here—back in Paris."

He told the detective lieutenant about his abrupt visit to the States, the circumstances of his trip, and about his daughter, who was going to be living with Gabriela and him in the French capital.

"Ouf, you've been a busy boy, but then again, so have I. You've no doubt heard about the apparent suicides of Monsieur Bisset and his wife. Well, during our investigations, we discovered a private laboratory in which the good chemist concocted a deadly poison. It was this poison, injected into him and Madame Bisset, that caused their unfortunate demise."

Nick was wondering how all of this had anything to do with him, or what he was working on.

The French police officer continued. "We conducted an autopsy on the bodies, and their blood tests confirmed that the poison that killed them was identical to the poison that killed the girl we were holding in prison..." The Frenchman paused. He had a flair for the dramatic and loved to use it whenever he could. "... and quite possibly the same poison injected into your friend, the professor, when you were in Madrid."

Nick quickly connected the dots.

"Then obviously Monsieur Bisset was somehow connected with the Serpents of Christ."

Alain sounded tired; the media frenzy surrounding the deaths was just another unwanted distraction in an already busy day. "I would most definitely say so. He has a tattoo of the serpent on his back, just like the girl's."

"Can I meet you at the morgue in the morning? I'd like to examine the bodies myself, if that's okay with you?"

"No problem, Nicholas. I'll see you at ten, okay?"

Just as he was hanging up, Gabriela walked into the cluttered room to see if he was joining them for lunch.

Nick was deep in thought, still standing motionless in the center of Henri's office.

She interrupted him. "What was that all about?"

He snapped himself out of his introspection. "Nothing. Nothing that won't wait until tomorrow."

He followed Gabriela into the kitchen, sat down, and joined his new little family for lunch, but his thoughts were elsewhere.

What the hell am I doing, dragging Lucy into this mess? Am I totally out of my mind?

The following morning, after Nick and Gabriela had left to go to the morgue, Madeline took Lucy out to introduce her to the sights and sounds of Paris.

ψ

Alain Moreau greeted Nick and Gabi at the front door of La morgue de Paris. He had his usual half-smoked stogie protruding from his mouth. The cigar smoke, and the horrible stench of dead and decaying bodies, quickly entered their nostrils and lungs.

Side by side, on stainless-steel tables, lay the bloated bodies of Jacques Bisset and his wife. A woman who'd known them had speculated in the media that "they're probably closer together now than they'd ever been when they were both still alive."

The tables on which the Bisset's were lying had slightly raised edges and were sloped downward to allow bodily fluids to run into the floor's drainage openings. The doctors had turned the chemist over onto his stomach, revealing the hideous snake tattoo. Like the others they'd seen, it was coiled along his backbone. Gabriela gagged and left the room. If she'd stayed a minute more, she was sure she'd have retched up her breakfast.

Nick and the detective lieutenant went into an adjoining lab where attending doctors explained the results of their forensic tests.

Alain turned to Nick and raised his arms, indicating puzzlement and concern. "The only thing we don't know is whether this is the end of the trail or just the first step on a long and arduous journey.

Nick nodded his agreement and went outside to find Gabi, and to fill his lungs with fresh air.

CHAPTER THIRTY-NINE

Angelina Rodriguez's flight from London was forty-five minutes late arriving at La Guardia Airport in New York. The delay made Hector furious. He wasn't used to waiting for anyone, or anything, let alone a commercial flight. The terminal was unusually busy, filled with what he considered to be unkempt and insignificant lemmings. Finally, the schedule board indicated his daughter's flight had landed. Now he just had to wait for her to pick up her luggage and pass customs and Homeland Security.

After what seemed like an eternity to the impatient man, his daughter swept through the double glass doors, entered the arrivals area, and ran towards him.

"Hi, Daddy! Sorry I'm late. The plane was delayed leaving Heathrow."

Hector did his best to look happy, but beneath his feigned joy, he was seething—still enraged at the airline's inefficiency and their total disregard for passengers and those waiting for them.

His thoughts, if they could have been heard, would have shocked most people within earshot: *This sort of fucking idiotic inefficiency wouldn't happen if I were running things.*

He hugged his daughter, smiled, and spoke in a voice that belied his rage.

"No problem, my little angel. The limo's been circling the terminal and should be outside in a minute or two.

ψ

Traffic on FDR Drive was bumper to bumper, which only added to the man's fury. His blood was boiling, and the only reason he didn't vent his anger at the driver was that his daughter was sitting beside him in the rear seat. He looked towards her.

"Goddamn New York traffic is getting worse and worse every day; soon you won't be able to move anywhere in the city, except in the dead of night."

Angelina was feeling the same way but didn't want her father to hear the venomous tirade welling up in her throat. She simply smiled and turned to look out at the East River, swirling gloomily below them. Her father was speaking, but his words were lost in the distraction caused by her foul mood.

"I want you to know everything about our business and about our family's heritage and obligations. I want you to be ready and able to succeed me when the time comes."

Angelina snapped out of her brooding. She was startled by her father's remark. She stared at him, sensing that something was troubling the man, but she knew that now was not the time to ask. That would come later, when she knew more about the demons that seemed to be haunting him.

ψ

When Nick and Gabi returned to the apartment on Ile Saint-Louis, Lucy and Madeline were waiting for them. He knelt in front of his little girl.

"So how was your day? How do you like Paris so far?"

Lucy rushed into her father's arms, and her voice exploded in a nonstop outburst of unbridled joy. Then, with an ever-so-slight moment of hesitation, she turned to Gabi and hugged her too.

If happiness could be measured on the Richter scale, Gabriela was experiencing a magnitude-ten earthquake. Nick didn't think she'd ever be able to wipe the smile off her beautiful face.

"Alors, ma petite famille, where should we go for dinner tonight?"

Three expectant faces turned towards Madeline, who cupped her hand to her chin and assumed a pose of deep thought.

"I think something French, mes amis. There's a pretty little bistro just across the river on Quai de l'Hôtel de Ville where Henri and I used to go. I believe you'll love the food, and it's just a short walk away."

"The papers, Detective Palmer, your path lies in my brother's papers."

Nick spun around to see where the voice of Margaux Deneuve had originated. The others were getting ready to leave for the restaurant, and there was no indication that anyone else in the room had heard the voice of Madeline's sister. Then it was Lucy's voice he heard.

"C'mon, Daddy. I'm hungry, let's go."

ψ

Inca Gold Investments' offices occupied six floors of a traditional limestone building in lower Manhattan. The spaces were tastefully decorated in a manner befitting an established financial enterprise. Behind the front desk, in the sixth-floor reception area, the firm's corporate logo was mounted prominently on a highly polished black marble wall. The brandmark resembled the snake god Quetzalcoatl. It was made of eighteen-carat gold and lit to dazzle any visitor entering the room. Similar logos adorned the company's reception rooms at their offices in London, Mexico City, and Hong Kong.

Hector and his daughter arrived at IGI's New York office at nine in the morning on the day following her arrival in Manhattan. He toured her through the firm's various departments, and later, after they'd had lunch in his private office, he escorted her to a posh office in the research department on the fourth floor.

"This is where you'll begin your education. Ask questions, dig into the files, find out what IGI is all about."

He turned away and left the girl to settle into her new office, get the lay of the land, and introduce herself to her new colleagues. It didn't take Angelina long to realize she was probably the brightest person on the floor. It also didn't take long before she was hit on by several of the young-buck analysts, anxious to make a good impression on the boss's beautiful daughter.

While Angelina was becoming familiar with her new surroundings, Hector was busy making calls and recording names of prospective council members on his secure laptop. So far, he'd heard from just four of the apostles. None of their nominees seemed promising or even acceptable. His frustration was overwhelming, and he began to question the long-established rules of the Order.

I'm El Cardenal. I'm the one who makes the goddamned decisions. Why do I need the others to tell me what to do?

He leaned back in his chair and began taking long, deep breaths. His thoughts turned to Jacques Bisset. *Why the fuck did he commit suicide? If he'd left well enough alone, nobody would ever have connected him to the deaths in Paris and Madrid. Stupid bastard. Stupid fucking bastard!*

At six that evening, Angelina knocked and strode into his office. She was angry, red-faced, and if the scene were in a comic book, there'd have been steam coming out of both her ears.

"Daddy, if I ran this place, I'd fire half of the fucking idiots on the fourth floor."

ψ

"The problem is that we're chasing ghosts; so far we've no hard evidence about any of this."

Nick looked up at Gabi. He and Madeline had been painstakingly searching through the voluminous piles of papers Henri had accumulated over the years. Most of what they'd seen so far consisted of handwritten scholarly theories and published papers. Most were in French, but some had been translated into English.

"I don't know about you guys, but it feels like my eyes are about to pop out of my head."

As soon as the words came out of his mouth, Madeline passed him an article by Henri, published years earlier in an English theological journal.

Nick took the paper and began to read the article. It was titled "God's Words: An Abridged Thesis on the Written Dissemination of Early Religions."

The article was just four pages long. It referenced the Bible, Quran, Tanakh, Torah, and other secular writings, but what caught Nick's attention was a paragraph Madeline had highlighted with a bright yellow marker that dealt with record keeping:

From earliest times until the present day, keeping records regarding the business aspects of religious orders has been carried out in much the same way as today's conventional commercial enterprises. General accounting practices, doctrine, and major faith-based activities have been found scribed onto clay tablets that predate the advent of Christianity.

Nick passed the magazine to Gabriela and asked her to read the paragraph.

After reading the piece, she handed it back to Nick. He reread it.

"If the followers of La Orden de las Serpientes de Cristo have kept records like the other religious orders Henri is describing, then this kind of information could lead us to the hard evidence we're looking for."

Lucy came out of her room to say goodnight, and after many hugs and kisses, the little girl went to bed.

Gabi took up the conversation they were having before Lucy's sweet interruption. "It's a big world out there, Nick. I wouldn't even know where to start looking."

Madeline stretched, glanced at her watch, and suddenly jumped up. "Mon dieu, regardez l'heure. I have to get up early and take Lucy to her new school—and then we have to visit l'avocat to sign all the transfer documents. Bonne nuit, you two."

She kissed each of them on the cheeks, and she too trundled off to her bedroom.

Nick and Gabriela were left alone in the room—their only company the troubled thoughts they shared.

CHAPTER FORTY

"Toutes nos felicitations! Congratulations, Monsieur Palmer, you are now a very wealthy man."

Nick had just finished signing the documents stacked high on the lawyer's massive desk. Madeline and Gabriela took turns witnessing various pages of the transactions. It was a bittersweet moment for all of them, bringing up fond memories of Henri while also highlighting his absence.

The lawyer reached over, shook Nick's hand, kissed each of the ladies on both cheeks, and handed Nick several boxes filled with his future.

"Au revoir, mom ami. I am delighted you've decided to keep me on as your lawyer. If there's anything you need, please don't hesitate to call."

"There's one more thing," Nick said, glancing over at Gabriela. "If and when we officially move to France, can you look into what we'll need to do get the necessary documentation for resident status?"

The woman smiled, "It would be my very great pleasure, monsieur. Consider it done."

ψ

When they got back to the apartment, Nick placed the boxes of legal documents on Henri's desk. Because most of it was written in French, he'd need Madeline's help to translate and decipher the pages. Gabi came up behind him and draped her arms over his shoulders.

"You know, I think living here in Paris would be great, but we also have to figure out what we're going to do about Chicago. We both have commitments there that we have to deal with."

Nick turned and looked at Gabriela. It was something he'd been thinking about for weeks. He knew what his decision was but was reluctant to impose what he wanted on his beautiful girlfriend.

He paused, but now that the issue was on the table, he felt it was time to declare his feelings. "The only thing left for me in Chicago is my job, and a few scraps of furniture and clothing in an apartment I've hardly ever been to. Here in Paris, I'm beginning to feel I have a life again, and a seriously big part of that life is you."

Gabriela rubbed her forehead and stared at him. "I love it here too, Nick, but we've got to do something. Chasing ghosts is one thing, but what do we do when it's all over? Lie around like a couple of wealthy vagabonds with no purpose?"

Nick understood what she was saying. He'd been wrestling with the very same question and had yet to come up with anything resembling a good answer. All he knew for sure is that he wanted live in Paris with Gabi, Lucy, and Madeline.

ψ

Hector smiled at his daughter. Perhaps now was the time to get her acquainted with another, deeply hidden, facet of his vast enterprises: La Orden de las Serpientes de Cristo. He methodically shut down his array of computers, placed his arm around the girl's shoulders, and led her towards the door.

"We'll eat at home tonight. I have important things I need to tell you."

Angelina looked up at her father. She somehow knew this was going to be a crossroad in their relationship, and very possibly, a decisive moment in the rest of her life. She was bursting with excitement and anticipation. She wished their dinner were over already, so he could share all the secrets she knew he held deeply in his heart.

ψ

To Angelina, the meal seemed to last forever, but finally, after the last dishes were removed from the table, her father turned towards her.

"Did you enjoy the salmon en papillote? It's one of Chef's specialties."

Angelina was getting impatient, thinking that her father should stop the bullshit small talk and get on with what he wanted to tell her.

Hector found it difficult to reveal his innermost feelings and didn't often say what he was really thinking, but he noticed the girl's obvious restlessness.

Another dangerous characteristic she's inherited from me. I'll have to speak to her about the importance of patience… even if I have difficulty with the concept myself.

He learned forward, and hesitatingly, began the conversation.

"There's another side to our family's history I need to acquaint you with. It's important you pay close attention to what I'm about to say, because one day, when I'm not here, you're going to assume a role our family has held for over five hundred years."

Hector went on to describe the history that had led to the formation of La Orden de las Serpientes de Cristo, and the responsibility he, and all their ancestors, had taken on as leaders of the Order.

He told her about the secret religious regime the Order's thousands of followers adhered to. He told her about the twelve apostles. He told her about the clandestine department, secreted away in the same building that held the IGI offices, that dealt exclusively with communications to the Order's many followers, and the business side of the religion.

He didn't mention the sacrificial murders or the detective from

206

Chicago who seemed intent on destroying him—that conversation could wait for another, more appropriate, time.

Angelina sat through the whole dissertation without saying a word. In her wildest dreams, she hadn't imagined this aspect of her father's activities and character. She hadn't imagined the tremendous power he held in his hands, hadn't ever conceived of the staggering wealth that would all, one day, be hers. She reached across the table and took her father's hand.

"I want to learn more. I want to know everything. I'm ready."

Hector didn't feel comfortable with the girl's obvious eagerness.

"All in good time, Angelina, all in good time."

Angelina was already contemplating her future, already counting the days to when she would lead both IGI and the secret religious order her father had just told her about. Her brilliant mind was spinning with opportunities—opportunities she believed her father hadn't considered... or even dreamt of.

ψ

Over the following days and weeks, Angelina immersed herself in all aspects of the family business, and within a few short months, it was acknowledged by most employees of both IGI and the Order that she would, upon her father's demise, be their boss. This meteoric rise in his daughter's stature didn't go unnoticed by Hector.

The time was right, he decided, to continue her education, and tell her about the other more repugnant aspects of the religion he headed.

When Angelina arrived back to the apartment, after another of her twelve-hour days, he called her into his office. "There's another, some would say, more unpleasant aspect of the Order I must tell you about."

"It's about the human sacrifices of young women, isn't it?"

Hector was taken aback. He knew she'd been combing through the records in the Order's secret offices but hadn't realized how much she'd found out. She didn't look at all concerned, nor did she show any signs of distress. In fact, she looked very pleased with herself.

"I know all about it, Daddy. It's part of our heritage, an important ritual that helps bind together all our followers."

Hector felt uncharacteristically uneasy. The girl had obviously inherited another of his attributes: the cold-bloodedness that made him impervious to the feeling of others. He wondered how she felt about him... and how long it would be before she decided he was also dispensable.

His next thought would remain his and his alone:

I'd better watch this devious little angel. Who knows what she's capable of?

ψ

The question of what to do about their lives in Chicago went unanswered but hung ominously in the air of the apartment on Ile Saint-Louis.

Nick, Gabi, and Madeline spent many more hours sifting through the hundreds of papers Henri had accumulated over the years. By the end of each day, all three of them were exhausted but somehow managed to pull themselves together and revive themselves for Lucy's arrival from school.

This evening, at the appointed time, the little girl burst through the front door of the apartment and threw her books on the floor of the foyer.

"How was school today, Lucy?"

"C'était merveilleux, Papa."

Nick and Gabi both had questioning looks on their faces. Madeline, noting their confused expressions, burst into laughter, then reached out and hugged the little girl.

"I believe she's getting on famously."

"The teachers are really nice, and I've met a lot of new friends. Everything is in French, but it's not really hard to understand what they're saying."

Madeline ordered pizza from Le Sarrasin et le Froment, an Italian restaurant on Rue Saint-Louis, and Nick went to pick up their dinner order.

"What are you guys doing?" Lucy asked, looking at the stacks of papers and journals scattered throughout the room.

Gabriela answered the girl's question. "We're searching for clues, but we haven't found anything yet, and I'm beginning to feel the whole thing is pretty hopeless."

Gabriela picked up a handful of papers they'd already checked and discarded, and dramatically threw them into the air. As the papers fluttered gently down towards the floor, Lucy pointed towards the boxes of documents they'd received from l'avocat.

"What about those? Have you looked through all the papers in those boxes yet?"

Gabriela paused and looked at Lucy. *Jesus, two trained detectives racking their brains for hours, and we didn't even think of looking at what's in the lawyer's boxes.*

"We'll start looking through those first thing tomorrow morning, smarty pants."

Nick arrived with the pizzas, and while they were eating, Gabriela told him about Lucy's brainstorm.

He heard the voice of Margaux Deneuve then. It seemed to fill the air, but nobody else appeared to hear her: *"Vous êtes les bienvenus! You're welcome."*

Nick smiled. Perhaps it wasn't so much Lucy's idea as one that had been conveyed to her by Margaux Deneuve.

CHAPTER FORTY-ONE

Alma Gonzales, the sixty-two-year-old master tattoo artist, practiced her art in a small one-bedroom apartment in Mexico City's Roma district. The only sound that interrupted the room's silence was the steady hum of a rickety air-conditioning unit that protruded over the street below from the apartment's grimy second-floor window.

Alma was scared. The man whose back she was facing was evil. Every pore of his body seemed to ooze with the sulfuric stench of hellfire. She completed the last few stabs of the tattoo and placed her instrument down carefully on the small round table that sat next to her rickety wooden chair.

"Señor, está complete."

The man rose and twisted his head to survey the woman's handiwork in the full-length mirror that leaned against the opposite wall. He grunted his approval, put on a scruffy denim shirt, and left the woman alone to contemplate the overwhelming sense of foreboding she felt crawling over her skin and throughout her entire body.

The depiction of the snake god Quetzalcoatl was the only image she was allowed to execute, and she'd spent many years perfecting it under the tutelage of her predecessor. She'd completed literally hundreds of similar assignments and was paid exceptionally well for her work—and her silence. But the man whose back she'd just pierced with a million tiny pinpricks was different from all the others. The tattoo seemed to come alive in the environment of the man's uneven, knife-scarred skin. Even when he stood motionless, the viper on his back seemed to move with a fluidity that belied its inked form.

Alma pushed herself up from the chair. The many years spent toiling, stooped over her work, had left her with a permanent and painful hump. She threw a colorful shawl across her bent shoulders and left the apartment. The man with the tattoo she'd just completed was waiting for her on the building's dilapidated landing. He pushed a long, evil-looking knife towards her throat.

"Tell anyone I was here, and I'll kill you… you and your whole fucking family. Entiendes?"

She simply nodded, pushed her way past him, and went out onto the busy, dusty street. If the gringo could have read her thoughts, he might have been more respectful.

Stupid young fool, you know nothing. If anyone knew what I do for a living, both of us would be dead.

ψ

Alma Gonzales was one of the Twelve Apostles of New Spain. She was a senior member of La Orden de las Serpientes de Cristo, and she took it upon herself to have the man whose back she had just finished carefully tattooing watched. Andrés de Córdoba was Alma's sacrosanct name within the Order, and de Córdoba wanted to know the man's every move.

The Uber she'd ordered from the dingy apartment in Roma dropped her off at a much more luxurious building in Polanco, one of Mexico City's most exclusive neighborhoods. The boy who was waiting for her in the spacious apartment she owned was her carefully chosen apprentice.

ψ

Miguel Perez was the son of an impoverished farm family in Usmajac, a small town south of Guadalajara. He was now just seventeen, but since his earliest days, while attending a small country school surrounded by dirt and cactuses, he'd shown a remarkable aptitude for art. It was this natural artistic talent the old apostle wanted to capitalize on, and she was teaching the boy the intricacies of the ancient art of irezumi, creating tattoos by using only handheld needles. Miguel didn't know it yet, but the only image he'd ever be allowed to create was that of the serpent god on the backs of the Order's believers.

ψ

Emilio Sanchez, the man whose back had recently been "inked" by the old lady in Roma, had a sixth sense, and he now sensed he was being followed.

He was born and raised in East Harlem, the tough-as-nails New York City neighborhood in Upper Manhattan. The hood, stretching from 125th to 155th off 8th Avenue, is sometimes called Spanish Harlem or El Barrio. The cultural mix of Latinos, African Americans, and others living in the densely populated towers of city-owned apartments, created a breeding ground for tough, often violent street gangs. Emilio was the leader of one such gang.

He'd been surprised when a man had contacted him and asked to meet him at a restaurant in the Upper West Side. The invitation, delivered by messenger, had come with a sizeable stack of hundred-dollar bills and the promise of more to come. Emilio couldn't resist the offer, though it was from a man he didn't know.

The meeting had taken place at the Chipotle Mexican Grill on Columbus Avenue. This Manhattan outlet of the fast-food chain was not the Ritz, but it was a vast improvement over what Emilio was used to. When he'd entered the restaurant, Hector was waiting and motioned the gang leader to come over to his table.

ψ

"Thank you for coming. I didn't know if you would."

Emilio slouched in the chair facing the man, with an evil sneer on his face that overtly implied that his meeting with Hector had better be worthwhile.

"I'm here, aren't I? What d'ya think? I'd just take the money and run?"

"To be perfectly honest, that possibility had crossed my mind."

Emilio was twitchy and impatient. He didn't want to be here for any longer than necessary. "So, what's the deal?"

"Two hundred thousand dollars. I want you to kill someone for me."

"Are you crazy? I get enough heat in this town, and I sure as hell don't need more."

Emilio stood and was about to leave the table, but Hector took hold of his arm with a grip that made the younger man wince.

"Not here, you idiot. In Mexico City."

Emilio sat back down; he'd never been out of the city, let alone out of the country, and was intrigued by the man's offer.

"So again... What's the fucking deal?"

Hector looked nervously around the almost-empty restaurant to make sure nobody was in earshot. This was his initiative and his alone. Nobody at IGI or the Order knew of the deal he was about to make.

"There's a man, a cop from Chicago, who's sticking his nose into my business. I'll give you the first hundred thousand up front and the second instalment when the jobs done. I'll get you to Mexico City—"

Defiant, Emilio interjected. "How the fuck are you going to get me into Mexico? I don't have a fucking driver's license, let alone a passport."

"Think about it for a second, Mister Sanchez. Thousands of Mexicans enter the States without a passport every year. It doesn't take much brain power to smuggle one man across the border the other way. Don't worry. I'll arrange everything. All I want you to do

213

is show up where and when I tell you. Understand?"

"Okay, I'm in Mexico City. What's next?"

"I own an apartment block in Roma—that's a neighborhood in the city. You'll stay in one of the apartments until your target arrives in the city—"

Emilio interrupted him again. "He's not in the city?"

"No, at the present time he's in Paris, but trust me, he'll be going to Mexico City very soon."

The conversation was beginning to annoy the gang leader. "And what the fuck am I supposed to do while I'm hanging around waiting for the pooch to show up?"

Hector reached into his jacket pocket and handed the man a folded piece of paper. "You're going to get a tattoo."

Emilio unfolded the paper and saw a photograph of Quetzalcoatl, the snake god, tattooed on the back of a woman. He stared at the image for about a minute, then handed the paper back to Hector.

"Fucking cool, man. It sure as shit beats the ink I've already got."

He pulled up the front of his dirty T-shirt to show his newfound benefactor the multitude of crude images scrawled over most of his body. Hector also noticed the numerous ugly knife and gunshot wounds on the man's torso. He reached out to shake the man's hand.

"Have we got a deal then?"

"Fucking right, mister—you didn't tell me your name."

"That's right, Mister Sanchez. But you'll be hearing from me soon, and you'll know who it is."

Hector got up and left the gang leader sitting alone in the restaurant. The hoodlum was already dreaming about his first trip out of New York, and what he was going to buy with all his newly found wealth.

CHAPTER FORTY-TWO

Since the arrival of Lucy, mornings at the apartment on Ile Saint-Louis had become a little more routine. Gabi or Nick made breakfast while Madeline fussed around, making sure her little princess looked neat and tidy before escorting her to school.

"Daddy, do I have to wear this uniform? In California, I went to school in shorts."

Madeline jumped in to save Nick from having to answer her. "Mademoiselle, in Paris, we women dress beautifully, and appropriately. Your school uniform is the first step in learning about French fashion, and the importance of dressing for the occasion. Today, your occasion is attending school, and you look beautiful."

Nick and Gabriela were still laughing at the elderly woman's tongue-in cheek berating as Lucy, accompanied by Madeline, left for school.

Gabi finished her last sip of coffee and pointed to the boxes stacked on Henri's desk.

"When Madeline gets back, we'll start going through those documents from the lawyer's office."

ψ

It hadn't taken Angelina Rodriguez long to stumble upon her father's other, more malevolent and highly illegal, business ventures. Her agile mind was churning a mile a minute as she dug through the seemingly endless number of files supposedly hidden from detailed examination. She was thinking about the tremendous opportunity lying there at her fingertips.

Holy shit, the old mans into human trafficking, prostitution, murder, extortion, drug smuggling, and a whole bunch of other very nasty stuff. Very, very cool. Pretty soon he's going to wish he hadn't given me carte blanche to rifle through all this stuff.

She was her father's daughter, but until now, she hadn't really known the man. Except for the infrequent times he visited her at school or when she saw him at her mother's Paris apartment, he was an enigma to both her and her brother. A mystery man who paid the bills and vanished, via private jet, into his world of business. She couldn't think of any reason she should be loyal to him. After all, he was just another stranger to her—a stranger who had just, inadvertently, handed her the keys to his kingdom.

ψ

When Madeline returned from taking Lucy to school, they sat down and began the arduous process of going through the boxes from Henri's lawyer. The pile of documents was formidable, but page by page, they began to make headway.

The first box contained papers pertaining to the transfer of Henri's assets to Nick. This pile of legalese held standard boilerplate agreements that included the transfer of ownership of the apartment, art, furnishings, and all other hard property. The second box contained tax receipts and returns from the previous years, meticulously filed by Henri's lawyer. In the third box were share certificates, investment documents, and banking information. This box, they decided, would be the most likely to provide the leads they were searching for.

"Mon dieu, that brother of mine certainly had a lot of irons in the fire."

Nick and Gabriela nodded at the elderly woman's remark. There was a huge pile of documentation to go through, and most of it was in French, a language neither of them was conversant in. They both looked at Madeline. She would be doing most of the heavy lifting on this one. She gave them an apprehensive smile and lifted a pile of papers from the box, just as Lucy breezed through the door. It was already lunchtime, and Madeline now had a diversion, and an excuse to postpone the inevitable. She jumped at the opportunity.

"Demain. Tomorrow. We'll start tomorrow."

She carefully placed the papers back into the box and rushed over to greet Lucy, the little girl she now considered to be her adopted granddaughter.

ψ

The following morning, the routine in the Ile Saint-Louis apartment was much the same as always—breakfast, Madeline taking Lucy to school, and once again all three of them diving into the box of documents. Nick and Gabi were mostly onlookers as Madeline read through the papers with her glasses perched perilously on the tip of her elegant nose.

She suddenly looked up. "Voila! This may be something."

She waved a share certificate in the air—a share certificate issued by Franco Pharma.

"These are shares in the company headed by the couple they found mysteriously dead several weeks ago. I think they've probably greatly depreciated in value."

Nick immediately went online to check on the status of the pharmaceutical company shares. He found the value of his shares had indeed gone down since the death of the company's founder, but they were beginning to rebound. The announcement of a new management group, initiated by Inca Gold Investments, one of Franco Pharma's major stakeholders, was credited with the quick turnaround. Nick clicked off the site and did a search on IGI. The home page of the company's website was emblazoned with their logo.

He couldn't believe what he was seeing. "Holy shit, take a look at this."

The two women stood behind him and looked over his shoulder at the computer screen. The stylized image of Quetzalcoatl, the snake god, was front and center, shimmering in gold on a black, marble-like background.

Madeline gasped and held her hand to her mouth. "Putain de merde a raison!" This could be the lead our mirror girls were telling you about."

Nick moved his cursor through the screen. He needed to find out more about the investment company with the snake logo.

"Shit! It's gated. I need a password to access the site."

Nick rubbed his eyes, placed his hand against his chin, and tried to come up with a solution to the problem. Then it occurred to him. He'd be given access to the site if he were a client of the firm. He called out to Madeline, who was in the kitchen busily making lunch.

"Madeline, could you please call Madame Agard to see if she'd be able to make an investment in Inca Gold Investments for us? We need to be clients of theirs to get into their website."

ψ

"I've checked. You'll need to put up a minimum of two million euros to participate in the IGI fund."

Madame Agard, the family's lawyer, was on the line to Nick, explaining the commitment he'd need to make in order to participate in the fund and to obtain access to the site.

"Can, you do it? Do we have enough funds?

"Oui, monsieur, you have enough to do that, and fifty times more if you wish."

The realization of what Henri had bequeathed him was still beyond staggering to Nick. It was like he'd won a lottery and then some, though whenever he thought about of the loss of his dear friend, he knew that none of this wealth was worth the deep pain he still felt inside.

He thanked the lawyer and asked her to proceed with the investment—with one small caveat: "Is there any way you can make the investment anonymously?"

"It may be difficult, Monsieur Palmer, but I believe I can arrange it through a blind trust administered by my firm. I will confirm all of this and let you know."

Nick hung up and turned back to his computer. He entered his password and the screen lit up, not with his usual wallpaper of the night skyline of Chicago, with its dazzling lights reflected in Lake Michigan's dark waters, but with the spectral image of Margaux Deneuve.

He was thankful Gabi had joined Madeline in the kitchen, out of sight of the ghostly image on his screen.

"Bonjour, Detective Palmer. Remember: The closer you get to the truth, the more dangerous the journey will be."

He stared straight into the girl's eyes. He wanted her to stay—wanted to ask her more questions he knew she wouldn't answer.

"Does that mean we're on the right track?"

"Gabriela Martinez. Protect Gabriela Martinez. She is vulnerable."

The image of the French girl faded and vanished, and he was left looking at a blank computer screen. He wanted to know more. She had told him to protect Gabriela. He wanted to know why the woman he loved was in danger. He wanted to know what the danger was. He realized his heart was pounding, and his palms were sweating. His level of anxiety was bursting through the roof. The chase was becoming all too real, all too precarious.

Then he heard a familiar voice from the kitchen. "Hey, big guy, come and get it. Lunch is on the table."

CHAPTER FORTY-THREE

Nick and Gabi were lying in bed. His mind was going a mile a minute, trying to figure out the cryptic message Margaux had delivered to him earlier in the day. His beautiful bedmate had something entirely different on her mind.

"Nicky, there's something important we need to talk about."

Nick snapped out of his thoughts. She'd never called him Nicky before, and he wondered what that was all about. What did she need to talk about that was so important?

Gabriela was sitting up, leaning against her pillow with her computer on her lap. Her voice, when she finally spoke, sounded strangely apprehensive. "I think I'm pregnant."

The four small words slapped him across the face like he'd been hit with a wet towel. He was totally surprised, dumbfounded, and utterly at a loss of words. As he stared at Gabriela, he could feel himself grinning so hard that he thought his face would break. Finally, she broke the awkward silence.

"So, are you just going to sit there like a big lump with a stupid smile on your face or are you going to say something?"

Nick still didn't say anything. He just sat there looking at her, until finally, he reached over and held her tightly in his arms.

Then came the barrage of questions. "When? Do you know if it's a boy or a girl? Wow, this is awesome. It's the best news I've heard since we left Chicago. I guess we'd better think about getting married."

She pulled away from him and began laughing at his awkwardness. "What and spoil all the fun? Let's just leave things as they are until we finish the job, and oh, let's not tell Lucy and Madeline yet. Not until after I see a doctor."

Sleep didn't come easily to the Chicago cop that night. His life was about to change again, and Gabi's news was another complication, albeit a happy one.

ψ

Emilio Sanchez was bored. He'd been hanging around Mexico City waiting for something—anything—to happen. He missed New York, missed his gang, and even though he had plenty of money and a nice place to stay, he craved action.

He'd left the apartment and had soon fingered the guy who was following him. He decided to confront the man, so he ducked into an alley off Calle Bajio, and as the man passed by, he grabbed him and pulled him into the darkly shadowed passageway.

"Hey, amigo, are you looking for me? Do you want to chat or something?"

The man struggled to release himself from Emilio's grip, but the more he struggled, the more provoked the New York gang leader became. There was a clicking sound, and an evil-looking switchblade appeared in Emilio's hand. A short struggle abruptly ended when the blade found its mark in the chest of the hapless hireling who had been employed by the woman who'd tattooed the snake god on Emilio's back.

Blood began to seep onto the rough ground beneath the man's body, turning the pavement a dark red, almost black. Emilio hurriedly left the alley and vanished into the crowds of people pushing their way along the street, all of them oblivious to the crime that had been committed just steps away.

ψ

Alma Gonzales heard about the death of her nephew the following morning. There were no witnesses to his murder, but she knew who the guilty party was and vowed revenge. This was her family, her city, and the fucking Americano would pay for his vile actions. She knew who to call to right this terrible wrong.

"Holiness, my nephew has been murdered. Murdered by the ungodly Americano hombre you sent to receive the sacred tattoo of Quetzalcoatl. I'm calling you as a courtesy, to inform you that my family is intent upon revenge, and it will soon be done."

Hector Rodriguez swore under his breath. He was furious about the idiocy and irresponsibility of the man he'd hired but adopted a conciliatory tone of voice for the old woman on the other end of the line.

"My sincere condolences to you and your family, Sister Andrés. I recruited the young man in good faith that he would be a devoted follower of La Orden. Obviously, my judgment was flawed. I promise I will personally deal with the man's evident shortcomings. So please, Sister, do not do anything rash until you hear back from me."

Alma Gonzales gave the man her word she would do nothing until after the funeral, but following that, all bets were off.

ψ

"Why the fuck did you kill the Mexican?"

Emilio Sanchez pleaded ignorance and innocence. He didn't know how the man in New York had found out so quickly about his deadly extracurricular activities.

"I haven't the slightest idea what you're talking about."

"Don't give me that shit! I know everything you're doing. Now I've got to get you hidden until your real assignment arrives. I'll get back to you, so stay put in the apartment, and don't move one fucking step until you hear from me."

Hector Rodriguez slammed down the phone, then called the man who headed his illicit business interests in Mexico.

"Hola, Manuel. I've got a little problem I need your help with."

Manuel Freeman was a Mexican of Jewish descent. He'd long abandoned his roots in Judaism and now worshiped in the temple of vast amounts of money, gained through prostitution, illicit drugs, and human trafficking. His boss, the man on the other end of the line, didn't seem to mind him skimming a little off the top, so helping the wealthy New Yorker with his dilemma was the least he could do.

Hector explained the issue, then gave the crime boss some very specific instructions.

"Pick up this Emilio Sanchez asshole from the apartment in Mexico City and get him as far away as possible. Set him up in Acapulco or somewhere... where he can return to the city when I need him. Then put guards on him twenty-four-seven to make sure he behaves. He's a belligerent little prick, so be careful."

"No problem, señor. Say, when are you coming back? We need to meet."

"Soon, my amigo, soon. I'll call you when I'm coming. Adios."

ψ

Nick tiptoed around Gabi as if she were made of the finest bone china. His unusual behavior didn't go unnoticed by the ever-vigilant Madeline.

"Qu'est-ce qui ne vas pas? What's wrong with you two? Did you have a fight?"

Before he could mumble an excuse, Madeline's cell rang.

Answering it, she listened for a moment and then held out the phone. "Nicholas, it's Delphine Agard. She says she has good news for you."

She handed the cell to Nick, but her look told him that, once he was off the call, she'd still be looking for answers.

"Madame Agard, Nick Palmer here. Madeline says you have good news for me."

"Bonjour, Monsieur Palmer. As you requested, I have deposited two million euros to Inca Gold Investments. Your investment is in a blind trust, registered to a numbered shell company, which is wholly owned by you. As soon as the investment is registered, they'll email me the codes you'll require to access their website."

"Merci, Madame Agard. I look forward to hearing from you."

When he hung up, he found himself looking straight into the stern countenance of Madeline Boucher. She had carefully corralled Gabriela so that she was now standing next to him, them looking sheepishly at the elegant Frenchwoman.

"Que se passe-t-il? What's going on with you two? What's your little argument about?"

Gabi looked over at Nick, shrugged her shoulders, and turned back to their French friend.

"I think I'm pregnant."

The elderly woman reached back to steady herself against a chair. It took several seconds for her to regain her composure, but when she did, the excitement spewed out of her mouth like a volcanic eruption of the French language.

They knew that being able to keep the happy news from Lucy would now be next to impossible.

CHAPTER FORTY-FOUR

Angelina Rodriguez was quietly plotting the overthrow of her father, finding out just how hated he was by most of the management—and by all the employees—at IGI. These same people were now being covertly wooed by the beautiful and seemingly innocuous daughter of their boss, and they loved every minute of attention the alluring and intelligent young woman lavished upon them. To complete the coup, she needed an ally, someone she could count on and trust explicitly.

She picked up her cell and placed a call.

"Philippe?"

Angelina's younger brother recognized the sugar-coated voice of his sister.

"Hey, Angie. To what do I owe the pleasure?"

"Can you come to New York? I'm working on something big, and I really, really need your help. Can you come soon?"

This was something new. His sister didn't usually need his help... or anyone else's. Caution signs started flashing in his brain, but as usual, he found it hard to resist her siren call.

"Okay, but can you give me a heads up? I'd love to know what I'm getting into—besides the usual stuff."

"I can't talk about it on the phone. I need to see you in person. Don't call Hector to send the jet, and don't plan on staying at the apartment. I'll check you into the Four Seasons. When do you think you can get here?"

ψ

Philippe Rodriguez and his sister had been raised by nannies. Their father was never around, and their mother was more involved in the social whirl of Paris, London, and New York than she was with them. When needed, the children were nothing more than fashion accessories to the glamorous woman. Because of their unorthodox upbringing, they had no friends but each other, and because of this, they'd developed a relationship that went well beyond the normally accepted notion of sibling affection.

Philippe enjoyed all the benefits that came with being the son of a wealthy father, but sometimes that was not enough. He loved his sister and conceded to himself that she was more intelligent than him, but he also knew that she lacked the street smarts he had. Perhaps that's why she was reaching out to him. One thing he knew for sure was that whatever she wanted, he'd have to watch his back.

ψ

Nick's cell rang. Checking the screen, he saw that the call was from Josh Nicholson, his boss in the Chicago. He didn't get a chance to say hello.

"Nick, what the fuck's happening with you two? I haven't heard a word from you in weeks."

"Hi, Chief. We were just talking about you. Got a minute?"

"No but go ahead and fill me in—and I hope it's worthwhile."

Without mentioning the ghostly young women who were helping and protecting him, he told the man about the string of murders, all of them, similar to the Susan Roberts case in Chicago they'd been following up on.

"There's a very strong possibility that all the killings are the work of a religious cult based in Mexico. Gabi and I are working with the cops in Mexico City, Paris, and Rome. It's like peeling an onion—a dangerous and often foul-smelling onion."

"Are you both okay? Are you still seeing those women in the mirror?"

Nick avoided the man's second question. "There have been several attempts to kill us, but we're both still standing and getting closer to closing in on the core."

"Well, for Christ's sake, be careful and call me more often than you've been doing so far—and try to wrap it up quickly. I need both you guys back here."

After hanging up, Nick turned towards Gabi and filled her in on the conversation he'd had with their boss in Chicago.

"Did you tell him I'm expecting?"

"God no, that would have really sent him over the edge."

He reached his arms around her and gently patted her tummy.

ψ

Delphine Agard called and gave Nick the password he needed to access IGI's secure website. He turned on his computer, called up the site, and was greeted with the image of the hideous serpent logo he'd come to hate. He began scrolling through headings on the navigation bar.

He discovered that the firm had been founded in Mexico City, in the late eighteen- hundreds by Señor Fulgencios Rodriguez. The privately owned equity and investment firm was now controlled by Hector Rodriguez, a descendent of the founder. There were portraits of the family's leadership hierarchy up to and including the present day. They looked, all in all, like a malevolent bunch of crooks.

Hector Rodriguez, IGI's current chairman and CEO, had two children at school in England and a wife living in Paris. He also owned what was believed to be the world's largest and most valuable collection of Mesoamerican art and antiquities in private hands. There was no mention of any charitable causes he or his firm contributed to or were patrons of.

Nick stopped reading and thought about the company and the man running it.

Just an ugly, evil-minded, money-churning machine with no compassion or conscience.

He spent the next several hours reading through the firm's management profiles, their capabilities, and their investment strategies. Next, he scoured the company's portfolio of investments.

"Gabi, come over here and take a look at this."

What he wanted her to see was IGI's substantial investment in Franco Pharma. It seemed to Nick that the firm was funding a company showing a minimum return on investment and couldn't possible justify the further ongoing financing from IGI that seemed to be taking place.

Gabriela quickly scanned the page Nick had pointed out and made her opinion very clear.

"I think that, as a new and significant investor in IGI, this is definitely something you should be looking into."

"More than that, I think we should take a closer look at Señor Hector Rodriguez. My gut is telling me what we're seeing here is just the tip of a big and very nasty iceberg."

ψ

"Bonjour, Papa. Bonjour, Gabi."

Lucy and Madeline tumbled into the room like they were being propelled by a miniature tornado. The little girl threw her books onto a chair and rushed over to where Nick and Gabriela were sitting. Her excitement was bubbling like cola poured too quickly into an ice-filled glass.

"Papa, can I go for a sleepover at Chantelle's house? Please say yes! Please say I can!"

Nick looked questioningly at Madeline. This little-girl stuff was new to him, and he didn't quite know to handle it.

"C'est bon." Chantelle lives in the building next door, and I've spoken to her parents. They would love it if Lucy could spend the night with them."

Nick smiled, grunted his approval, and his little daughter ran happily from the room to pack a bag for her great new adventure.

ψ

Philippe Rodriguez had unpacked and was lying on the bed in the sumptuous Manhattan suite that his sister had arranged for him. His first-class seat on British Airways had not been like the ones in his father's private jet but had been a whole lot better than those farther back in the plane, behind the curtain. He'd poured himself a scotch from the suite's minibar and was waiting for Angelina to arrive. There was a soft knock on the door, and he jumped up to answer it. He'd almost forgotten how beautiful his sister was.

"Hi, Philippe. How are you? How was your flight?"

He exaggerated his response with smiles and arm gestures that smacked of indifference.

"The flight was terrific, and the accommodation here is beyond belief. What do you want me to say? Everything was shitty?"

"Don't be such an ass. You're here for a reason."

She hugged her brother and kissed him full on the mouth. He kissed her back with an ardor that belied most people's understanding of sibling love.

ψ

. They lay next to each other in the inordinately large bed, their clothing scattered in untidy tangles on the suite's lushly carpeted floors.

229

"So, sis, what else do you have on your evil little mind?"

She elbowed him in the ribs and jumped out of bed. "Get up, stud. We'll order dinner from room service, and I'll fill you in."

He reluctantly climbed from beneath the covers.

CHAPTER FORTY-FIVE

Nick called Alain Moreau to see if his friend had any information regarding Hector Rodriguez. The detective lieutenant instantly remembered the conversation he'd had with Bryan Evans, the man from the New York Times He was beginning to wonder why the American billionaire was becoming such a hot topic.

"You're the second person who's asked me about Monsieur Rodriguez. Give me a day or two to check it out, and I'll get back to you. Oh, and please give my love to the beautiful Gabriela, and to the equally beautiful Madeline."

He laughed and hung up, leaving Nick with a cautiously optimistic feeling that they were getting close to the head of the serpent.

Alain called Bryan Evans at the New York Times and asked if he'd had any further contact with Hector Rodriguez. The newspaperman lied again. He'd called Rodriguez several days after Nigel Thomas's death had been confirmed by the police and told him about the murder of the Australian killer.

"No, Alain. He hasn't contacted me yet, and I don't know how to contact him. Don't worry; I'll call you if I hear anything—anything at all."

The next call the Parisian cop made was to the American financier's wife at her opulent apartment in Paris.

"Bonjour, Madame Rodriguez. This is Detective Lieutenant Alain

Moreau of the Paris police. I'm sorry to disturb your day, but I'm calling about your husband, Monsieur Hector Rodriguez."

Claire was alarmed. She had a strong belief that not everything her husband was involved in was legal or aboveboard. She hid her fears and sounded nonchalant.

"Ah, Detective Lieutenant, what can I tell you?"

"First, madame, I would like to know if your husband has been to Paris lately, and if so, for what purpose was he visiting? I would also like you to come to the police station to look at some photographs of people your husband contacted while he was here. Hopefully, you may be able to help us identify them."

Claire Rodriguez tried, with difficulty, to conceal her concern. "Non, monsieur, I haven't seen my husband in many months. We live quite separate lives, you know, but if you wish me to come and look at some photographs, then so be it."

Alain Moreau had carefully phrased his questions to contain a verbal trap. If she denied Hector had been in Paris, as she just had, then why would she be willing to visit the station to identify photographs of the people he'd met with?

"Merci, madame. I will be in touch with you shortly to arrange an appointment, and in the meantime, if you hear from your husband, please call me."

ψ

Nick turned away from the computer screen and looked at Gabriela.

"I think Hector's been taking serious kickbacks from his deceased friend at Franco Pharma. Why else would he dump so much of his investors' cash into the company?"

Gabi looked thoughtful. In her police days, she'd run into people like Hector and not understood the lengths to which they'd go to amass power and money. This kind of twisted motivation just wasn't part of her psyche. She shook her head, not having an answer for him.

Nick sighed. "There's always been good people, bad people, and people who skirt the edges. I think Hector Rodriguez falls firmly into the category of bad people, and we should do our best to find out how he fits into this whole mess of things."

"Do you think he's got anything to do with the murders of all those innocent girls?"

"Don't know, but I wouldn't put it past a guy like him. I just can't figure out how it all connects."

Nick leaned back in his chair and stretched his neck upward towards the ceiling. He'd been leaning over his computer for too long. When he looked back down at his computer, the face of Margaux Deneuve seemed to be floating above and over Franco Pharma's conflicting financial statements. Gabi was looking over Nick's shoulder. She still had a difficult time believing in the apparitions, but Margaux smiled at her, and Gabriela felt a surge of warmth spread throughout her entire body. It was as if a blessing was being bestowed on her, and she immediately felt like the girl on the computer screen knew she was expecting a child.

"Be careful. The man you have identified is evil and immoral and will stop at nothing to prevent you from discovering his hidden world. He is Satan incarnate and impervious to our powers and influence. We ourselves cannot stop him, but you can. We are only here to guide and protect you—when we can."

The image of Margaux Deneuve faded, and they were left looking at the financial statements of the company they'd just recently invested in. Nick turned towards Gabi with a look of concern.

"When we can? That sounds ominous, but it certainly sounds like Hector could be our man."

ψ

Angelina and Philippe thoroughly enjoyed their room-service dinner. She'd chosen the salmon and her brother had virtually inhaled his steak.

Following their meal and some sibling flirtation, they'd ended up in bed, resuming their previous activities.

Angelina was propped up against the headboard, soft pillows cradling her back, the sheet she'd pulled up barely covering her breasts. Philippe laid back on his pillow with a smug look of satisfaction on his young face. Angelina's expression suddenly turned serious. This was the moment her brother had been waiting for.

"I want to take over Father's businesses, and I need you to help me do it."

Philippe, who was as ambivalent about his father as she was, had somehow known this was the direction his visit to America was going to take. He pushed himself up on his elbows and tried to not to sound too cocky.

"I'm assuming you have a plan?"

"I do, but first I have to swear you to secrecy. After that, I'll tell you the extent of his operations."

She shot him a look that said, *"Don't even think about fucking with me or I'll kill you—brother or not, lover or not."*

Philippe got the message loud and clear. His sister had a way with words, whether she was speaking to him, or not.

"Okay, consider me sworn. I'm all ears. What's your plan?"

Ψ

"Where have you been? It's almost midnight."

"Sorry I'm late, Daddy. I've been out for dinner with a friend."

"Do I know this friend of yours?"

Angelina smiled to herself, then bounced over to the man and kissed him on the cheek.

"Let's just say he comes from a very wealthy family. Good night, Daddy."

Ψ

Emilio Sanchez felt like a caged tiger. His guard had arranged for him to have frequent visits from some of the local ladies, but that distraction offered him only temporary respite. What he needed was to fulfill his assignment, get the hell out of Mexico, and make it back to his friends and home turf in the Barrio. He stood up and turned to the man sent to guard him.

"Hey, Chico, I'm going out for a walk."

"No, señor. I was told to keep you here."

The burly Mexican stood in front of the door, a veritable roadblock at 350 pounds of solid muscle, covered in a picture-book spectacle of tattoos.

The New Yorker was insistent. "Come with me. I just want to walk around the block, and then we can come right back afterwards."

Chico thought about it. He too was getting bored with this seemingly endless assignment.

"Okay, amigo. Just around the block, and we come right back here."

The two men took the stairs to the ground floor and went out into the busy street. Emilio waved goodbye to his guardian then and took off running, zigzagging through the hordes of people on the crowded streets, soon completely out of sight of the man whose duty it was to keep him under wraps.

ψ

"Give me a triple tequila."

The bartender poured Emilio the drink and watched as his customer downed it in one gulp. Emilio slammed his empty glass down on the crude wooden bar.

"Give me another."

Two tough-looking Mexicans noticed the wad of cash Emilio pulled out each time he paid the barman, and after the second drink, when he got up to leave, they followed.

Emilio turned into an alley, then turned to face the street and the men who had followed him from the bar. This was exactly the kind of action he needed. He pulled out his knife and waited for them to close in.

Unfortunately for Emilio, the two thugs had been followed into the alley by his erstwhile bodyguard. After a brief skirmish with the mountain of a man, the would-be thieves ran from the scene.

"Fuckhead, gringo, you're coming back with me."

Chico grabbed Emilio by the back of his jacket, manhandled him back to the apartment, and pushed him down into a chair.

"Try anything like that again, and I'll cut your fucking legs off."

He grabbed another chair, placed it in front of the door, sat down, and folded his tattooed arms across his massive chest.

CHAPTER FORTY-SIX

Hector strode through the opulent reception area of IGI's New York headquarters. He ignored the friendly greeting from each of the two receptionists and went directly to his office, settling into his chair and calling Angelina to come to him.

His daughter had arrived at the office earlier than him and was already happily berating a junior analyst when the call from her father came in. She picked up the phone, listened for a moment, then sent the frightened young woman—the recipient of her needless ill humor—scurrying away.

When Angelina entered Hector's office, she found him staring out the window.

"I'm going to convene a conclave of the apostles, and I would like you to accompany me." He turned to face his daughter and tried to judge her reaction to his sudden request. "It's an important meeting. We need to designate three new members to the assembly, and I will be putting your name forward for inclusion."

The young woman had had a premonition that this was what her father was going to say. Ever since she'd been made aware of their family's connection to La Orden de las Serpientes de Cristo, she'd thought about it often and had secretly reached out to the remaining apostles to gauge their feelings about Hector's leadership.

Her exterior demeanor didn't change, but if her thoughts had been visible, Hector would have seen his daughter flipping cartwheels of joy.

"Thank you, Father. Thank you for offering me such a great honor."

Hector smiled. With his daughter's involvement, his plans for succession and his continued leadership of the Order would be assured.

After Angelina left, he placed a call to Acapulco.

"Hola, amigo. Get that son of a bitch New Yorker you're guarding to Mexico City pronto. Give him a cell and email me the number."

The man on the receiving end of the call was happy his unpleasant assignment was over, so he could return to his family.

ψ

"You took Angelina out of university and didn't even consult me?"

Claire Rodriguez was on the phone to her husband. To say that she was upset would be a massive understatement. She paced back and forth across the living room of their plush Paris apartment like a mother lion who'd just lost one of her cubs.

"You stupid inconsiderate asshole. She's just months away from graduation, and you pulled the rug right out from under her?"

Hector shrugged. He was used to the occasional rant from his wife. It was the only time he got any kind of real emotion from the woman.

"She's happy, she's engaged with the work, and she's fast becoming an asset to the firm. And besides that, why the fuck do you think she needs a degree when she's ten times smarter than anyone else in that goddamn school? Have you seen her test results lately?"

Claire backed off. She hadn't followed her daughter's academic records. It hadn't seemed important to her, and now Hector's words were hitting her right where it hurt. She felt ashamed and somewhat admonished by the man's reasoning. Instantly, she regretted her earlier outburst.

Hector liked to win, and his wife's sudden silence confirmed he'd hit the jackpot.

"I'm taking her to Mexico City next week for some important

meetings. I'm sure she'll be a huge asset to our future growth."

Claire wasn't going to let her husband off that easy, and after Hector hung up, she placed a call to Alain Moreau at the Paris police.

"Bonjour, Lieutenant Detective. Claire Rodriguez calling. I have just heard from my husband and thought you might be interested in knowing he'll be traveling to Mexico City from New York next week on business."

"Merci, madame. Thank you for letting me know."

New York and Mexico City were so far out of Alain Moreau's jurisdiction that they didn't even register on the map, and even if he could do something to help his American friend, getting assistance from those distant police forces, without any hard evidence, would be next to impossible. There was nothing he could do about the billionaire's movements, but he still felt obliged to inform his friend from Chicago about what he'd just heard from Hector's wife. He placed a call to Nick's cell.

ψ

Philippe Rodriguez spent the day in Soho. He liked the vibe of the Broadway south of Houston neighborhood. He liked the shops, the restaurants, and the people. Most of all, he liked that it was an area of Manhattan his father seldom ventured into.

He was going in for lunch at one of the city's most famous French restaurants when his cell rang. It was his sister, wondering where he was.

"I'm just going in for lunch. Why don't you grab a cab and join me?"

"No, I can't right now. I'll meet you later back at the hotel," she paused, "and I've got great news to tell you."

Philippe shrugged and waited to be seated at a table in the busy restaurant.

ψ

Nick turned to Gabi and Madeline. He'd just hung up from Alain Deneuve and had determined what his next step would be.

"Hector Rodriguez is going to Mexico City. I think this may be the endgame, so I'm going there too. I need to finish this off, once and for all."

The two women spoke, almost in union. It was as if they'd rehearsed the line beforehand.

"We're coming with you."

Nick threw his hands in the air in feigned exasperation. What he didn't need was a woman who was expecting her first child, and an elderly French lady, tagging along on what could be a very dangerous trip.

"No, neither of you can come. Who'd be here to look after Lucy?" The women exchanged glances and agreed between them that Madeline would be the obvious choice to stay in Paris, and because Gabriela was of Mexican descent and spoke fluent Spanish, she should be the one to go with Nick. The exasperated Chicago cop quickly realized he had no choice but to take his pregnant partner with him.

"Okay, Gabi, I don't like it, but you can come, but only if you promise you'll back off if things get out of hand. I don't want to take a chance on you getting hurt."

Madeline hugged Gabriela. The younger woman was like the daughter she'd never had, and she too was concerned about Gabriela being a part of what could be a perilous undertaking.

Nick went online to check the availability of direct flights from Paris to Mexico City, as Gabriela leaned over his shoulder and pointed out her preferences from the list of departures on the computer screen.

"I like the Aeromexico flight. We don't have to get up before daybreak, and we arrive in Mexico City at a reasonable time in the evening."

Gabi started walking away from the desk but then turned back towards Nick.

"You know, business class would be nice."

Nick smiled, booked their flights, and placed a call to Alain Moreau to let him know their plans.

"I met a woman in the Mexico City police department at a conference last year," Alain said. "Let me look up her name and contact info. I'll call her and let her know you're coming and text you her contact info. You never know if, or when, you'll need to call in the cavalry."

ψ

When Philippe got back to his suite at the Four Seasons, his sister was waiting for him. She was uncharacteristically nervous and looked as if she'd been pacing around the room for hours.

"Where the hell have you been? I've been waiting here since just after we spoke."

Her brother always seemed to have the ability to calm her down. "Relax, Angie, and tell me what your great news is."

His sister seemed to relax a little. She walked over to him, draped her arms over his shoulders, and barraged him with kisses.

"I'm going to Mexico with Hector. He wants to make me an apostle in the Order. This is his weak spot. It's our opportunity to take over everything,"

Her brother pushed her away and held her at arm's length by the shoulders. "Are you sure you can do it?"

"Absolutely. Never been surer of anything in my life. I've been in contact with the existing apostles, and they'll support me. They believe Hector is becoming psychotic and ineffectual. They want a younger leader, and that, my darling brother, will be yours truly."

She spun away from Philippe's grip and executed a perfect pirouette in the center of the room.

Her brother looked at her in feigned admiration. "Wow, all those expensive ballet lessons seem to have paid off."

CHAPTER FORTY-SEVEN

After a pleasant and uneventful flight, Nick and Gabriela arrived at Mexico City's Benito Juárez International Airport. They passed easily through the formalities of customs and immigration and found themselves in a frantic cacophony of travelers racing aimlessly around in search of everything from missing loved ones to toilets. Despite his earlier misgivings, Nick was happy that his beautiful traveling companion was there, and that she spoke flawless Spanish.

They picked up their luggage and pushed their way through the crowds to the line of taxis and limousines parked outside the arrival's terminal. Their driver, a young man with a touch of larceny in his demeanor, thought he'd be able to overcharge the turistas for the fare. He quickly became angelic when Gabriela asked him in flawless Spanish to take them to the Four Seasons hotel.

Unbeknownst to them, the suite they had reserved was virtually identical to the adjoining suites, just three floors above them, that Hector and his daughter now occupied.

ψ

Hector called Emilio Sanchez and told the New York gang leader to meet him in the hotel lobby. He needed protection for himself and Angelina. He also wanted to give the gang leader the description and photograph of the Chicago cop, which he'd managed to get from his friend at the New York Times. He didn't mince words.

"For Christ's sake, clean yourself up and dress like you belong at the Four Seasons. I don't want anyone here thinking I'm fraternizing with a fucking street thug."

ψ

Angelina was in her own suite, oblivious to fact her father had hired a hit man to take out the worrisome cop. She had her own agenda, and even though she'd carefully planned every step in her seizure of power, she worried she might not be able to carry out her own part in the plan. She needed reassurance, so she called her brother in Manhattan.

"Hi, you, I'm in Mexico City. The conclave is planned for day after tomorrow. I'm scared, so please tell me I'm capable of doing this."

Philippe listened. He'd never heard his sister have any misgivings before and knew he needed to bolster her confidence.

"Listen, Angie, the guy's a total asshole and an ineffectual prick. He's never really cared about you, or me, or Claire. It's always been him taking advantage of the Order and fucking people in business deals. He has no friends, and nobody at the firm gives a rat's ass about him. If it wasn't for his money, neither would you. What you have to do isn't hard when you think of him that way."

"Thanks, little brother. Things always get better when we talk. I'll call you later, when it's done."

Angelina knocked on the door to the adjoining suite, went in, and looked at her father in the way her brother had just described him.

This is going to be easy.

ψ

Nick called the number for the Mexican police officer referred to him by Alain Moreau. He got through to the Secretaría de Seguridad Pública (SSP) and asked to speak to Inspector Francisca Ramirez Flores. The woman answered after one ring.

"Buenas tardes. Habla el inspector Ramirez Flores."

"Do you happen to speak English?"

"Sí, señor. What can I do for you?"

Nick quickly told her who he was and explained that Alain Moreau had given him her name in the event he required police assistance.

"It would be my pleasure to help you, Detective Palmer, but please remember, Mexico City is out of both your and Alain Moreau's jurisdictions. I represent law enforcement here, and I strongly suggest you contact me if you run into any illegal activities, or conversely, if any illegal activities run into you."

Nick thought he heard her chuckle.

He assured the officer he would call and keep her informed if he found anything illegal going on. Before hanging up, he asked if she would check to see if a man named Hector Rodriguez had entered the country within the last few days, and if so, if there had there been any hotel reservations made under the same name.

"That shouldn't be too difficult, Detective Palmer. I'll get back to you first thing in the morning."

ψ

The coincidence of timing couldn't have been more precise. Nick and Gabriela walked out of the elevator and into the hotel's sumptuous lobby at the very time Hector and Emilio Sanchez were in their meeting. Hector looked up and did a double take. He hadn't expected his nemesis to be staying at the same hotel.

He pointed towards Nick and whispered to the gang leader from New York. "That's him! That's the prick who's been fucking up my life."

Emilio looked at the couple walking towards the front door. He stood and followed them out onto the street.

"Be careful, Señor Palmer. Someone evil is following you."

The warning voice that only he could hear stopped Nick dead in his tracks. He looked around the crowded streets and saw nothing out of the usual. He whispered softly to the woman who was warning him.

"Juliana? Who? Where?"

Gabriela sensed something was wrong and, also began surveying the crowds surrounding them. She saw the glint of a gun emerge from under a man's jacket. She yelled and pushed Nick to the ground just seconds before a hail of bullets shattered into the wall behind them. Nick felt a searing pain in his arm from one of the bullets but managed to get up. He was on his feet just in time to see the departing gunman vanish into the melee of frightened people. Gabriela lay on the sidewalk, a pool of blood beginning to spread from under her prone body. Nick knelt beside her, frantically looking for any signs of life. A gut-wrenching wave of nausea spread throughout his whole body, and his head began spinning, locked in a living nightmare, desperately hoping he'd wake up and everything would be okay again.

He fought through the pain in his arm and found Gabriela's wound. It was in her shoulder, in her brachial plexus, and she was losing a lot of blood. His rudimentary first-aid training with the Chicago force clicked in. He knew exactly what he had to do.

"Got to stop the bleeding… got to stop the bleeding…" he kept saying, over and over to himself.

He pushed down hard on the wound. He saw her blood covering his fingers and almost cried out in anguish. Through the fog that clouded his mind, he heard himself yelling and pleading to anyone who'd understand him.

"Help me! Please help me! Somebody, call for an ambulance! Please call for an ambulance!"

Eventually, the sound of approaching sirens reverberated in his head. He was still on his knees. Blood was still seeping through the fabric of her jacket. He was in a daze, still pushing down on the shoulder of the woman he loved, still trying to stop the blood that seemed to be flowing everywhere. Someone touched his shoulder and gently lifted him to his feet. Everything was happening in torturous slow motion. The paramedics injected Gabriela with a painkiller, dressed her wound, placed her gently on a stretcher, and rolled her into the waiting ambulance. Another medic dressed his wound, and tried, unsuccessfully, to corral him towards a second ambulance. He watched the ambulance carrying Gabriela drive away, uncertain if he'd ever see her again. His wretchedness and helplessness were overpowering; then he heard the voice of Juliana Cortez float above the hubbub of the crowd.

"Protect her... her and her baby too."

The voice in his head went away, only to be replaced by the voice of another woman, a voice he recognized from his earlier phone call. He somehow managed to unscramble his pain and the chaos in his head and looked towards the source of the person speaking to him.

"Inspector Ramirez Flores?"

"Sí, señor. How is it you know my name?"

"I'm Nick Palmer. I spoke to you earlier about Hector Rodriguez."

"Oh, sí, I remember. Does this madness have anything to do with him?" She swung her arm around, indicating the scene of carnage and the numerous police officers cordoning off the area. At that moment, Nick's thoughts were elsewhere.

"Please take me to the hospital where they took Gabriela. Please..."

The woman took him by his uninjured arm, led him to one of the police cars surrounding the scene of the shooting, and they were soon on their way to El Hospital de Urgencias Pediátricas in the exclusive Polanco neighborhood near their hotel.

When they arrived, Nick was informed that Gabi was in intensive care and about to undergo emergency surgery. Nick told the attending doctor that she was expecting their child and pleaded with him. "Don't let her die. Please don't let her die. I'm begging you."

The doctor, who'd checked and applied a new dressing to the wound in his arm, reassured him that she was in good hands and not to worry.

Easier said than done, thought Nick.

He sat in the waiting room with Francisca Ramirez Flores, his new friend in the Mexican capital's police force. She wanted answers, and he was more than ready to give them to her.

CHAPTER FORTY-EIGHT

Several witnesses came forward and reported to the police that they'd seen the shooter leave the hotel shortly after Nick and Gabriela. Other witnesses, in the hotel lobby, confirmed the shooter had been in a meeting with Señor Hector Rodriguez, a guest at the same hotel. This information was communicated to Inspector Ramirez Flores at the hospital.

She turned to the distraught man sitting in the chair next to her. "It seems your Señor Rodriguez is up to his ears in trouble."

She filled him in on the details she'd just heard from eyewitness accounts and saw an anger rise in the man's face that was terrifying. She took hold of Nick's good arm, looking him squarely in the eye.

"This is my jurisdiction, Nicholas. I know how you're feeling but taking things into your own hands would be a huge mistake. Trust me!" Then she became more consolatory. "But... because of the circumstances, and because you're a fellow police officer, I will let you assist in the investigation."

ψ

As Emilio Sanchez was running from the scene, he was stopped dead in his tracks by the mountain of a man Hector had hired to guard him.

"Quick, señor, into the back seat, and get down so no one can see you."

The New Yorker did as he was told, and soon the car was speeding away from Polanco, towards the much less affluent Roma district and the apartment there.

Emilio was afraid. He had just committed a serious crime in a city he knew little about. This was much different from his home turf in Spanish Harlem. There he knew where to hide and where he'd be safe from the authorities. Here he was a pawn in a game controlled by a man he hardly knew and absolutely didn't trust. After they got to the apartment, Emilio went into the bathroom and splashed water onto his face. He needed to think things through—needed to figure out how he'd get out of this mess. He looked up from the sink, and into the mirror, and saw the reflection of the man Hector had sent to guard him. He was standing right behind him. The big man was smiling, and his stained, uneven teeth exacerbated his fearsome countenance.

"Time to go, señor."

He pulled a multicolored rope from behind his back, swung it over Emilio's head, and pulled it tight. The punk from New York struggled, but he was no match for the massive Mexican and soon lay dead on the filthy floor of the bathroom. The Mexican picked up his cell and placed a call.

"It's done, Holiness. The gringo is dead."

"Gracias, my friend. You shall be rewarded in the afterlife. Dispose of the body as you see fit."

ψ

Gabriela came out of surgery and was resting in a recovery room not far from where Nick and the Mexican police inspector were waiting. Her doctor informed them that her surgery had gone well, the baby was fine, and that he expected the beautiful detective to make a full recovery.

"I think, señor, when she's well enough to travel, she should go home."

ψ

When Nick went into the recovery room, Gabriela was still asleep. He kissed her gently on the forehead, then went back to the waiting room. Francisca was just completing a call. She hung up and spoke to Nick in hushed tones.

"I believe we've found the shooter. A man matching his description was found, impaled on a spike on the fence surrounding the Metropolitan Cathedral in the Plaza de la Constitución. The body was naked, but there is a tattoo of a snake on its back. Strangely, even though the square is always busy, there were no witnesses."

Nick eyes narrowed, and he was clenching his teeth. He was like a bloodhound now, hot on the trail of a mass murderer.

"I need to see his body. Where's he been taken?"

Nick and the Mexican police officer left the hospital and drove to the morgue.

"I hope, Señor Nicholas, you have a strong stomach. Unfortunately, most morgues in Mexico are seriously overcrowded. Many of the bodies are unidentified and later buried in pauper's graves. Numerous others are stored in refrigeration trucks, and many are left to rot. The man who tried to kill your friend has recently arrived, so his body may still be available to see."

The morgue lived up to the description. The smell of dirt, death, and chemicals the overworked pathologists needed to perform autopsies was overbearing and brought them to the brink of retching. They were shown into a room where the body of their recent arrival was lying. Fortunately for Nick, the woman in charge spoke English.

"We've lifted his prints, taken photos, and sent them up to see if he can be identified. We've taken blood samples to see what drugs or medication he was on. Other than that, all we can do now is tag and store him."

The doctor was obviously impervious to death. She'd seen far too many dead bodies in her short career and looked upon them as large lumps of meat sent in to fuck up her already fucked-up day. Nick wondered what her home life was like.

"Can you flip him over? I'm interested in seeing the tattoo on his back."

Two assistants complied with Nick's request. Once again, he found himself staring at the hideous image of the snake god. The only difference between this one and the others was that this one was newly inked and much clearer.

"Do you have a magnifying glass I could use?"

The doctor opened the top drawer of a small white cabinet and handed Nick a well-worn facsimile of what he'd requested. He began scanning the tattoo from the snake's head all the way down to the small red box near the end of the reptile's tail. Suddenly, he stopped and leaned in to take a closer look.

"Holy shit, this isn't a fucking signature! It's a map."

He handed the glass over to the policewoman, and she too looked closely at the tiny image.

"This looks familiar. I think I know where it is."

Francisca took a photograph of the tiny red box with her cell. Then she turned excitedly to Nick. Her enthusiasm was contagious.

"C'mon, Señor Nicholas. Let's get to the station and confirm my theory."

Nick's response was exactly what the woman had expected.

"Drop me off at the hospital. I'll catch up with you later."

ψ

When Nick arrived back at the hospital, Gabi was awake. Her face was pale, and she had dark circles under her eyes. Nick bent down and gently kissed her cheek, having a difficult time holding back the tears welling up in his eyes. She managed a weak smile and then whispered, so softly he had a difficult time hearing her. "You should see the other guy."

Nick wanted to take her in his arms and hold her tightly, overjoyed that she retained her deliciously sick sense of humor.

"Once they let you out, I'm shipping you off to your parents' home in Texas. You'll need lots of R and R before you'll be ready to hit the streets again."

Her face took on the pugnacious, stubborn look he knew meant trouble. "No, my home is in Paris with you, Lucy, and Madeline. That's where you can ship me."

Nick realized there'd be no point arguing. Deep down, he was thrilled she wanted to go back to Paris.

"Okay, have it your way, but I'm sure you'll soon get sick and tired of all the care and coddling those two girls will subject you to, and then you'll wish I'd sent you to Houston."

He kissed her once more and said goodnight.

"Oh, and, by the way, the other guy you mentioned earlier is dead."

ψ

Hector heard about how and where his guard had left the unfortunate New Yorker. It wasn't hard to miss. Photographs of a naked man impaled on a spike in front of the cathedral were all over the news and internet. His thoughts about the henchman who had killed the New Yorker were anything but kind.

Stupid fucking bastard doesn't have a goddamn brain in his tiny moronic head.

He threw the remote at the television and stormed into the adjoining suite to see his daughter. He had a difficult time controlling his anger.

"Are you prepared for the conclave? Do you have your speech ready? Do you want me to go over it with you?"

Angelina was calm and controlled. One look at the enraged man confirmed that taking control of his enterprises was justifiable—and long past due.

"I'm fine, Daddy. Really fine and more than ready."

ψ

When Nick arrived at the police station, he found Francisca leaning into the screen of her computer. She was scanning a map of Mexico City, trying to match the lines in the small box in the victim's tattoo with corresponding streets on the map.

"It's here somewhere. I remember similar lines from a class on Mexican geography at university." She paused and looked confused. "Or was it history?"

Nick couldn't help himself. He spoke up. "Perhaps we should be looking at a much older map. This cult we're looking for has been around for a long, long time."

CHAPTER FORTY-NINE

Nick left the policewoman and returned to his suite at the Four Seasons. He had a lot of calls to make—calls he wasn't looking forward to making.

"Bonjour, Madeline. It's Nick."

The elderly Frenchwoman obviously picked up on the wretchedness in his voice. "Oh non! What's wrong? What's happened? Are you alright? Nothing's happened to Gabi, has it?"

Nick told her about what happened in Mexico City, including the news that he and Gabriela had been shot.

The elderly Frenchwoman was apoplectic. "Do you need my help? Is the bébé okay? Should I fly to Mexico?"

Nick assured her that his wound was superficial, Gabriela was recovering well, and that everything was under control.

"Don't worry, Madeline. She's in good hands, doing well, and will be returning home to Paris as soon as she's able to travel."

The Frenchwoman calmed down a little. "I know some excellent doctors here, Nicholas, and don't worry, Lucy and I will take good care of her. I promise you."

Nick asked her to break the news gently to Lucy and assured the distraught woman that he'd call her regularly with updates on Gabriela's prognosis.

Next, he called Gabi's parents and bought them up to speed on the shooting and subsequent condition of their daughter. Gabi's mother repeated, almost verbatim, the words he'd heard earlier from Madeline.

The last call was to Josh Nicholson, his and Gabriela's boss in the Chicago Police Department.

This one wasn't going to be easy. "Hi, boss, it's Nick. I've got some bad news, and some good news. What do you want to hear first?"

"Always the bad news, Nick. That way I have something to look forward to."

Nick didn't quite know where to start, so much had happened since he last spoke to the man. "Well, sir, to start with, Gabriela's been shot."

His boss's reaction was at odds with his normally stern behavior. "Shot! Fuck! What happened? She isn't dead, is she? What—"

Nick cut him off. "She's fine but still in the hospital. A gunman, hired by this Rodriguez character, took shots at both of us. Gabi pushed me out of the way and was hit for her troubles. I got away with a minor flesh wound."

"Anything I can do?"

"Nothing right now, sir. We're getting very close to the people who murdered Susan Roberts, and I believe it's the same crowd that's been killing young women all over the world for more than five hundred years."

"Has this got anything to do with the women you've been seeing in mirrors?"

Nick still felt uneasy talking about the apparitions, especially to Josh Nicholson, and he desperately wanted to change the subject. "So boss, now do you want to hear the good news?"

"The only good news I want to hear right now is that you've closed the file on the case and are on your way back home to Chicago."

"Yes, sir, but there's something else I should tell you. Gabi's pregnant."

"She's wounded and pregnant? Is the baby, okay?"

"The doctors say the baby's fine."

There was a long silence on the other end of the line. Finally, Nicholson said, "I guess I won't be seeing Gabriela anytime soon."

Nick didn't feel it was the right time to tell him about their planned move to Paris. Nicholson had enough to digest. Laying more news on the man didn't feel right or appropriate.

"Got to go, boss. I'll keep in touch."

Nicholson hardly had time to get in his next words. "About everything, understand? About everything."

Nick knew the man well enough to know his parting remark meant he not only wanted to be kept abreast of the case but also wanted regular updates on Gabi's condition and progress.

Nick went into the bathroom then. He felt like he hadn't had a shower in weeks and needed to get the clarity he hoped the steaming-hot spray would provide him.

"Hola, Detective Palmer. All of us are greatly saddened about what happened to Detective Martinez, but her sacrifice will get you closer to the conclusion of your journey."

He wiped the steam off the mirror just in time to see the image of Juliana Cortez fade into nothingness.

ψ

The following morning, a well-armed riot squad of Mexican police, all dressed in camouflage uniforms, arrived at the reception desk of the Four Seasons hotel. Guests who were lingering in the lobby either scattered like scared sheep or gawked unashamedly at the frightening spectacle of firepower. The officer in charge of this show of force, Inspector Francisca Ramirez Flores, strode up to the frightened girl behind the counter and asked her for Hector Rodriguez's room number. The girl quickly scanned her computer screen, then turned her terrified eyes back to the imposing woman officer.

"Señor Rodriguez and his daughter checked out at 6:15 this morning, señora."

"Mierda! That's two fucking hours ago. They could be anywhere by now."

Francisca pulled out her cell and dialed Nick's number. "Where the fuck are you?"

"Buenos dias to you too, Francisca. I'm just about to leave the hotel."

She ignored his allusion to her curt manner. She sometimes forgot the pleasantries others felt were important, especially when she was up to her neck in police business.

"I'm in the lobby. Get down here! I'll see you a minute!"

To Nick, her last remark sounded more like an order than a polite invitation.

The elevator doors opened, and Nick was confronted by a company of tough-looking police officers with Francisca front and center of the pack. She didn't mince her words.

"They're gone."

She explained to Nick what had happened, and that she'd issued an all-points bulletin for the suspect couple to be arrested and held. He looked at the assembled force of police officers and was more than happy he wasn't one of the people they were looking for.

The fleet of armored police vehicles stood outside the hotel's front entrance and were blocking the comings and goings of guests.

The harried hotel manager was pleading with the officer guarding the front car. "Could you please move your vehicles to a less conspicuous location further down the street? You're making our guests feel uneasy."

His plaintive request fell on deaf ears.

Francisca ushered Nick to the front door. "I've pulled some old maps of the city. Let's go to the station and check them out."

The police contingent left the hotel, piled into the convoy, and roared off, leaving the poor hotel manager surrounded by guests peppering him with questions he couldn't answer.

On the ride to the station, Nick called the hospital to check on Gabriela. The nurse who answered explained that she was still sleeping, and her condition was improving.

"People came to visit her earlier this morning, a man and his daughter. I didn't let them see her, though, because she was still resting."

Nick's brain exploded. With everything that was happening, he hadn't thought to request that guards be stationed at Gabriela's hospital room. Guilt spread throughout his body like a massive tidal wave, threatening to engulf and drown him. If anything happened to Gabriela, he would vanish forever into a deep dark well of unspeakable pain. He turned to Francisca; the look on his face conveyed anguish, anger, self-condemnation, and unspeakable guilt.

"Get a fucking detail of guards over to the hospital! Rodriguez and his daughter tried to get into her room."

The police inspector picked up her phone and screamed instructions to the person on the other end of the line. When she hung up, she turned to Nick. This time her voice was more consolatory, and she reached over and touched the arm of the distraught man sitting next to her.

"Don't worry, Nicholas. They're on their way."

CHAPTER FIFTY

The Catedral Metropolitana lies on the north side of the Plaza de la Constitución, also known as the Zócalo, at the center of Mexico City's historic district. Home to the Catholic Archdiocese of Mexico, the cathedral is the oldest church in the city. Construction began in 1573, and it took over 250 years to complete the magnificent structure that stands today. Unbeknownst to virtually all the devout pilgrims and tourists who troop through the venerable edifice, the church was built on the site of Templo Mayor, the religious and social heart of the Aztec empire. More specifically, it was built atop a temple dedicated to the snake god Quetzalcoatl.

For La Orden de las Serpientes de Cristo, the duality of the building, being both a Christian church as well as the historic temple of Quetzalcoatl, made it the holiest of holy places.

Hundreds of years ago, when the cathedral had been under construction, a secret chamber was excavated and built by native men and women conscripted to hard labor by their Spanish overlords. This hidden room was zealously guarded by trusted members of the Order and used only when a full conclave of the twelve apostles was called by El Cardenal.

Fernando Garcia, the present-day guardian of this secret chamber, was fully prepared for tonight's conclave. His wife had carefully washed the holy black robes, and they were now hanging on designated hooks along the chamber's ancient stone wall. He'd purchased new candles and incense and made sure that the entrance and exits of the apostles, through a seldom-used rear door or a hidden portal inside the church, would go unseen. Tonight's duty was the most important undertaking that Fernando, the lowly church handyman, could do, and he would make sure there would be no intrusion on the unholy gathering.

ψ

"The conclave of apostles of La Orden de las Serpientes de Cristo meets tonight."

The urgent voice of Juliana Cortez seemed to come out of nowhere, and the realization that time was no longer on his side alarmed him. Nick wanted answers, and he knew they wouldn't come from the ethereal voices in his head. It was up to him, and his newfound colleague in the Mexico City police force, to find the key to the puzzle of where the gathering of evil would occur.

"Nick, I've got it! I recognize the location on the map."

The sudden, jubilant whoop from Francisca snapped him out of his thoughts, and he leaned over and stared at her computer screen. She pointed at the map.

"It's the fucking Zócalo! We didn't need the old maps. It's here today just like it's always been. It was just too obvious for me to notice."

Nick was puzzled. He was a stranger to the city, and the name didn't ring a bell.

"What's the Zócalo?

"It's also known as Plaza de la Constitución. The top line on the map is a street, the Republica de Guatemala, and the shape in the top left hand is the Catedral Metropolitana. It's the most important square in all of Mexico. All major celebrations are held there."

Nick looked closer. It was all beginning to make sense, and he felt the rush of excitement growing in his chest. He swung around to face Francisca.

"That squiggle where the cathedral is looks like a snake. It couldn't be that obvious. Could it?"

The Mexican police officer shrugged.

"This little square in the tattoo has been around for a long time. I'm sure, back in the old days, it had more relevance to the cult's followers than it does today. What, I don't know is why they've picked the cathedral?"

Nick did a Google search on the ancient cathedral and quickly discovered that the snake god Quetzalcoatl's temple was buried beneath the venerated church.

"I bet the conclave will convene at eleven tonight, somewhere in the cathedral."

He quickly explained the significance of the number eleven to the Mexican police officer, and she agreed Nick's reasoning had merit.

"I don't know how they're going to pull off a meeting at that time of night. The Zócalo is usually teeming with people, and there's also always a large police and military presence in the plaza."

Francisca stopped, but Nick could almost hear the gears in her head turning. "I think we should set up a special task force to monitor the situation, and just to be on the safe side, I think we should get there early, around eight."

Nick left Francisca to mobilize her force for the evening's take-down, then hitched a ride to the hospital in the police vehicle he'd ridden in earlier. The hard-looking guards on duty at Gabriela's room were dressed in camouflage battle fatigues. They wore body armor, helmets, and carried enough firepower to stop a small revolution. The guards wouldn't let Nick enter Gabriela's room at first, and it wasn't until they got clearance from Francisca that he was finally allowed to see her. She looked up and gave him a million-dollar smile.

"Well, it's about time. I thought you'd forgotten all about me."

Nick laughed out loud, elated to see that she was getting back to her old self. This was shaping up to be one of the better days.

ψ

Following their unsuccessful attempt to harm the already damaged Gabriela, Hector and his daughter left the hospital to prepare for the conclave, scheduled for later that night. They hid, in plain sight, at a roof-top restaurant overlooking the Zócalo and the cathedral where the conclave was set to happen. Hector drilled Angelina on the protocol of the meeting and asked her, once again, about the speech she would be expected to deliver upon being accepted as an apostle.

"Don't worry, Daddy. I have it all figured out. I know exactly what I have to say and do."

Hector wasn't worried. He had too many other things on his mind to be concerned about his daughter's accession to the ranks of the apostles.

ψ

At eight that evening, Mexico City police officers began taking up hidden strategic positions inside and around the cathedral. The men and women in this group were dressed like street vendors, tourist guides, office workers, and the like. Armored vehicles with an elite squad of fiercely armed officers were hidden in the courtyard of the Palacio Nacional building on the eastern side of the plaza, ready to deploy as soon as the order was received from Francisca.

None of this seemingly usual activity was observed by either Hector or his daughter.

The first sighting came through from a police officer, cum tour bus guide, at 8:47 p.m.

An elderly woman was seen stealthily entering the cathedral through a small door hidden in the rear facade of the building. Other officers soon began reporting in. Several potential suspects had mysteriously vanished inside the massive structure, and yet another person had entered through the same small rear door that the elderly woman had gone through earlier. Nick and Francisca were stationed with the small group of officers hidden in the Palacio Nacional.

She whispered into her handheld radio.

"Don't do anything until all the suspects have entered the cathedral."

A scratchy voice on her device broke the stillness of the night: "Señor Rodriguez and a young woman are entering the cathedral through the main entrance."

Nick jumped up and turned to the woman in charge of the operation. "Let's go! He'd be the last in and first out."

Francisca gave the order, and the convoy of police four-wheelers shot out of the Palacio's center doorway and into the plaza. People scattered everywhere to get away from the imposing police presence. Seconds later, the armed convoy screeched to a halt in front of the cathedral.

ψ

Hector and Angelina crept silently through the nave of the enormous church. The shuffle of their footsteps on the hard stone floor was the only sound. Candles, lit by the faithful to remember loved ones, flickered and threw foreboding shadows against the opulent, gold-festooned ornamentation surrounding them. In a far corner, a man almost hidden in the shadows gestured for them to follow. They made their way past the Altar de los Reyes to a secret doorway and followed their guide down a steep stairway into the very bowels of the cathedral. They continued through the dusty crypt, past the tombs of departed archbishops, and entered a small, long-forgotten chamber with a lone chair set against an ancient stone wall outside the entrance.

"Por aqui, santidad."

Fernando Garcia bowed to his exalted guests and pushed his hand against one of the stones. Several seconds later, an opening appeared in the seemingly solid wall, and Hector and his beautiful daughter entered the sacred chamber. The opening quietly closed behind them, and Fernando sat back down on the lone chair to guard his eminent guests.

The chamber was lit by a profusion of candles, and an overpowering smell of incense filled the enclosed space. An ancient wooden table surrounded by thirteen chairs stood at the center of the room. The chair at the head of the table was larger and more ornately carved than the others. This was the seat of El Cardenal, the hereditary leader of La Orden de las Serpientes de Cristo, Hector Rodriguez.

Hector and Angelina took their robes from the hooks and slipped them over their street clothes. There were nine others in the chamber, all similarly dressed in black robes tied at the waist with multicolored rope. The assembled apostles were standing in small groups, murmuring softly among themselves.

They acknowledged the presence of their leader and quietly took their seats. Angelina was the only person who remained standing.

Hector got right to the point. He motioned towards his daughter and introduced her to the assembled hierarchy. "This, my esteemed colleagues, is my daughter, and the only candidate worthy for inclusion into this sacred council."

All heads turned towards Angelina. No words of disagreement were uttered.

As Hector continued, his voice sounded arrogant and dismissive, as always. "If we are all in agreement, then so it is done."

Hector smiled and turned to Angelina. It was time for her to speak to her fellow apostles.

Angelina walked slowly around the table, as if she were trying to find the right words, finally stopping behind the chair at the head of the table—the chair occupied by her father.

She untied the knot on the rope around her waist, released the cord, and quickly swung it around her father's neck. The two apostles who were seated closest to Hector jumped up from their chairs and held the startled leader down as Angelina slowly tightened the rope. No one moved or spoke. Finally, Hector's head dropped onto his chest, and Angelina pushed his limp body off the chair. Angelina replaced the colored rope around her waist and sat in the seat recently vacated by her late father.

"It is time, my dear friends, for new leadership. Time for the next generation to advance the syllabus of our order. I am, like my father and my venerable ancestors before me, a direct descendant of Christina de Delgado and Coatl, the high priest of Quetzalcoatl. Leadership of La Orden de las Serpientes de Cristo is my birthright—a birthright I now claim."

Suddenly, a gentle breeze was felt in the enclosed space. The candles flickered, and the men and women in the room looked nervously around. It was as if the god Quetzalcoatl was troubled and rallying against them. The breeze strengthened and the candles illuminating the dank room began, one by one, to flutter out. The depth of the darkness and the mysterious breeze that precipitated the candles being extinguished was enough to send all those present into a state of frenzied fear.

The apostles rushed around in the darkened room, bumping into each other and into the table and chairs. The massive entry door was immovable, and their cries for help never reached the unhearing ears of Fernando Garcia, their guardian outside. It was as if each of them was living in a nightmare, a hideous cloak of deprivation and terror from which there was no escape.

The ghosts of angels were smiling.

CHAPTER FIFTY-ONE

Nick and Francisca were among the first wave of Mexican police to enter the semi-darkened cathedral.

"Equipo, sepárense. Cubran toda el área."

Her order to spread out was quickly obeyed by a dozen or so officers. Members of this elite force were dressed in somber gray combat fatigues, had submachine guns at the ready, and were soon making their way through the same space crossed earlier by Hector Rodriguez and his daughter.

On each side of the processional were sixteen chapels, each dedicated to a different saint, each brilliantly festooned in gold, and each with its own altar. These chapels, the main cathedral, and the adjoining Sagrario church were thoroughly searched, but no sign of the fugitives could be found.

"Francisca, get over here! I think I've found a stairway."

The urgency in Nick's voice spurred her and several of the heavily armed officers towards him. Francisca ordered the armed men to precede them, then she and Nick followed hard on their heels. Their flashlights showed row upon row of ornately carved sarcophagi. A heavy cloak of death permeated the air and sent shivers down their spines. Nick was looking at the multitude of large, stone caskets.

"This must be a crypt."

"And you must be a brain surgeon," quipped the woman in charge.

The squad of heavily armed police officers quietly passed the sarcophagi and found themselves in a small stone room with a strange little man sitting alone on a chair. His eyes were closed in prayer, and he was twisting a length of colored rope around in his fingers. One of the officers prodded him with the barrel of his gun, and the man leaped to his feet. The look of terror in his eyes was palpable, and he threw his arms into the air.

"Quien eres tu? Que deseas? No se nada."

Francisca translated the man's frightened reaction to Nick. "He wants to know who we are and what we want and says he knows nothing."

"If he knows nothing, then what the fuck is he doing here by himself, fiddling with that evil piece of rope? And—"

Nick stopped dead, raised his head, and sniffed the air. Francisca did the same.

"Do you smell incense?"

"Yes, and it seems to be coming from that stone wall."

Nick went over to the wall and put his face close to a small crack where the mortar seemed to have fallen from between the slabs of stone.

"There's a room behind this fucking wall."

Nick's blood started boiling and all his pent-up fury was directed at the man who was evidently guarding the room. He turned, reached out, and grabbed the unfortunate Fernando by the scruff of his shirt.

"Open it, or I'll break every fucking bone in your slimy, scrawny little body."

Nick's words were quickly translated by Francisca, and the terrified man pushed his hand against the keystone. A large section of the wall swung open, and the cadre of armed officers turned their flashlights into the dark cavern.

The scene before them was what they imagined hell would look like. Dirt-encrusted bodies dressed in black, hooded robes. Men and women of varying ages with their fingers torn and bleeding from desperately clawing at stone walls in their futile attempts to free themselves from what would have been their hideous grave.

As they stumbled out, one by one, the officers unceremoniously herded them into a corner of the room at gunpoint.

When Nick and Francisca entered the secret enclave, the candles miraculously relit themselves. Nick smiled. He knew the ghostly women he'd been seeing, and hearing had something to do with the night's events. Francisca was terrified. She thought it was a miracle from God.

I'll tell her later, Nick thought, *or maybe not.*

They discovered the body of Hector Rodriguez on the floor next to an overturned chair. A cursory examination showed he'd been strangled. The image of Susan Roberts sprung into Nick's head, and he was sickened by it. They went back to where the apostles were being held at gunpoint.

"She's the one who did it. She's the one who murdered El Cardenal."

The old woman was pointing her crooked finger towards Angelina. "She wanted to take control, wanted to be the one, and she killed her father do get it."

The others nodded their agreement.

Angelina stood her ground, arrogant, defiant, and totally remorseless. "Fuck you! Fuck you all. I did what I had to do, and you know it."

Francisca stood in front of Angelina. Her utter contempt for the evil young woman was evident in her tone of voice.

"Angelina Rodriguez, I am arresting you for the murder of your father, Hector Rodriguez."

She turned her attention to the other black-hooded detainees. "And I'm arresting all of you as accomplices to the murder."

There was no hesitation, no reading of rights, and no sign of mercy on her face.

ψ

Nick left the cathedral and went back to the hospital. It was now well past midnight, but he desperately needed to see how Gabi's recovery was progressing.

"Buenas noches, Señor Palmer.

I think she is waiting to see you."

Nick smiled at the guard and silently entered the room. Gabriela was sitting up reading, the light above her bed casting long shadows on her face, so Nick wasn't sure if she looked better or not. When she smiled, he felt sunshine enter his soul. He bent over and gently kissed her forehead.

"Jesus, Nick, is that all you've got?"

Then and there, he knew she was going to be okay. He pulled a chair up to her bedside and recapped the evening's events at the cathedral.

"Okay, so what's still bugging you?"

"We still don't know who actually murdered Susan Roberts. That's what's bugging me. That's how this whole shit-show started."

He buried his face in his hands. Something was missing—something he felt he knew but couldn't retrieve from his brain. The frustration was disheartening. It was as if a tiny filament of his thoughts had taken a hike to God knows where. Silently, he began at the beginning, retracing every step, every minute, of his path from Chicago. Then it hit him. It was something they'd learned from Henri weeks earlier. He jumped up from the chair.

"It's the records! It's the goddamned records. Remember what Henri wrote about every religion keeping records. Jesus, even the Bible is a record of sorts."

He turned to Gabriela, bent over, and kissed her. Not like the previous peck on the head but a full-on, full-throttle kiss on her beautiful lips.

"We've got to call Nicholson and bring him up to date. If he can corral the cops in New York, maybe even the Feds, to raid Hector's offices and homes, they may find the records we need. Hell, he may even be able to win brownie points for the department."

He placed his cell on Gabriela's hospital bed and made the call.

"Nick? Jesus Christ, do you know what time it is? This had better be good, or I'll have your balls for breakfast."

Gabriella laughed out loud, and their boss in Chicago realized he was on speaker phone.

"Why the hell didn't you warn me you've got a woman on the call? Nice hearing your laugh again, Gabi. I've missed it around here. Okay, fill me in. What's so damn important that you got me out of bed?"

CHAPTER FIFTY-TWO

Philippe was worried. He still hadn't heard from his sister after the previous night's conclave of the apostles. He contemplated calling her cell but knew that, if he disturbed her when she was doing something important, there'd be hell to pay. Instead, he called the assistant at Hector's office.

"Sorry, Mister Philippe. I haven't heard from either your father or your sister today."

In his gut, he felt something had gone terribly wrong with his sister's plan. He began pacing around his luxury hotel suite. *What the fuck happens if everything goes sideways? What if Hector's still alive? What if Angelina's dead? What the fuck am I going to do if everything falls off the rails?*

He called his mother in Paris. Perhaps she'd heard something. Claire Rodriguez answered on the second ring.

"Hello, darling. Where are you? I've been trying to get hold of you and your sister for days."

The woman obviously knew as little, or less, than he did, so after exchanging some ineffectual banter, he hung up and went back to worrying.

ψ

Josh Nicholson wasted no time calling his colleagues in New York and his contacts in the FBI. He explained what had happened in Mexico City and requested that they obtain a search warrant for both of Hector's residences, and for his offices in lower Manhattan. He gave them Francisca Ramirez Flores's contact information in Mexico to confirm the particulars, and within hours, several squads of FBI officers descended on Hector's offices, his Manhattan apartment, and his home in Bedford. Staff at all locations were told to go home, and the Feds began their methodical search of files and records of both IGI and La Orden de las Serpientes de Cristo, the religious order that Hector had carelessly, and unlawfully, incorporated as a charity so he could benefit from numerous tax exemptions.

Hector's assistant called Philippe, apoplectic. Between her sobbing and her terror that she would somehow be implicated in what his father had been doing, he could hardly understand a word of what she was telling him.

"The police are here. They're everywhere, looking at everything. They told us all to go home."

An hour or so later, news of the raid in Mexico City and the subsequent raids at Hector Rodriguez's offices and homes were all over the internet and on news reports throughout the world.

Josh Nicholson requested any information pertinent to the murder of Susan Roberts be sent to him immediately, and because of his tipoff and initial involvement in the investigation, both law enforcement services agreed to his request.

ψ

"So, big boy, what're we going to do now?"

Gabi looked pale and tired. It had been a long night for her too, so Nick decided to sidestep her question.

"Well, as soon as I can get you out of here, we'll go home to Paris, and then figure it out from there."

She nodded, closed her eyes, and pretended to fall asleep. Nick kissed her forehead and left the room.

ψ

Philippe saw what had happened. The news of his father's death and his sister's role as the prime suspect in his murder was everywhere: on the television, on the internet, and on the grim faces of staff and guests at the hotel. He loved his sister, loved the way she looked, loved the heady scent of her perfume, loved her smile, and her voluptuous body. He loved her soft touch, her animal-like carnality, and their secret hideaway weekends in the English countryside. But now he hated her too. Hated her for what she'd dragged him into. Now he and his self-indulgent mother were the only ones left. Claire had called him a dozen times in the last hour, leaving desperate messages for him to call her back. He chose to ignore her pleas. His cell rang again. This time it wasn't his mother, and he didn't recognize the number. He answered it anyway. *What the fuck else could go wrong?*

"Philippe? This is Jonathan Bloom. I'm your father's attorney. We need to talk."

ψ

"Josh, I think we've found what you need."

Josh Nicholson walked over and closed his office door. The man on the other end of the line was the FBI agent in charge of searching Hector Rodriguez's various homes and offices.

"It's unbelievable, fucking unbelievable. We found a set of books in the old man's safe. Each page contained a detailed record of the murders of young women. Names of the murdered women, their executioners, and names of the people who witnessed the ceremonial executions—dates, times, the whole fucking thing. Almost five hundred pages dated from the sixteenth century right up to your Susan

273

Roberts case—all neatly handwritten. I've never seen anything like it. This could be the biggest murder investigation in history."

The Chicago cop was temporarily speechless as he tried to digest the scope of evil his friend had just described to him.

"Look, Josh," his friend said, "this is much bigger than all of us. It's your detectives who led us to all this, so you guys should take the first round of glory. I hear your balls are being hung out by the bigwigs upstairs, and this bust could help you out a lot."

The cop in Chicago took a deep breath. What the FBI man was offering would take a ton of heat off what the whole department was getting from above, but it somehow didn't feel fair.

"Thanks, Chuck, but you're the guys on scene. It's your game now."

"Believe me, Josh, we've got a ton of other shit here. Drug smuggling, human trafficking, robbery, prostitution, extortion, illegal armaments, tax evasion, you name it, and our friend Hector was into it up to his asshole. Believe it or not, he kept detailed records of all that shit too! We're going to be up to our eyeballs in this crap for years, so take what I'm giving you and run with it. You can buy me a couple of beers next time I see you."

True to his word, the following morning a package arrived on Josh Nicholson's desk with copies of all the record books about the cult from Hector Rodriguez's safe.

ψ

Angelina Rodriguez didn't know where she was, but her filthy, rat-infested cell felt more than a million miles away from her usual luxurious accommodations. She stalked around the confined space like a caged lioness. She was angry at the insolence of the police officers who'd arrested her, and the fury she felt for the Chicago cop who put her here ate at her gut like a gluttonous parasite.

She didn't know the name of her Mexican guard and didn't want to know it. He was disgustingly dirty, his sweat-soaked shirt reeked of cheap tequila, and his salacious smile displayed a row of rotten brown teeth. He usually just threw the food at her through the rusty bars that separated them, but today was different. Today he slid her meager meal, which had been placed on a small round tray, under the cell door.

"A gift from your devoted followers, Señorita Angelina."

He strolled back along the corridor smiling, humming a little Spanish song, totally oblivious to the yells and insults being hurled at him by the other prisoners in the cell block.

Angelina lifted the tray from the cracked concrete floor. It felt heavier than it should have. She threw the piece of stale bread and rancid cheese onto her bed and turned the tray upside down. There, stuck to the bottom and coiled up like a snake, was a length of multi-colored rope. She stifled a gasp, but the message was loud and clear.

ψ

Josh Nicholson didn't quite know where to start. He called the chief of police, gave the man a brief synopsis of what he was holding in his office, and asked if he could schedule a meeting.

"Jesus Christ, Josh, if what you've got is real, and I'm not saying it isn't, we've got a fucking tiger by the tail. C'mon up right now and bring the copies of the books with you."

Josh Nicholson and the chief spent the better part of the morning going through the handwritten entries and formulating a plan on how best to handle the huge pile of incriminating evidence they held in their hands.

"Step by step, Josh, step by step. I'll brief the mayor; you and your people start contacting Interpol, and all other police jurisdictions where the murders occurred. This is big, Josh. This is fucking global-manhunt big. Say, tell me again, who're the detectives who got the ball rolling on this thing?"

"Detectives Nick Palmer and Gabriela Martinez, sir."

"They're going to be heroes, Josh. Fucking heroes, I tell you."

CHAPTER FIFTY-THREE

"Where the hell are you guys?"

Josh Nicholson was happier than Nick could ever remember him being. The man sounded like he was on the verge of being jubilant.

"We're at the hospital in Mexico City, just getting Gabi ready to be discharged. We should be back at the hotel in no time."

"Well, my friend, there may be a crowd of people from the press waiting for you guys."

Nick pulled back a corner of the blinds, peeked out of the window, and sure enough, the sidewalk in front of the hospital's main entrance was teeming with reporters and cameramen, all waiting for Gabriela and him to exit the building. For a moment, Nick was speechless.

"What the fuck is this all about, boss?"

The cop in Chicago brought Nick up to date about the FBI's discovery of the books in Rodriguez's office, and the subsequent global manhunt set in motion with the release of their contents.

"The mayor wants to give you and Gabi the keys to the city, the president of Mexico wants to present you with the Order of the Aztec Eagle, whatever the fuck that is, and we've been stickhandling more calls to the precinct than I can ever remember. I won't even tell you what the chief said."

"Why not? Might as well hear it all."

"He, said you're both fucking heroes, and the whole world seems to be agreeing with him. I think you guys better get your asses back here as quickly as you can."

Gabi was sitting on the edge of her bed; she'd managed to lift the hand that wasn't in a sling, and raised her eyebrows in a universally understandable look that said, *"What the hell's happening?"*

"It looks like we're famous."

He flicked on the television hanging above the bed and scrolled to an English news station. The lead (and much repeated) story showed photographs of him and Gabriela below a large headline: OVER 500 MURDERS SOLVED BY CHICAGO COPS.

The announcer went on to describe details of the case, as scenes of the crowd of reporters stationed outside the hospital were flashed across the screen.

Gabriela's Mexican guard knocked and entered the room. He was accompanied by four additional, and equally intimidating, police officers. One of them, an attractive woman who looked to be in her early twenties, smiled and spoke to them in broken English.

"Señor, señorita, we will accompany you to your hotel and place a guard on your room. Our mayor, the American ambassador, and other important people wish to meet you there."

Gabi was helped into a wheelchair and the little procession went through the halls of the hospital and out to the cars waiting for them on the far side of the crowd.

ψ

Angelina was more afraid than she'd ever been in her life. She'd been in trouble before, but never in a situation like this—never in a spot she couldn't buy or talk her way out of. The total darkness of her cell and the foul bile that kept rising from her gut exacerbated her terror. She fiddled nervously with the length of colored rope smuggled to her by the foul jailer. She knew it was virtually impossible for her to escape the prison, and even if she did get free, the rope delivered to her was a death sentence from the disgruntled and dangerous followers of Quetzalcoatl.

Seeing no other option, she tied a noose at one end of the rope and slipped it over her head. Turning over the disgusting bucket that served as her toilet, she climbed up on it. Then, standing on the tips of her toes, she tied the other end of the rope around a bar in her tiny window. After a final long breath, she kicked the bucket out from underneath her.

They found Angelina's dangling body the following morning. Her beautiful face was drained of blood, looking like she'd been sucked dry by a vampire.

ψ

Jonathan Bloom's sumptuous law offices occupied nine prime floors of a tower in the Upper West Side of Manhattan. Philippe stepped off the elevator into what seemed like the hushed realm of a posh London gentleman's club. He wasn't kept waiting very long before a tall, well-dressed, silver-haired man came out to greet him.

"Philippe? Very nice to finally meet you. I'm Jonathan Bloom, your late father's attorney. My sincere condolences on your loss."

He was led through a maze of corridors, past numerous cubicles, to a spacious corner office overlooking Madison Avenue. There was a large stack of file folders and documents spread out on a small conference table in the corner of the room.

"Your father's will's pretty cut-and-dried, but because of the unusual circumstances surrounding his death, the funds will be tied up for what I estimate to be many, many years."

Philippe's emotions were running wild, but his expressionless face was a mask of stoic indifference. "What are my sister and I supposed to live on?"

"The good news is that your father set up some extremely generous offshore trust accounts for you, your sister, and your mother. In my opinion, these trusts will not be construed as assets of the companies, wholly owned and controlled by your father. Further to this, I've taken steps to ensure that these trusts will remain secret and hidden."

Philippe was beginning to feel much better about his future.

"How much are we talking about?"

The lawyer looked very pleased with himself. He leaned in towards the young man, and in a voice slightly louder than a whisper answered the question.

"You and your sister each have a trust valued at three hundred and fifty million dollars. Your mother's is worth seventy-five million. Your father's instructions further state that, in the case of either your death or your sister's, the funds from the deceased sibling's trust will automatically transfer to the surviving sibling. Your mother's trust, on the event of her death, will transfer equally between you and your sister."

Philippe smiled. *The crafty old fucker. This was a game of survival of the fittest, and so far, only me and the lawyer have the advantage of knowing about it.*

There was a soft knock on the door. Bloom's assistant slid quietly in and handed the attorney a note. He quickly read it and handed it to Philippe.

"Condolences and congratulations, Mr. Rodriguez. Your sister has just committed suicide in her Mexican jail cell. Now you're twice as wealthy as you were a minute ago."

ψ

Nick and Gabriela were jostled through the crowd of reporters and onlookers. Cameras and microphones were shoved towards their faces, and questions in at least four different languages were being yelled at them. The whole melee, as they were to find out later, was being broadcast live throughout the world.

Their reception at the Four Seasons was equally tumultuous but somewhat more subdued, and when they finally reached their suite, they found every spare inch of space festooned with flowers. Gabriela slowly got out of her wheelchair and sat on the edge of the bed.

"We've got to call Lucy and Madeline to let them know we're okay."

Nick agreed and made the call. He put his cell on speaker mode so they could both be in on the conversation. Their elderly French friend answered tentatively.

"Nicholas?"

"Oui, Madeline, and Gabi too."

"Dieu merci, Lucy and I have been worried sick about you two. We've seen you on the news. Why is Gabi in a wheelchair? Is she okay? Is the bébé, okay? When are you coming home?"

The questions from the elegant Frenchwoman kept coming, so quickly and furiously they couldn't get a word in edgewise. When Gabi finally inserted herself into the conversation, the smile in her voice was obvious.

"Arretez, Madeline. We're fine. I'm fine. The baby's fine. We'll be home soon, and when we get there, we'll tell you the whole story."

Nick was standing at the window, looking out at the crowds of reporters in front of the hotel.

"You know, none of this would have happened if it weren't for my mirror girls, my guardian angels."

He turned and faced Gabi. The adrenaline rush that had been pulsing through his body for more days than he could remember was wearing off, and he suddenly felt more exhausted than he'd ever been in his life. He was also deeply troubled that he couldn't say anything about the ghosts of the martyred girls who were the real heroes. He waved his arms around the room.

"They did it all. They guided and protected us. All these flowers, all this praise… everything should be theirs."

Gabriela slowly stood and walked over to him, reached up and gently kissed him.

"You need to get some rest. Go and take a shower, then crash for an hour or two. Believe me, things will look much better after you clean up and have a nap."

ψ

Nick looked in the bathroom mirror. The steam from the shower was beginning to cloud the glass. He wiped it clear and stared at himself.

"Where are you? How can I thank you? Please say something… anything."

The face of Susan Roberts appeared. She looked different. This time her features were soft and almost transparent. This time she was ethereal. She had a ghost-like quality on her face and her voice was like a sweet whisper.

"There's no need to thank us. No need to reveal our presence. We are finally at peace, and that is thanks enough. Enjoy your life, Nicholas Palmer. Love and protect those who are close to you. Goodbye."

The young woman's image slowly drifted away. She had a Mona Lisa smile that radiated a warm, peaceful glow throughout his whole body. Once she was gone, he slipped out of his clothes and stepped into the hot shower.

CHAPTER FIFTY-FOUR

Nick and Gabriela were required to make a stopover in Chicago before continuing to Paris. This "request" had come from both the mayor and the chief of police. In truth, it was an order they couldn't ignore.

Their flight landed at O'Hare, and they were greeted by the dignitaries. A large crowd of aggressive reporters, hell-bent on getting the first words from the harried couple, were jostling for prime positions near the gate. Members of the press were disappointed. Nick and Gabi were hustled through the airport to waiting limousines and taken to the police station where the whole thing had begun.

Josh Nicholson greeted them, and following a huge round of cheers, applause, and hand pumping from their fellow officers, they were ushered into the beige-walled, bare-boned conference room. Public relations staff from both city hall and the police department were waiting to brief them on the press conference the had planned for the following morning. Then they were left alone to debrief their superior officer.

After two hours of intense interrogation, they were driven to Gabi's apartment, where they collapsed onto the bed, too tired to think of anything except sleep.

ψ

The press conference was held at city hall. The huge room was packed with reporters from local and national print and broadcast media, city officials, and representatives from the state capital.

Nick and Gabriela were front and center at the podium, with the mayor, the chief of police, the governor, and Josh Nicholson standing alongside them. Except for Nick and Gabriela, who weren't used to this level of attention, the assembled group were all smiling and waving at the enthusiastic crowd.

Introductions were made, speeches given, and finally the podium was given over to Nick, who nervously approached the microphone. He looked apprehensively around the mass of smiling faces. This wasn't something he'd ever expected to be doing. His heart was pounding. His palms were sweating. He glanced towards Gabi, hoping for some sign of moral support, but she was engrossed in a conversation with the police chief. Wiping his sweaty palms against his pants, he looked nervously out at the hushed crowd, and began.

"This wasn't a one- or two-person investigation."

He looked lovingly at Gabriela, who turned a brilliant shade of red.

"This was a collaboration of police officers, here and in many other jurisdictions."

He turned to Josh Nicholson.

"I would like to thank Josh Nicholson, my boss here in Chicago, who believed in my theory. I would also like to thank Detective Lieutenant Alain Moreau of the Paris police, Inspector Silvio Bianchi in Rome, Police Inspector Javier Ruiz in Madrid, and Francisca Ramirez Flores in Mexico City. There were numerous others who wish to remain anonymous, but without their help and guidance, none of this would have been possible."

Nick paused and wiped away the beginning of a tear.

"I would also like to thank my very dear friend Professor Henri Deneuve, who died in the cause of the investigation. I know he's watching over us. I would be remiss if I didn't also thank his brilliant sister Madeline Boucher for her unfaltering support."

He lifted his head and faced the crowded room.

"Lastly, I would like to thank Detective Gabriela Martinez, my partner in crime, and life, who took a bomb blast and a bullet during the course of our investigation."

He reached over, took Gabi's hand, and gave it a soft squeeze.

"This is a great day for justice, and a great day for the Chicago cops, America's finest police force. Thank you all for coming."

The room exploded with cheers and questions being yelled at him from the press corps.

Josh Nicholson stepped up to the microphone and spread his hands attempting to quiet the noisy crowd.

"A full statement and press package will be released shortly that should answer all your questions. Thank you all for coming. We're going to get these two heroes someplace where they can get some rest."

ψ

Philippe Rodriguez was watching the press conference on the television in his Manhattan hotel suite. His world was collapsing around him. His father's investment firm, ICI, was crawling with FBI agents, and under investigation by everyone and anyone who thought they had a claim against it. Likewise, daily arrests were being made and charges laid from a long list of his father's criminal associates. And to compound everything, La Orden de las Serpientes de Cristo was also under intense scrutiny. His mother alternated between being weepy and being furious. She'd been scorned by her coterie of friends in the French capital and was threatening suicide. Most of all, Philippe desperately missed his sister.

He felt an overwhelming sense of anger towards the man at the center of the podium. An intense, insatiable rage permeated his whole being. He clicked off the television and paced around the room, punching out at everything within his reach. Furniture didn't escape his wrath. He used chairs and tables to knock holes in the walls, and finally, after throwing a lamp through the television, he collapsed crying onto the floor. He swore to exact his revenge… not right away but sometime in the future, after he'd rebuilt the empire stolen from him by the cop from Chicago.

He called his lawyer and told the man to settle his account at the hotel, then packed and caught a limousine to Kennedy Airport and a flight to London.

ψ

Nick and Gabriela tendered their resignations to Josh Nicholson and gave notice to Jake Murphy, the affable superintendent of their Gold Coast apartment building. Their sudden celebrity status would make their police work in Chicago untenable, and the siren call of their new life in Paris was impossible to resist. Their goodbyes were short and emotional. Nick thought he saw tears welling up in the corners of Josh Nicholson's eyes, but the man quickly brushed them aside.

When they got back to their apartment building, Jake Murphy didn't hold back. As Gabi wrapped her arms around him for a long goodbye hug, he cried like a baby.

They packed what they needed or wanted, told Jake to dispose of everything else as he saw fit, and a few days later, left for O'Hare and their flight home to Lucy and Madeline in Paris.

There was a going-away contingent at the airport: Josh Nicholson, Jake, some of their colleagues from the police department, and a few reporters who'd somehow gotten wind of their departure. They passed through security, boarded their flight, and were soon flying over the skyline of the city where they'd first met. It was a bittersweet farewell.

TWO YEARS LATER

Nick woke up. It was the middle of the night, and something was wrong. There was a strange glow coming from the living room of their Paris apartment. He shuffled into the room to see if they'd inadvertently left a light on. The glow was coming from a large mirror occupying place of pride near the front door.

"She's with us now. Madeline is reunited with Henri and me."

Nick couldn't take his eyes off the image of Margaux Deneuve. She was beautiful beyond words, and an aura of soft golden light surrounded her whole being.

"Remember her fondly, but do not weep. She's happy and content with us."

The image faded, and Nick felt an overwhelming sense of calm engulf his entire body. He tiptoed to Madeline's room and went in. Her eyes were closed, and she had a beautiful and peaceful smile on her face. He lifted the sheet and gently covered her face.

Nick returned to his bedroom and Gabriela, gently waking her and telling her what had happened. She nestled her head onto his shoulder and silently wept.

TEN YEARS LATER

Mornings at the apartment on Ile Saint-Louis were usually a madhouse of happy chaos, and this morning was no exception. Young Henri was a boisterous nine-year-old, and little Madeline was a precocious seven-year-old showing signs of being as beautiful as her mother. Eighteen-year-old Lucy was studying medicine at the Sorbonne, and tomorrow was to be her nineteenth birthday. Nick and Gabriela were busily preparing the speech they were scheduled to deliver at a conference of police chiefs in New York City later in the week.

Nick had almost finished shaving when the image of a woman appeared in the mirror. It was a face he recognized, but it was older, grayer, and more haggard than it was the last time he'd seen it. He stepped back, uncertain what to say to the woman, who looked like one of the druggies he'd rounded up in Chicago when he was a rookie cop.

It was Lucy's mother—the wife who'd left him so many years ago in Clarendon Hills.

"Protect Lucy. Please protect Lucy."

Dull gray tears ran down her ghostly sunken cheekbones. Her deep-sunken eyes were pleading with him, begging him to keep watching her. The wretched image of Isabela turned, and as she did so, the robe covering her frail shoulders dropped to reveal the half-completed tattoo of a multicolored snake.

"I'm sorry, Nicholas. I'm so very sorry."

A bone-chilling shiver ran down his spine. Never in his most terrifying dreams had he ever considered that the cult of evil he'd helped destroy a decade ago would return to inflict their odious revenge on him and his family. He dropped the shaver into the sink and rushed toward a window overlooking the street below. He saw his daughter turn around the corner and screamed at her at the top of his voice.

"Lucy! Lucy! Stop!"

The girl didn't hear him. She was bouncing along listening to her favorite tunes on the headphones he'd given her as a birthday gift.

Nick raced out of the apartment, taking the stairs three at a time. He ran frantically down the street, desperately pushing people out of his path until he turned the corner and saw Lucy ahead of him. She was completely oblivious to the dark gray van with blacked-out windows parked halfway down the block in front of her. Nick screamed at her again, and this time she turned and stopped to wait for her father.

The three men sitting in the van didn't move, watching and waiting.

"Holiness, what do you want us to do now?"

The man they'd questioned smiled—a cruel, twisted grimace that distorted the features of his handsome face, making the son of Hector Rodriguez virtually unrecognizable.

Nick caught up to Lucy and wrapped his arm around her shoulder.

"Gabi and I want you to come to Manhattan with us. Is that okay?"

"Is it okay? Wow! Yes, that would be beyond awesome. I've never been to New York before."

The man sitting in the front passenger seat of the van turned to the driver.

"Get me the fuck out of here."

Nick heard the van start up. He turned and watched it pull away from the curb.

I'm probably being paranoid. It's just a van, for Christ's sake.

A solitary breeze wafted off the Seine and blew down the street towards where Nick and Lucy were standing, but only Nick felt it.

He tightened his hold around his daughter's shoulder and leaned in towards her.

"You know, honey, I think the whole family should go to New York."

ABOUT THE AUTHOR

A.E. Lawrence is a pen name. The real person lives with Vickie, his wife of forty-plus years, and a couple of dogs on a small farm in the beautiful hills of Caledon, slightly northwest of Toronto.

In a parallel life he's the founder and Chief Creative Officer of a successful advertising/design agency in Toronto, and has won numerous awards for writing ads, commercials, brochures, and the like for a wide variety of clients.

When he's not doing chores or writing (hopefully blockbuster) novels, you'll find him doting on Emily and Natalia, his two granddaughters, or fly fishing for trout at his club or in the many neighboring rivers.